Darkster, Even the Gods Tremble

Part of Hyades Wars,
Book 3 in the Orcs series

Michael Ryan

Hyades Wars Publishing
Hyadeswars.com

ISBN-13:
978-1-7329292-2-7

Body of Work

Path to the Gods
book 1 in the Orcs series

Darkster, Even the Gods Tremble
book 3 in the Orcs series

The Troublemakers
book 1 in the Humans series
book 2 in the Orc series

The Troublemakers, Halfling
book 2 in the Humans series
book 4 in the Orc series

Schula and Downs, Love Triangle
book 1 in Life's Mysteries

Tales of Hyades Wars
book 1 in Short Stories

Acknowledgments

This book is dedicated to all my fans, and all readers of sci-fi/fantasy everywhere. Without you reading my works, and joining the Hyadeswars universe, the fulfillment of writing would wane significantly. Thank you.

Special thanks to Nathan Rosario for Artwork created. Font for cover page was created on cooltext.com.

This book has been edited by Sandra Ely from Polished Pearl Author Services.

Content

Prologue

Ucktock trudged forward over this cold, barren world, cursed with the dead rising, and the live dying. He checked his coordinates on his wristwatch as he plotted his course, ever onward passed a vast nothingness.

Marshil was once a thriving world, rich in culture and technology, as much as orcs were capable of, anyway. But now, it was stricken with a disease that ravaged souls and brought even the hardiest orcs to their knees, praying to their gods for salvation from the evil cloud that enveloped it. To Ucktock, everything looked the same - abandoned and ruined; he knew nothing of a curse.

He wondered what had happened to this planet; his reports were all wrong. He should have come upon the outskirts of a city by now, but everything lay in waste. It didn't help that wind-driven sand pelted him relentlessly. He rechecked his position, stopping this time to make sure he wasn't in err. He wiped away sand that encrusted the corners of his eyes. "Summa bitch," he muttered.

Also, he decided to contact Muddy, another orc from his homeworld who he was supposed to meet up with. So far, communication from Muddy was nonexistent. Perhaps it was the storm that made communication impossible. Perhaps it was electromagnetic interference. It really didn't matter why. Ucktock tried again. "Muddy, dis Ucktock. You der?"

Once again, there was no response. Ucktock wondered if his partner had gone off course. He speculated that the storm may have confused the instruments, giving bad coordinates as a result.

A putrid smell assailed his nostrils, urging him to squint his red eyes against the sand storm that further wore down the structures around him and bit at his nose. The smell was vaguely familiar. *Like roadkill,* he thought. He felt uneasy – very uneasy. He didn't even know why. As far as he could tell, there was no life anywhere around him.

He instinctively dropped to the ground and rolled for cover, keeping low until he was sure there was no danger. Several minutes of peeking his head up so his nose could snort the waft of stink, and confirm without doubt that its current harmlessness matched what his eyes observed, he slowly lifted his body and carefully continued onward.

He made a bit of a left turn where his nose brought him to a cluster of buildings. *This* was the city he anticipated coming across. But it was nothing more than lumps of stones, arranged in what appeared to be dilapidated walls. Some signs of windows and door frames were visible, but no doors or glass remained, and the structures were roofless. Sand dunes rose thirty feet in every direction.

Ucktock had a strange feeling. He became cautious as he crept along a stone wall to his right. He drew his sidearm and looked around, the scent of rot and decay becoming stronger. He came to a stop to read a carving that caught his attention. He rubbed across it with his right hand, revealing: "Bromstead semetery."

He entered a gate that hadn't been covered in sand and found a building with a monument in front of it; this was clearly the mausoleum. Headstones ran in rows along its sides, giving obvious passage to its large, iron front doors.

The smell that brought him this far was overwhelming at this point. Through the howling wind, Ucktock heard cries and gods-awful moans. He slowly crouched and quietly approached the burial chamber.

Just then, an arm burst through the wall where glass used to be. The rotted hand that was attached grabbed Ucktock in a mad frenzy to pull him inside. Ucktock shot his gun into the arm, separating it from the unlucky soul who previously owned it. Yellow and green rot splattered, hitting Ucktock in the face. The vile substance made him sick.

Thirty cursed souls surged forward and took up position where the armless assailant had been. One creep couldn't bust through the iron framework that surrounded the doors, but this many would surely do so from their combined weight. Moans of agony became violent howls as the mass pushed against the bending barricade that sought to contain them in their tombs.

Ucktock backed up, shocked at what he saw. He had heard about creeps, but it was very different to experience them first hand. Their appearance was gruesome, their existence grotesque, their ferocity unmatched, and the psychic blow they dealt was indescribable. How could he kill something that was already dead? And if he died, would he turn into one of them? Shivers ran up his spine.

He turned and ran to the cover behind the wall, hoping he was at a safe distance. Maybe this would deter the creeps from pursuing him if they broke out of the tomb. He slumped behind the wall and watched intently, praying to his gods, but visibility was down to zero. The creek of twisting metal informed him of death's advance.

The decision was made to flee the area as fast as possible. He didn't want to face thirty of the beings that haunted his mind. He jumped up and rotated in the opposite direction. He ran into another being and screamed in horror, "Garrrrrr. Get away!"

"What da hell da matta wit' you?"

Ucktock's heart was in his throat, beating like a drum in his ears. He had never been so happy to see Muddy. "Don't evva do dat again!"

Muddy laughed. "You look lika you seen a creep."

"I saw lots a dem and dems comin' dis way! Run!"

One
Curse the Damned

The female concocted another brew, much like the one used the day before to blind some old male orcs. She took particular pride in what she did, for there weren't any others that were capable of making potions. Sure, there had been lore of an old hermit named Grim, but that was so long ago that most orcs had forgotten about his writings.

Even though her husband was away, she was intent on using the potion as soon as possible. The orcs in the valley were contestable cuds and she wanted to rid herself of their meager existences. Resources were scarce, and as far as she was concerned, it was her right; the strong shall survive.

"Mama," came from Cracka. She hated being interrupted when she worked. She wondered why she ever went through with having the little bastard. As an infant, he cried, ate, pooped, and not much else. Now that he was a bit older, he asked so many stupid questions that she longed to drop him off somewhere, never to be seen again.

"What you want? Mama's busy." She continued moving liquids and parts of sacrificed animals from pot to pot, perfecting her witchcraft, as well as her potions.

The boy wiped his runny nose with a forearm and questioned, "When Papa be home?"

"Dunno. He wit' Warchief Boppa in Bigtown. It far away. Dunno."

"He far away?" the curious tot quizzed.

"Yes, now shutta up and go a sleep." The witch went back to work, her beady, red eyes fluttering as she passed from one conscious plane to the next. She closed her eyes and rocked, reciting words in some ancient tongue. Then, she wrapped her hands in tree oil-soaked cloth; it resisted moisture and heat. She worked the boiling potion from pot to beaker, muttering more ancient prayers as she did.

When finished, she dressed in a worn cloak, marked by dirt and blood. She grabbed a dagger by the front door, some potions, and headed for the valley. She left the boy behind.

The journey only took around forty minutes on foot; it was a bit longer than that under the cover of darkness, however. When she arrived, she was careful not to be seen; she clung to the hedges and tall grasses that outlined the village by the creek. She spotted her first victim with anticipation from the cover of the foliage that hid her. Chills as a precursor, caused the victim to rub his arms, trying to eliminate the goosebumps she brought with her.

It was typical for orcs to sleep during several periods per day in the valley, four to six hours at night and the same during daylight. Life was relaxed and somewhat carefree. She hated the way these useless orcs acted. They may as well have been tree stumps or rocks. Yes, she hated them indeed. At least the sporadic sleep cycles meant that individuals would wander out into the night to use the outhouses or the woods to relieve themselves.

This night was marked by her casting spells on unsuspecting orcs that simply rolled out of bed and rushed to empty their bladders. As a result, many

11

would go blind, mute, or mad. They would have blamed it on the water being contaminated or even a work of the gods, but someone caught a glimpse of the female, leaving no doubt as to the culprit. She had tempted fate, throwing just one more spell, and then another as dawn approached.

The spellcaster fled into the morning dew and holed up in a nearby cave. She covered the entrance with sticks and foliage to conceal her during the witch hunt. She didn't want to lead the mob that followed her to her house; if her husband found out that she had failed so miserably, it might have been worse to face him than the angry mob.

She had little thought about her son; not even the slightest acknowledgment crept into her heart. He slept that night, not realizing that she even left the house until later that morning. To him, it was just another time his parents weren't around. Like usual, he got into mischief by stealing food from someone in town and throwing rocks through windows.

Hotta's small moon sought solace; it searched for company amongst the ever-present darkness. Even when the light came out, it was lost – hidden from view. It was set on a cyclical course, always spinning, never changing in its hopeful path around its mother. Perhaps it would never realize its importance on this world, for it couldn't see its impact on those around it. Yet, it continued on.

***

"I home," Nuttybomb yelled as he entered his home. He threw his arms up to welcome his wife or his kids into his waiting arms. And sure enough, Uhra and the children came from several rooms away.

Uhra burst out in elation, "Younut!" She ran into his arms and squeezed him as hard as she could. She kissed his face again and again, then looked into his eyes. "I miss you."

Nutty smiled. "Me, too."

The twins were almost three now and each clung to one of Nutty's legs. Joy, his girl, hollered, "Hi, Daddy!"

Nutty released Uhra and bent down to pick up his little prides and joy. Uhra took a step back so the kids could see their long-lost father.

Uhra watched the interaction between father and children. Nuttybomb was massive compared to the peanuts he picked up. He was a killer, too, taking the lives of over two thousand enemies with his bare hands over the last several years. But he was gentle with his little ones, his love shining through.

Nutty asked, "How are you, Crazybomb?"

His son simply growled and beat his father's torso as hard as he could. Then, he hid his face in Nutty's chest.

Nutty exclaimed, "Wow! Yer strong!"

The boy laughed and said, "Dat nuttin'. I gonna kill a carnidawg wen I gets a lil bigger."

Nutty chuckled. "I bet you will."

Although she was ecstatic to have her husband home and to see him handle the kids so well, Uhra was concerned with his appearance. His coloring was off a bit and she noticed he was clammy when they hugged. His breathing seemed loud to her, too, but maybe he was just excited to see his family. She waited for Nuttybomb to put the kids down before she spoke. "You ok?"

"Ya. Why?"

"You looka funny. You sick?" Uhra queried.

Nutty didn't want to worry his wife, and he certainly was more of a male than to give in to being a little run down. "I fine."

Uhra wasn't so sure, but she went along with her stubborn husband. All the same, she asked, "Want me to maka hot bath fo' you?" She figured this would give her time to talk with him while he relaxed. Maybe he would open up.

Nutty obliged. "Sure. Dat would be great."

The two walked into the bathroom, leaving the kids to play with some items Nutty brought back from the other worlds he had visited. Nutty looked around fondly at his residence. It wasn't really a palace, but big enough to keep guards on staff to protect his family in his absence. He brushed a finger along the marble walls and smiled. He thought to himself, *An orc wit' marble walls*.

Uhra grabbed some towels and started the water in the tub. There was actual running water now. The little village named Bigtown had blossomed into a metropolis, sporting running water, sewers, and electricity. Its population grew to almost a million. She turned to see Nutty getting undressed.

Nutty moaned as he lifted his arms above his head to pull them out of the sleeves of his shirt. His back was littered with scars from bullets and knives. He bent over to take his boots off and groaned, his knees cracking and popping as he did so. He sighed as he sat down to pull off his socks and pants. He was riddled with pain and it showed.

Uhra was horrified at the sight of her husband's mutilated body. His chest and abdomen looked worse than his back, something she thought to be nearly impossible. She didn't care what it looked like; she loved him no matter what, but to see the abuse his poor body had taken in such a short amount of time gave her pause. She held back tears as she fought to dismiss the thoughts of pain he must have suffered.

Nuttybomb stood up and grunted as he straightened. He eased his way to the tub, but stopped when he saw Uhra's concerned look. "What wrong?"

Uhra didn't know how to address the one thing that was so insignificant as compared to the rest of his wounds. She pointed to his groin and questioned, "Umm...What a happen to you a pee?" Somehow, she just blurted it out.

Nutty was unfazed. He, too, didn't give much thought to how his body looked as long as it functioned. He responded nonchalantly, "Oh, I fight a human and I get all cut up."

"But" Uhra paused before asking the inevitable, "why it look lika puppy dawg wit' ears?"

"Dunno. Doc said it healed ok and it work good. Da ears? Eh, whatevva."

"Do it hurt?"

Nutty shook his head, "Nope, not no mo'."

"Anda you sure it work ok?"

"Yup."

Uhra felt a little odd. Maybe she shouldn't have said anything, but she always seemed to have a knack for putting her foot in her mouth. He didn't seem to care, so she was fine with his appearance. "Ok."

Nutty jibbed, "Why? You not lika puppy dawgs?"

Uhra bit her lip and snarled. "I wuvs puppy dawgs." She disrobed and entered the tub with her husband.

***

The crazed woman made a break for it as the cave offered little cover from the mob that sought to destroy her. If it was a little darker, she may have been safe, but not with the morning light shining. She cast a spell or two in the direction of the mob and took off in the other direction. She cursed in an ancient tongue and hissed in modern hysteria.

Orcs cried out. Several were reduced to mumbling masses of convulsing, babbling lumps, the result of spells taking hold. Others shrieked in terror over what they witnessed. The sight of the evil spells and how they affected their other villagers was ungodly. They weren't accustomed to seeing such witchcraft and didn't know how to combat it. They scattered momentarily.

The witch attempted to deceive the angry mob by heading in the opposite direction of her house, and then, doubling back around them to go home. She understood how hard it was going to be to evade capture and basically gave up on saving the location where she lived; she was now in a life or death struggle. She took the time they dispersed to run.

Her plan seemed to work. Even as the confused mob regrouped, they followed her original path to nowhere. They wielded swords, pitchforks, and guns. Some held pieces of wood or iron bars – whatever was laying around that could be used as weapons. She saw them wave their arms above their heads and run off into the distance, their shouts becoming silent as they left.

She backpedaled, carefully covering her tracks. Her hood was down so her eyes could look around her without being blocked. Her cloak waved behind her and seemed to get caught on every thorny branch she passed. She had to tug on it repeatedly while her lungs pumped more oxygen to her brain than necessary. She was lightheaded with adrenaline racing through her, her heart carrying amped-up blood to her extremities.

The front door flew open and was flung shut just as quickly. The house was dark and quiet, perfect for her to hide for a while. She deadbolted the door and scampered toward the back of the house.

"Hi, Mama," came from the lonely boy.

The witch snarled, "Shutta up or I killa you. Go a bed!"

"But Mama..."

The crazed woman swung her arm and landed a backhand across the child's face to quiet the problematic bastard. The boy flew to the other side of the room with the wind knocked out of him. He whimpered as he tried to force air into his lungs.

He cried, "I sorry."

"I said, shutta up!" The job of barricading the windows was underway. The large eating table was stood up on end; dishes crashed to the floor. It, along with a bookcase, was pushed to cover two of the vulnerable openings. Other pieces of furniture followed.

Cracka didn't want his Mama angry with him. He hated the sound of her voice when she spoke in anger. He reasoned that she must have found out about the fires he started, for angry voices were becoming clearer. He ran to his bed and hid under the covers once more.

A voice bellowed from beyond the front door, "Come out! You come out or we gonna burn you out!"

The witch growled. She gathered some beakers and rushed some potions into production. She tried to dissuade the crowd that gathered outside her home in a lovely voice. "One minute. I not dressed."

The voice added, "We know who you be. You not foolin's us. Open up!"

"I almost dressed," was her response. She ditched the cloak beneath the house through a hole in the floor that she covered with a rug. She brushed her hair and went to the door. She kept the potions nearby.

"Dis da last time. Open up!"

She obliged. "Ok." She wouldn't escape again, that much was clear. At least, she wouldn't escape by being stuck inside. She lifted the deadbolt and slowly opened the door. "How I help you?"

Several orcs burst in and grabbed her. They pushed her to the floor and began interrogating, "Why it so dark in here?"

She sweetly offered, "I wus sleepin's."

"Sleepin's, Huh? Why you got all da windows blocked?" One of the orcs shivered, another rubbed goosebumps on his arm.

"'Cause my husband be away at war. I gots a boy I keeps safe."

A tall orc, obviously in charge, smacked her across her face. "You lyin' bitch! Wer you hide da cloak?"

The witch cried ever so fearfully in a state of forced confusion, "Wut cloak? Why you here?"

18

"You not foolin's me. We gots you anda you gonna hang!"

She bit one of the orc's legs and jumped to her feet. In an instant, she grabbed some vials and spat in unintelligible utterances. The orcs were immediately disfigured. She turned and splashed liquid through the doorway, covering a few more orcs just outside. They were her next victims.

She screamed as she leaped from within and tossed beakers at other orcs' feet. Some were inflicted, but others weren't, and they rushed her. They fought to grab her wild, thrashing body, her eyes rolling back in her head. She bit and clawed anything that touched her in a furious and desperate frenzy. Like a cornered animal, she fought almost unrealistically to escape.

She physically mauled an orc that tried to hold her; she bit his throat and slashed him repeatedly with her dagger. In all, five orcs were cut and/or bitten while containing the witch. She screamed out, "Headhunta gonna killa you all!"

This gave pause to orcs familiar with the great warrior's name. Her ranting threats only sealed her fate; she was brutally hauled away to the village in the valley and her house was set afire.

Cracka crawled out of the burning building to see his mother being abducted. He assumed she was being taken because of him, because of his atrocities. He choked from the thick, black smoke that filled his lungs, unable to help her. He couldn't even call her name or say goodbye. He collapsed some eight feet from the blaze that leveled his refuge and he slipped into unconsciousness.

***

The two orcs fled south, trying to hide from the creeps that they envisioned following them. They made their way through the abandoned city, once grand and full of life. Sand and dust still hung in the air, even though the winds had died down and the storm had passed, giving a slightly better view to the buildings they passed.

Muddy stopped along an outcropping of stacked stone and brick to pick up one of millions of leaflets that Nuttybomb had ordered dropped on the planet several weeks before. He handed it to Ucktock and asked, "Wut dis?"

Ucktock studied the worn paper, turned it several times, and began to read out loud. "Da times of evil are nearin' a end. I am Wargod Nuttybomb and I am comin's to kill Darkster. You will be free fro' his ruthless ways. Join my army and help to defeat him!"

Muddy questioned, "Nuttybomb a god now?"

"I guess," came from his bewildered partner. Then, he admitted, "I not know him a god, either, but dat wut it say, so a must be true."

The travelers discussed Nuttybomb's accomplishments over the next few hours, his victories, and how he brought his world from chaos to a powerful, space-faring empire. They admitted that he should have died many times over, but always slipped from death's grips. Perhaps he was a god indeed.

With nightfall nearly upon them, Muddy got his partner's attention. "Ucktock, we close I tink. Looka." Muddy pointed to a row of single-story buildings to their south.

Ucktock rubbed his stomach and licked his lips. "I smell boarcakes."

The smell came from within one of the buildings they encountered. Ucktock led Muddy to the front door that emitted the glorious aromas from behind its threshold. His nose could find boarcakes from miles away.

Ucktock knocked on the door and waited. Inside the building, silence fell, a curiosity to the two travelers. He muttered, "Maybe dems hidin' da boarcakes so we no eat dems."

The boards that protected the windows spread and large gun barrels poked through the openings revealed by their parting. The front door flung open as well bearing arms to defend against the orcs that startled the occupants.

Ucktock yelled, "Whoa, whoa! I come in peace."

A voice replied from within the dark confines of the makeshift fortress, "Who a you?"

"I Ucktock. I travel far lookin' for udder orcs."

The concerned voice sought comfort, "You hurt?"

"Nope."

"What 'bout da udder orc wit' you?"

Ucktock repeated, "Nope."

The guns lowered, and the voice inside invited, "Come in, but hurry, hurry. It almost a dark now."

The two orcs outside looked at each other. "Ok?" They cautiously stepped inside, their eyes adjusting to the pitch-black interior.

They were met by a handful of orcs that weren't quite right. One blinked incessantly, another twitched. They crouched or hunched to stay as low as possible while they moved around, taking up positions around the newcomers. One spoke after they all settled down. "I Todwick, rula of dis house. Wut you want here?"

21

Ucktock explained, "I come fro' Hotta to tell all dat Warchief Nuttybomb..."

Muddy corrected, "Wargod Nuttybomb."

"Right, Wargod Nuttybomb is comin' to save all fro' Darkster."

Todwick appeared agitated and his tone confirmed it as he said, "Darkster? Him gone. Him no problem anymo'."

Ucktock implored, "Gone? Wer?"

"Dunno. But him kill dis world befo' he leave."

"Why?" Ucktock pried.

"How da hell should I know? We just left behind, tryin's a survive."

Ucktock admitted, "I see all da sand and lika no animals fo' food. Must be hard a live here now."

Todwick's irritability grew. "Sand or no sand, don't matta. It da creeps dat da real problem."

Ucktock got goosebumps. "Ya, I saw some near da old city at da semetery."

"Some? You lucky you only see some. Anda da city? Stay away fro' dat place. Der be thousands a creeps der."

Ucktock found himself chuckling. "Thousands?"

"It not funny. You stupid or sumptin'?"

"I don't tink so. Why?" Ucktock asked.

Todwick couldn't believe he had to elaborate to the noobs that interrupted his dinner. He snarled, "'Cause da creeps is serious, and most orcs were killed in da city fro' dems. Den, dems became creeps, too. It not funny."

Ucktock argued, "But why I not see lots a creeps in da city den?"

"Dems mostly come out a' nighttime. Dat's why."

Muddy turned to Ucktock and pleaded, "We should travel a' daytime den."

Todwick scoffed, "You still gonna travel afta wut I tells you?"

Ucktock stated, "A course. We troops anda we follow Wargod Nuttybomb. He will keepa us safe."

"Can he stop da creeps?"

"Yup. I tink so. He comin' to kill Darkster anda we have udder orcs dat can help da creeps back to da udder side if he too busy."

Todwick became wild; the other occupants threw themselves to the ground and began to shake. He asked as quietly as he could, "You hear dat?"

Ucktock, unaware of the levity of the situation spoke loudly, "Nope."

Todwick grabbed Ucktock and pulled him to the floor as he cried, "Shhhhhh! Dems will hear you."

Ucktock whispered, "Who?"

Between gulps, Todwick cried, "Creeps."

"Maybe dems comin' fo' da boarcakes."

A hammer seemed to hit Todwick between the eyes. He jumped to his feet and scrambled to the fireplace sighing, "Oh no, da boarcakes. I fogots dem still cookin's and makin' a smell. Creeps don't want dems, but dems will come here 'cause dems know we cookin's. We in trouble now."

Muddy sounded off, "So? We can just fight dems."

"Shhhhhh!" came from the fearful Todwick. "No, we can't justa fight dems. Get down anda shutta up."

Ucktock and Muddy went along with Todwick, even though they couldn't fathom some creeps being so dangerous. Their senses began to confirm creeps approaching in large numbers. Although all creeps

23

smelled of the same dying tissue, they each had some distinct odors they carried with them. The orcs' noses differentiated dozens of unique scents, each belonging to a creep. Fifty or more were encroaching upon the little house.

Childhood stories told of creeps as fairytale-like snippets; sometimes even used as bedtime stories. The harsh reality of the creeps' capabilities was glossed over, or all together omitted to soothe children. However, modern stories from within the military shed some light on the true nature of these tortured souls. Ucktock knew orcs were prone to embellish, so he assumed the truth to be somewhere between what he recently heard and lore from the past. He couldn't have been more wrong!

Deafening pounding erupted around the house, creeps throwing their bodies against the doors, windows, and even block walls. Blood curdling screams cut through the darkness, their shrillness biting into the weary souls that awaited their fate. Indigenous orcs in the building hunkered down in hopes of the impending onslaught to simply disappear; they hid behind furniture and trembled.

Ucktock jumped to one side of a window when he saw the wood barricade crack and splinter. Muddy followed, briefly guarding the opposite side of the barricade until he witnessed the front door coming apart. He left Ucktock and readied himself to deal with the threat at the entrance.

A board was ripped away from the front door and rotten bodies fought to gain access to the interior of the building. Muddy fired into the crack where wood was missing and hit several creeps. He was only delaying the inevitable as creep after creep pushed forward, their collective weight snapping the thick boards that sought to keep them out.

Screams were louder than ever as the tortured souls battered every area of the building, each weakness giving way to the overwhelming strength of the undead. Bullet after bullet tore the creeps apart, but they kept coming; several making their way inside the front door. Another burst through a window, his power and the unbelievable speed at which he moved taking the orcs by surprise.

Unfortunately, the smell of boarcakes led several dozen creeps to their prey. Their horrid screams and the noise from guns prompted many more to gather. They were relentless in their maddening intrusion, for they knew not any comfort; they were devoid of thought. They were simply driven by an empty promise of salvation if they killed...and so they did. Now, they numbered in the hundreds.

Five creeps bolted through the front door. Muddy shot two and Todwick managed to catch another, but two were on Muddy in an instant. He fell backward, pulling his sword as he hit the floor. He swung wildly; unimaginable fear crippled his rational thoughts as he decapitated a creep. The other one bit down on his left bicep and shook its head violently, tearing flesh from bone. He screamed in pain.

Ucktock left the window and ripped his sword through the creep's skull, severing half of it from the spine that previously supported it. He yelled out, "Stop shooting," as he realized the noise of the guns was probably drawing too much attention. He begged,

"Use blades!" He turned just in time to catch two more creeps as they pushed through the front door's opening.

The smell of Muddy's fresh blood increased the already ferocious frenzy. Like a drop of blood in a sea of sharks, it aroused the monsters and enhanced their cravings. The frame to the front door collapsed, and with it, a fairly large opening was created as stone and blocks exploded into the house. A window at the back of the house was now large enough for creeps to force their way in as well.

The orcs fought, not only the physical bodies that attacked them, but the psychological horrors that haunted each one. Ucktock's hair was up on his arms and the back of his neck. He was hypersensitive to the possibility of dying and becoming a creep. He trembled as he swung his sword.

Muddy was losing blood fast. He was all too aware of succumbing to unconsciousness and possibly passing away. He fought with a heightened fear that quickened his strikes, brought reality to the forefront, and slowed the battle around him.

Todwick fought to keep nausea from inhibiting his actions. The putrid smell of death assaulted his nostrils and plagued his throat, pushing food up and into his mouth. He swallowed time and again to clear his airways.

The other orcs dealt with much the same. The sight of dead, dismembered orcs, their lifeless eyes, and the ferocity of their attacks were daunting to say the least. The creeps' haunting screams were horrifying to the untrained occupants that fought for survival. They fought as best they could against the nightmares that swarmed them.

A young orc was distracted by the sheer number of creeps that were busting into the place. A momentary lapse cost him an arm...and then...his life as the mob tore into him. A nearby friend tried to save him, but he was ripped apart in seconds, far too quick for rescue.

The volume of bodies that was piling up had actually begun to cause a bottleneck. The front doorway was littered with them and the creeps beyond raged against their fallen, but to no avail. One of the windows became blocked as well. This brief respite gave the orcs a chance to regroup and better block the other areas that hadn't faltered yet.

The orcs fought furiously, dropping the creeps that were stuck in the clogged openings. They struck at will, each creep they stopped further inhibiting those behind from entering. Not only did the creeps block the entrance to the building, but less of them pushing inward reduced the weight that had been buckling the walls. Perhaps the battered orcs stemmed the tide.

Two
Marshil's Plague

The flames died down days ago and the smoke disappeared, leaving a slow, smoldering frame of what was. The house was gone, save for some low-lying blocks that marked the perimeter and a mound of soot. Everything else was eviscerated.

Headhunta raced to the spot his dwelling once stood and hollered for his wife and child, desperately seeking an audible response to confirm their survival. He picked up cries from his boy, who was hiding in the hedges nearby. "Cracka," he called out.

The troubled child didn't run to his father as one might expect. Instead, he methodically wiped his eyes and walked to Headhunta in a slow, deliberate manner. He stopped in front of his father and looked up.

Headhunta questioned, "Where Mama?"

"What you care? You nevva here wit' her."

"Where she be?"

Cracka was in defiant silence.

Headhunta ordered, "Tell me where she be, boy."

Cracka answered through gritted teeth, "Dems took her." Tears streamed down his face.

Headhunta's panic was immediately accompanied by anger. "Who? Who took her?"

Cracka wailed, "Da valley orcs."

Headhunta's eyes widened, the levity of the situation ringing between his ears. "When?

"Lika ten days ago."

Headhunta surveyed the damage for several minutes as he mumbled to himself, "Ten days longa

28

time. She prolly dead. Why dems taka her? Wut she do?" He turned to Cracka and commanded, "Stay here lika you did. I be back tonight."

He left the boy again to go off and fight, but for the first time, Cracka understood why. His dad was gonna try to save his Mama. If it was too late and she was dead, then his dad would enact revenge like the valley orcs had never known.

Headhunta hid among the growth that covered everything on the town's outskirts. The hot, wet climate allowed every kind of thorny vine to take root and they did. He used a hardy vine to climb into a treetop where he observed the valley orcs' movements throughout the day. To his surprise, there were a dozen orcs that had been stricken by disease or something crippling enough to mangle their bodies. He thought, *Did my wife do dis*?.

As night fell, he moved. He did so with minimal sound and virtually no effort. Hiding and striking the enemy while being unseen was his forte, even though it was generally frowned upon by orcs. Most chose a head-on fight.

His heart sped up when he found one of his wife's shoes in the center of town. They had her alright, but what did they do with her?

He quietly approached the first house to his right and evaluated the best way to enter, do what he wanted, and leave without being seen or heard. He already knew to enter in the rear of the house as he observed the occupants all day. He was in and out in minutes, having slain the two adults that lived there.

The next dwelling was similar. However, this time he eliminated a mother before killing two children. He had no remorse for what he had done and what he was still about to do. Not only did he harbor feelings of hatred for the orcs that abducted his wife, but he was desensitized by years of war; there wasn't anything he hadn't bore witness to.

Over the next hour, he killed every orc that lived on the main road. He had two accidental encounters with individuals who ventured out to use outhouses, but they too were eradicated without incident. The only time he gave pause was to study the words *Witch* that had been painted on a sign in the center of town along with his wife's bloody garments that were tossed in the street like rags. He became enraged.

Each dwelling he entered, he killed silently like the night itself and checked for signs of his wife. But she couldn't be found over the next four hours. Fully confident that all residents had been handled appropriately, Headhunta wandered into the graveyard to see if he could uncover any hints there. But to his disappointment, none were discovered.

He backtracked into town to find the place where corpses would have been prepared for burial. It only took fifteen minutes to find it and begin looking around. The building wasn't remarkable in any way and it didn't stand out from the other structures. However, once inside, he found rickety stairs that led to a basement.

His hand rubbed the cool stone walls as he decreased in elevation into the damp cellar. His mind took note of the drop in temperature and registered as the type of place where bodies would be processed. While his nose led him through the misty series of rooms, his face led him to a string that hung from the ceiling. More precisely, it was to a drop light that he pulled to light the dank catacomb. And there she was.

He closed his eyes before traversing across the cold, hard floor to where the body lay. It was already decayed beyond recognition and the horrific odor that emitted from it was choking. He went to it to search for any recognizable markings to let him know if it was indeed her.

The female had long dark hair like hers, but that wasn't enough to verify who it was. Her finger nails were long and her height, although difficult to determine with certainty, was also a match.

Headhunta hoped to find some marking that would clearly reveal that this was a valley orc and not his wife. He looked closely at her feet and worked his way upward, scanning her legs and torso. He examined each arm and came to her neck, and then, he found it.

A leather string had untied from around her neck and slid under her head. Tied to the string was a carnidawg tooth. Headhunta had fashioned this piece of jewelry himself as a gift to his wife. He cut the leather and ran it through the tooth he drilled.

A varied plethora of emotions filled the distraught husband as he slammed the table with his fists. He assumed was his wife, his mate, and the mother of his only child. Until recently, they had shared great experiences together. His constantly being away precipitated tension and he even found himself leaving so he wouldn't have to deal with her at times. Her witchcraft was all she concerned herself with before her death and it had been tiring. But he also recognized that it was he who introduced her to dark magic. He stood there, numb and shocked, partially blaming himself for her demise.

***

Nuttybomb laid on his bed, just waking from the best sleep he had in seven months. He rubbed his eyes and sat up. He stumbled to the bathroom as he yawned. Then, he coughed to clear his throat. He smiled when he saw Uhra standing at the doorway to the bathroom beyond, but soon saw concern on her face. "Wut wrong?"

She gasped and held her mouth. She pointed to an area just below Nutty's head. She lacked words, emotion freezing her mouth, concern gripping her brain.

Nutty looked down and realized he had spat a pile of blood all over his bare chest and stomach. His eyebrows dropped over his nose, causing a ridge and wrinkles that confirmed his concern as well. He coughed again as some fluid found its way into his airway. A large spray of red and green liquid erupted from his mouth and ran down his chin, expanding coverage on his upper torso and surrounding areas of the floor.

Uhra found the words, "Nutty, wut wrong wit' you?"

Nutty reasoned, partially lying to himself and to his wife, "Dunno. But it no hurt, so I ok."

"You gotta go to da doc, Nutty."

A reluctant and proud orc agreed, "Ya, I go tomorrow, I guess," not showing worry over the bloody incident.

Uhra wasn't satisfied, "No, get you a butt up and go now."

Nutty sighed and obliged, "Fine." He urinated, washed up, and waited for the doc to arrive that Uhra called. He walked passed the rooms where his kids slept and smiled. He hadn't seen them in seven months and was elated that he was so lucky to have them. He only wished he had more time to spend with them, but as the leader of Hotta, he had to protect them. That meant going wherever war brought him.

Nutty briefly thought about war and decided to summon Moonoak, his spiritual mentor. The two had become good friends and trusted each other without question. They had several short conversations over the last seven months while Nutty was off planet, but now it was time to discuss Darkster in detail and in person. Moonoak was scheduled to arrive later in the evening, a good while after the doc to allow ample of time for both appointments.

A quick call was made to Nutty's generals and admirals to receive updates; there was nothing remarkable reported. Nutty asked the general in charge of Marshil if he had any information yet from the scouts that were sent to her surface. Again, nothing worth noting was forwarded.

Doc Cutstick arrived much sooner than Nutty anticipated. Perhaps Uhra had rushed the doctor, or perhaps he simply understood the importance of tending to the leader of millions on multiple worlds without hesitation. Either way, he was invited into the bedroom where he began examining Nutty. He began listening to his chief's heart and lungs. He sighed, "Hmm," several times as he moved a stethoscope from side to side.

Uhra quizzed, "Hmm, wut?"

Doc Cutstick waved his hand as he tried to hear clearly. "Please, Mrs. Bomb. One minute. I sorry, but I needs to hear."

If Nuttybomb wasn't so understanding, the doc would have been eaten alive right there and then for showing even the slightest bit of disrespect to a warchief's wife. But Nutty understood and actually respected Cutstick for his bold statement and determination to do the right thing, which in this case was to evaluate Nutty, regardless of interference. The fact that the interference came from Nutty's wife was inconsequential. The doc understood that the patient's health came first. However, Doc Cutstick was on a short leash.

After a minute or so, Cutstick addressed Uhra. "I apolgy, Uhra. I hear sum stuff dat concern me."

Uhra impatiently asked, "Wut stuff?"

Cutstick looked from Uhra to Nutty and back, making sure to show respect by speaking to both. "I tink you gots holes in a lung. Maybe sumptin' in yer lung, but dunno. Need to take pictures."

Uhra inquired, "Dat were da blood come fro'?"

"Ya, prolly. But der be mo'. Nutty heart gots problems."

"Wut problems?"

"Dunno. Need pictures fo' dat, too."

Nutty argued, "But der no time for dat, Doc. I gots to go to Marshil."

Cutstick warned, "Please, shutta up and open yer mouth." He shoved a thermometer in Nutty's mouth as he went to disagree with wasting time to have scans of his heart and lungs. Then, he turned to Uhra and

34

pleaded, "Maybe he no listen to me, but you must have him do pictures."

Uhra asked, "You tink it serious, Doc?"

"It might be. Him lung bleeding...and pretty bad, too. One sec." With that, Cutstick removed the thermometer and found it to his disliking. "Gots a feva. Gots a infection."

Nutty hastened, "I fine."

Cutstick refuted, "I let you know if you fine. How long you sweat lika dis?"

"Dunno. Maybe since fight wit' humans. Lika three or four months."

"Feva only come to orcs who got da feva, a bad sick...or when der be a real bad infection."

Uhra pleaded with her husband, "Nutty, you gots to take some time to get checked."

Cutstick added, "Might be poison in yer body, too."

Nutty disagreed, "I no eat or drink poison."

"No, yer body might have stuff in it lika bullets or stuff lika dat. Dems could poison you. You got newer scars near yer heart. Bullets?"

"Yup," Nutty divulged.

Cutstick pressed, "Did docs take bullets out?"

Nutty elaborated, "No. Dems said too dangerous."

"Why?"

"Cus da bullets stuck in my heart."

Cutstick shook his head in some disbelief and obvious disgust. "Any udder bullets dat be in yer body?"

Nutty felt a little stupid as he made excuses, "Ya, but der be no time to get dems out or dems too dangerous to remove."

"How many bullets you still gots in you?"

"Dunno. Ten? Maybe twenty?"

Uhra gasped, "Oh my gods, Nutty."

Nutty tried to explain, "It not lika you can see doc when you in a battle, Uhra. Sumptimes, I just wrap up da hole or stitch it and continue da fightin'."

Uhra put her foot down as she crossed her arms. "Well, dis time you gonna see a doc."

Nutty tried to make light of the situation with, "I seein' doc right now." He forced a stupid looking grin, hoping to elicit a favorable response from his wife. Some missing teeth added to the perception that his whole body had been suffering from lack of care.

Uhra looked away from her belligerent husband and asked, "Doc, can Nuttybomb have pictures now?"

"No, but I can have dems set up fo' tomorrow mornin'. Den, I can looka dem and see Nuttybomb tomorrow night. We can talk den."

Uhra concurred, "Ok. Dat fine."

Cutstick asked his leader, "Anyting hurt, Chief?"

Uhra answered for Nuttybomb, "Ya, evvyting."

Nuttybomb felt like he was being castrated by his wife and her accomplice at this point. Still, he sat there quietly and waited for Doc Cutstick to leave before he said anything to Uhra – if he said anything at all.

Cutstick wrapped up the examination with, "Ok. See you in da mornin' at my office." Then, he left.

Nuttybomb decided to address Uhra without upsetting her, although he didn't really know how. He asked her, "Why you not let me talk and worry 'bout my own body?"

Uhra explained, "I nevva hear you complain or ask fo' help. Do you worry 'bout yer body?"

36

"Well, ya. Sorta."

"Sorta?" Uhra questioned as she folded her arms and tapped a foot on the floor.

Nutty justified, "I do ok, so I just keep goin'. I said I fine."

"But wut if you not fine? Wut if dis stuff kill you? Den, der be no warchief – and der be no husband to me and dad to da kids. Dat not important to you?"

"You know it important to me."

Uhra pried, "Den, when was you gonna go to a doc?"

Nutty sighed. "Dunno." He really had no intention of seeking medical help. He didn't like being told what to do or have decisions made for him. He was the warchief for gods' sake. It was embarrassing for his wife to fight his battles for him. "It embarrass me when you talk fo' me."

Uhra understood. "I sorry, Nutty, but maybe you should talk fo' yerself den."

He didn't like it, but she had a point. Deep down inside, he liked her caring for him; her speaking up on his behalf somehow validated how tough he really was. In the eyes of his troops and his citizens, he was a legend. He chuckled to himself as he thought the ramblings of an overprotective wife wasn't him giving in to medical attention. He was just appeasing her. He reasoned that, in this case, it was okay for Uhra and the doc to push him a bit. He softened and said, "Uhra, I know you worried. Sumptimes, I keep pushin' to save evvyone and evvyting. You right."

"I know." She chuckled.

***

Why Marshil wasn't as warm and wet as reported was a bit of a mystery. Instead, it was cool and windy with little vegetation. Life had taken a turn on the planet due to conditions similar to a nuclear winter. But why?

The newcomers from Hotta were too busy fighting for their lives to give the planet's strange climate much interest and they had no time to think about how the creeps came into existence. If they survived the onslaught, Ucktock and Muddy might have time later to surmise the hows and whys, not to mention whether or not Darkster actually left the world. But first thing was first.

Ucktock swung his deadly blade over his head in a downward motion, struggling against the limited height of the ceiling. Adjustments were made quickly in these close quarters, otherwise survival would have been short. He swung on an angled arc, severing a creep's arm and spinning, his momentum bringing him full circle. He swung upward in the same reverse angle and removed the other arm. A final thrust through the creep's neck brought just one of several hundred attackers to the floor.

Part of the ceiling fell through, not by any fault of high swinging blades, but by sheer weight. Creeps were everywhere, and with them, the dust from dead tissue filled the air and lungs of the orcs! Two dozen creeps fell awkwardly, piling on top of each other as they slipped between a nine-foot hole as the roof gave way toward the front of the house.

Muddy was pinned. He screamed in terror as he was confined by the vile mass that dropped abruptly upon him. Then, he screamed in pain. A deep bite into his leg and another in his shoulder brought home the reality of the situation. He yearned for fresh air and open lungs to welcome it.

The other orcs, led by Ucktock, used their swords to kill and their free hands to pull the writhing dead off their trapped brother. Each cut by a blade threw more dust, like smoke from a pipe into the eyes of those around them. A few more creeps fell from the opening to the floor. Eight on top of the pile ravaged the orcs as they sprang into helter-skelter hunger. They were free to wreak havoc!

Todwick was rushed by a few. He sidestepped the first one and brought his sword to bear, but another leaped onto his side and buried its gnarly teeth deep into his throat. He dropped his sword and pulled the creep from its bloody intentions, but another grabbed his waist and dug its mangled jaws into the pained orc's abdomen. He screamed out in agony.

Two indigenous orcs came to Todwick's aid, beheading the busy creeps that were too occupied to even notice while fighting off attacks upon them. Todwick lay on the floor, conflicted between holding in his intestines or stopping the seemingly endless blood flow that pumped out of his throat in time with his overworked heartbeat. He crawled on his back, into a corner as the desperate fight continued in front of him.

Muddy wasn't faring any better. Even while the creeps that bit him were confined, they clung to any body part available to them and ate like wild dawgs that hadn't eaten in weeks. They shook their heads violently, removing flesh from bone.

Ucktock was fighting to remove the layers of undead from his friend by himself while the other orcs helped Todwick. Finally, they all engaged the creeps that fell into the room. It was now that Ucktock wished he knew what drew the creeps to the orcs for he needed a plan to end the melee before he and the other orcs were all dead. Did they have the same senses that orcs had while alive? Some were so badly decayed that they didn't have noses, ears, or eyes. Yet they searched and attacked without handicap.

He wondered if the screams of his fallen or the scent of their blood brought other creeps from miles around. He just didn't know. However, he did know that he would have to come up with answers, and quick. Instinctively, he fought on, displacing any other thoughts from his mind. He grimaced as a creep ripped its wretched claws across his chest before falling upon his blade.

The smell of rot was nauseating. More and more death had added to the already unconscionable and debilitating odor. Gray powder, mixed with green and yellow, permeated everything; the once-live flesh was reduced to a fine dust that found its way into the smallest openings. Like water seeking its own level, so too did the rotted flesh of the undead. It tasted like poison on the tongues of the queasy orcs.

The pile of creeps tipped unevenly, falling toward one of Todwick's house mates. The orc stumbled, just long enough to drop his sword while gaining his balance. It was an act of defense, not ever thought out which was better – to fall and stand back up or to lower his blade. Nobody would ever know if it would have been better to fall and recover; he was ripped apart in an instant as several invaders overwhelmed his staggering and defenseless body.

Muddy, now able to move as the weight shifted above him, bore his blade into the top of a creep that had ravaged his other shoulder. He quickly sat up and decapitated the one that severely wounded his thigh. He couldn't stand up, but got to his knees and resumed the job of living. He knocked two creeps from their feet and cut through them like a knife through hot butter.

Ucktock jumped next his partner and fought alongside him. Within several minutes, the influx of creeps falling from the roof halted. More pushed through a window and the front door, but their bottlenecking slowed their advance enough to handle their reduced numbers as they entered the house.

It took nearly an hour to eliminate the last creeps. There was so little room to navigate over the heap of bodies that stacked to the ceiling in spots. The orcs searched for each other, whispering just feet from their comrades. They stepped upon and over the dead and sometimes still twitching creeps, eventually ending up in the corner where Todwick was.

The chore of stopping the heavy bleeding of Todwick and Muddy was underway. The two finally collapsed and let their guards down as high levels of adrenaline and endorphins diminished in their bloodstreams. Todwick, thankfully, lost consciousness while being stitched up and put back together. Muddy wasn't so lucky. He bit down on his gun barrel to avoid making loud noises while Ucktock stitched his shoulder. Nothing could be done to repair his leg without proper medical tools and knowledge. Ucktock repaired one artery and simply packed the missing muscle and skin with cloth and wrapped it up; it was all he could do.

Ucktock whispered to the remaining orcs, "Any udder orcs live nearby?"

Todwick's housemate looked up from the friend he attended to and responded, "No. Lika fifteen miles south, I tink."

"How many orcs der?"

"Not many. Most be dead."

Ucktock urged, "We should go der and be stronger."

The orc snarled. "You crazy! We get dead if we try."

"I might be crazy, but creeps gonna find out dat der be holes in da front door, da windows, and da roof. It not safe here."

"We no move at night. It mo' dangerous dan to stay till mornin'."

Ucktock didn't like sitting and waiting to be hunted, but maybe the other orc was right. He offered, "Only three a us can fight now. I hopa you right."

"Me too."

***

"Da child killed all my chicklens!" the old orc complained.

Headhunta laughed. "It good dems only chicklens. Betta dat no orcs die."

The old orc was aghast. The carcasses wouldn't last long in the oppressive heat on Hotta. He could eat a couple of them, but the others were all wasted. He wanted reparation for his losses, but he also knew that Headhunta was a killer, and a vicious one at that. He had been an elite guard for the warchief, and as such, had developed skills that were far beyond the average orc. "You gots any chicklens you could gimme fo' my loss? I just askin'."

Headhunta gritted his teeth, "No. I not in da chicklen business." He turned and walked away. He grabbed his son by his ear and tugged him all the way home.

When they arrived at their little hut, Headhunta prodded, "Why you kill da chicklens, boy?"

The boy shrugged his shoulders.

"I ask one mo' time. Why you kill da chicklens?"

The boy shrugged his shoulders again, but this time he was met with his father's backhand.

Headhunta demanded, "Tell me, now!"

"Dems just stupid chicklens. Mama died and she not a stupid chicklen."

"Boy, stop maka trouble fo' youself. I gonna be gone fo' ten moons, so I can get da bastids dat taked her. You stay outta trouble. Got it?"

The contemptuous child agreed, "Ok." He crossed his arms and pouted.

Headhunta grabbed his things and left without so much as a goodbye.

The boy didn't understand the war that took his mother from him. Her inability to have other children before her death left him without siblings, further complicating his ability to socialize. So, here he was- six years old, alone and troubled. He wanted to enact revenge on anyone and anything he could. At the very least, he was crying out for attention – something that would elude him.

That's the way it was back then. Darkster thought about the loss of his mother and that day he slaughtered the chicklens. Thirteen chicklens weren't compensation for his mother, far from it. He remembered disliking the old orc on that day too. The old bastard had the audacity to ask for replacement chicklens.

Because of that old bastard, Cracka had to stay in his hut while his father went off to war. He hated that old orc!

***

"Dis da mostest stupidest assignment I evva beed on," Quicklip scowled.

Nubbs offered, "Maybe you should drink lika me." He pulled a flask of shlogger from a pocket in his jacket and extended it to his friend.

"Ya, I keep gettin' dese jobs and I be a drunk. Anda you stupids fo' volunteering fo' it."

"I not drink 'nuff to get drunk. Just 'nuff to take da edge off fo' me. Anda I not stupids. I beed promised shlogger fo' doin' dis," Nubbs admitted.

Quicklip asked, "Not stupids? You did dis fo' shlogger?"

Nubbs admitted, "Well, I not know it be lika dis."

"You not da dumbest orc on da planet, but you betta hope he don't die."

The two walked northward, having already covered two hundred miles, but not recognizing any landmarks that their reports indicated they should have come across. It was becoming dark now. Quicklip asked, "Dis maka any sense to you?"

"Nope. It all looka da same. It all just sand and wind."

"Right? I tought it be warmer."

Nubbs added, "Anda it stinks on dis planet, too."

44

Quicklip had tried to place the smell for the last three days. It was disgusting, but vaguely familiar. Without any provocation, his mind drifted to a fight that he was in several years before. It was a battle that he, Nuttybomb, and the other elite guards were in against Darkster and his father, Headhunter. That was a fight of fights. The smell registered in his brain. "Hey, I know da smell."

"What smell?"

"What we just talkin' about, you boob! Dis planet smells."

Nubbs raised his flask and smiled, "Oh ya. What it smell like?"

Quicklip replied, "Dat fight with Darkster, remember?"

"Wait...Darkster smell lika dis?"

"No, da creeps did," Quicklip snapped as he smacked Nubbs' shoulder.

Nubbs sniffed the air as he trudged on. "Ya. Ya, dat wut it smell like."

Quicklip was thinking out loud as he spoke, "Why evvyting smell lika creeps?"

"Beats me," Nubbs replied without giving much thought.

The memory banks in Quicklip's brain went into overdrive. "Dat fight wit' Darkster was bad. Biggabomb had da bad lungs, Guthrak was cut real bad, Gunza too; all a us was hurt real bad. Thunda died soon afta dat."

Nubbs apologized, "He was you a good friend. I sorry."

"Ya. Him was so stupid. It was great talkin' wit' him and maka him mad. I used to pick on his mama."

"Wut did you say?"

Quicklip said with a smile, "Oh, just yo' mama jokes. Lika, yo' mama so oogly, her portraits hang demselves."

Nubbs smiled.

"Or yo' mama so hairy dat you got rugburn wen you wus born." Quicklip smiled before falling silent in thought.

Nubbs waited for Quicklip to say more, but upon nothing being spoken, Nubbs changed the subject. "Ok, but why it smell on dis planet lika dat?"

The two orcs came to a ridge and looked down into a valley below. The sight was unbelievable. Thousands of creeps wandered aimlessly, stuck in between the cliffs that kept them from escaping.

Quicklip gulped as he pointed to the unsightly scene. "Dat why."

Three
The Troubled Boy

Once again, Cracka wandered into trouble just after dark, hoping not to be seen by the old orc. He snuck around the vacant chicklen coop and came upon a barn.

He peered through the slats that gave partial protection to the animals inside from the harsh storms that struck every day during the wet season. He leaned against one of the creaky boards and looked around to make sure no one saw him. He looked up as well, not really noticing the rusty, metal roof that hung above him. He slowly pushed one of the doors open and entered this home of livestock.

Once inside, he partially emptied a container he brought with him, dousing as much of the straw that laid on the floor as he could cover and the old, tinderbox posts that framed the walls. The top layers of straw were dry, perfect for what he had planned. For good measure, he sprinkled some on the animals, too; he couldn't hurt the old orc enough.

He sparked a small flame near the barn door and hurried to the main house. He worked along the perimeter of the dwelling- carefully, but quickly-pouring the last of the fuel he had with him. This time, he lit the house in full, not worrying about the old orc coming out to intercept him at the barn as he did just seconds before.

The boy ran for cover behind the property and stayed close enough to hear what was transpiring. He looked on. As animals screamed from the barn, so too did the old orc as fire covered his house. Both structures were ablaze, all flammable items igniting from the heat that erupted in mere minutes.

The old orc would never insult the boy or his father again. Furthermore, he would never ask for chicklens as repayment for those lost. He would only hear his animals, and then himself, in their last few minutes.

The troubled child cursed the old orc and snickered under his breath. It wasn't enough to bring his mother back, only the villagers from the valley could do that...if she was even alive, but it was revenge. He sought to make things right however he could. Revenge was the only way he could think of, regardless of who did what to his mother. That was inconsequential. He needed to relieve stress and the lack of love that plagued him.

He raced home to his parent-less dwelling; back roads and overgrown paths were the ways he used to avoid being seen. Cracka hid, like his dad, among the shadows. He dashed in spurts, dropping to his belly when he heard voices or saw villagers that scrambled around the fiery commotion.

His temples were pounding, his heart was racing, his lungs were burning, but he made it to where his home used to be without being caught. He hid under makeshift blocks that previously supported the house for protection.

He began to think about what he did and how he escaped. Mostly, he thought about his mama. Revenge was his!

It was brief relief. Cracka heard the approach of the remaining villagers and local farmers. He spotted the flickering of lit torches in the distance. He decided to move on.

***

Morning light began to shine as a deep red hue appeared along the top of the interior walls. The opening in the roof helped dissipate the darkness that encompassed the beleaguered orcs the previous night. But now, the light danced, and along with it, hope that came with the new day.

Todwick wasn't doing well. His wounds needed medical attention from trained medical technicians, not those of battle-fatigued soldiers. Docs with surgical equipment were necessary for him to survive and it was apparent. The bandages that wrapped his wounds were soaked in blood and some sort of green, mucus-like scum. He began to smell like the creeps that infected him the evening before.

Muddy had regained some strength, although he was still hobbled by his wounds. He asked, "We gonna barricade dis place again tonight or we gonna travel?"

One of the indigenous orcs stated, "I stayin's here."

Another concurred, "Me, too. I not leavin' Todwick and he can't travel."

Ucktock pleaded, "It betta if we all go. I have orders a go. We can go now dat it light out. We be ok."

The orcs refused. One sat at Todwick's side while the other pushed through the pile of creeps and began gathering wood to block the openings before the next night.

Muddy urged, "We shoulda go, Uck. I can walk."

Ucktock smiled. Being the consummate warrior, he relished being partners with an orc who would carry on in the face of adversity. He respected Muddy like never before. "C'mon, my friend. Letta us go den." He helped Muddy to his feet, said his farewells to those he respected less, and left the broken building.

Muddy limped a whole mile before Ucktock offered to help him. He reluctantly gave in to an arm that wrapped around his back and under his arm that took some weight off his bad leg. He joked, "Carry me, Mama."

Ucktock quipped, "Screwa you!"

The hobbled orc retorted, "You lika dat. How 'bout a piggy back?"

Ucktock laughed. "I don't tink so. But boarcakes or any kinda piggy sounda good. Dis planet gots no damn food. Now, shutta up. We gots longa way to go."

"Wer we headed?"

Ucktock pointed in the general direction they were heading and joked, "Dat way."

Muddy didn't understand the joke and asked, "How far?"

Ucktock was so happy with himself and proudly stated, "Til we gets der."

"Wer?"

"Der."

Muddy was befuddled. "Wer is der?"

"Dat way."

Muddy growled, "You too much. Not can gimme a simple answer."

Ucktock scoffed, "I tought it gots no simpler dan dat." He busted a gut as the two took each labored step through the wasteland that surrounded them and kissed the horizon.

Muddy realized he was being played. It took a minute, but he finally laughed, well after Ucktock. His brain just needed time to catch up with the information it struggled to process. And when it did, he was hysterical.

Ucktock questioned, "Wut da hell so funny?"

Muddy pointed and squeaked, "Der."

Ucktock asked, "Wer?"

Muddy blasted, "Dat way!" He dropped to the ground and held his stomach as laughter buckled him.

"Shutta up," came from Ucktock once he understood the joke was reversed on him. "You can walk da rest a da way by yerself."

"Wer?"

Ucktock smiled and said, "Der."

***

Moonoak and his followers were closing in on the troubled boy, as were a group of angry and well-armed townsmen. They had gathered to bring in the one responsible for the fires that shattered their lives. The boy was the culprit, and now, they were close to capturing him. Upon stopping at a valley below the hiding boy, the shaman turned to his tribe and instructed, "You stay here. I talk to da boy alone."

The angry mob waved torches and weapons in the air, their voices crying out for justice. They couldn't bring back their loved ones, nor could they erect their burnt dwellings, lost to the sinister child in flames, even by killing him. Still, they wanted to get their hands on him, no matter what. Eventual calm found them through the words of their spiritual leader. "He can't get away ova mountains. Hims has to come dis way. Be ready fo him."

51

With that, Moonoak made his way through the brush and over a ledge. The short climb only tasked him for a minute or two. He surveyed the somewhat familiar landscape in search of hiding spots, lowering his hood to see better. Another minute of walking, and his eyes led him to an opening in the rocks, a hole to a small cave within. He cautiously crouched to gain access to the entrance and went inside.

The shaman brought to life a flame on the end of his staff with a snap of his fingers. The flickering light showed the boy, clinging to the wall like a goat on a cliff. There was nowhere for the child to fall, but he stuck to the rock anyway, maybe to hug the mother that never returned in kind. More importantly, there was nowhere for the boy to escape. The entrance to Moonoak's rear was also the only exit.

Moonoak asked, "Who are you?"

The boy didn't respond. His wild eyes pierced the darkness and elicited something in Moonoak's subconscious.

Moonoak felt the boy's fear. He felt his fear and he felt something else – an unease he couldn't fully understand. Did he feel the boy's fear and uneasiness, or did he feel his own? Maybe it was just the look in the boy's eyes; they were dark and cold, not the eyes you would expect from a scared child.

Nevertheless, a second attempt was made to elicit a response. "Why you hide here?"

But again, Cracka refused to reply. Instead, he snapped his fingers, imitating Moonoak's previous actions. At first, Moonoak didn't understand the boy's intentions. But soon it became apparent. Instantly, and to the surprise of both, flame burst onto Moonoak's

52

cloak, temporarily startling the older orc. While he removed the burning cloth, Cracka pushed passed him and into the light beyond, leaving the confines of the cave behind.

Moonoak, dropped the material, turned, and pursued, but the boy was gone. He hurried in the only direction the boy could have gone, back toward the place where the angry mob waited. He yelled, "Boy, it ok. I no hurt you." He stumbled when his robe got caught in some branches. His left knee took the brunt of his fall, but he was okay. However, he lost another few valuable seconds in reaching the boy before the mob did.

All the while, the shaman thought about the boy's powers. Orcs were notoriously mischievous as children, and could be downright barbarians as adults. Additionally, very few had the ability to summon fire, lightning, or any kind of potentially deadly force to use against others. Even Moonoak had his limitations, primarily using abilities of healing for good. A troubled boy with rare powers could be a massive problem for all later in life.

Moonoak rushed back to his followers, but...

They were all dead! Their guts had been opened and spread out across the landscape, littering the surroundings with their putrid bowels. Not only were the armed, angry orcs murdered, but the kind followers of the spiritual leader were, too. Who could have done such a thing? Not only was it overly vicious, even by orc standards, but highly unlikely such a great number of prepared hunters could have been so overwhelmed so quickly and quietly. Yet, here they laid.

Moonoak dropped his staff and fell to his knees. He prayed to his gods for the souls of the fallen to find peace in the realm beyond. He stayed for several days, burying the bodies and asking those who passed by to spread the word about what had happened.

Nearby orcs would later speak of a dark warrior who moved among the shadows lurking in the area. Rumors told of him freeing his wife from captivity and butchering the hundred or so orcs on the ridge. None of this was ever confirmed, nor was the fact that they left the area with their troubled child, never to be heard from again.

Years later, Moonoak, along with Nuttybomb, would link the killings to Headhunta, the witch as his wife, and Cracka as being Darkster.

***

Quicklip urged Nubbs to steer clear of the valley for obvious reasons; neither yearned to be food for the creeps they encountered. This lengthened their expedition by several hours, but the alternative wasn't really a true consideration. Their hearts raced in their chests.

Along the ridge they hugged, the shadows in the valley aiding the creeps in staying active. The orc's eyes rarely strayed from the incredible sight that tampered with their nerves. But soon, something else got their full attention.

They stumbled along a burial site, a cemetery of sorts, with rows of head stones. Quicklip questioned, "Why dems all dugged up?" referring to the deep crevasses, opened in front of each grave marker. The sand was littered with debris and bandages. Old, worn linens were also strewn about, full of holes and marked with encrusted, bodily fluids.

Nubbs cautiously came around to Quicklip's right and added, "Anda look. Da boxes dems all buried in are brokes."

"Wit' no bodies."

Nubbs eluded to the obvious as he said, "I tink we saw da bodies in da valley."

"Dis bad," Quicklip grumbled. "Dis real bad. Dems was dug up or did dems get out on der own?"

"Hey, der a town dis way, right?" Nubbs pointed northeast.

"Umm, ya. I tink."

Nubbs urged, "So letta us go der and find out what goin' on."

Quicklip agreed, "Good idea, fo' a drunk."

A wide smile was returned from the happy-go-lucky Nubbs. "I not a drunk. I just lika drink lots a shlogger.

"So, wut dat maka you den?

Nubbs answered, "Very happy." He laughed and hit his gut with an open hand.

Soon, happiness would end. They walked for fifteen minutes before entering the battered town by way of the main road. Something caused them to stop, though, before going into the heart of the forsaken refuge.

The hair on Quicklip's neck rose and he growled under his breath. His nose reached upward to take in the smells that changed his demeanor; he caught the whiff of danger in his nostrils. He looked around to find the cause of uneasiness.

Nubbs also sought to find the cause of his heightened heart rate and defensive oncoming that confused him as well. His eyes found movement in a building down the road. He whispered, "Ova der."

They crept toward the suspected area, clinging to the edges of buildings and hiding amidst the shadows cast by their silhouettes. Quicklip scoffed, "Quiet, you drunk. You gonna alerts dem to us comin'."

"I'm not sharin' my shlogger."

Quicklip insisted, "Shutta up."

Just then, several figures sprang from the building. "Stop or we shoot!" came from the orcs that confronted Quicklip and Nubbs.

Quicklip offered, "Don't shoot. We be friends."

"I don't got friends!" one of the figures claimed.

"You do now. My name a Quicklip and dis is Nubbs. We travel longa time, but only see creeps so far."

The agitated voice shot, "You no bring any wit' you, right?"

Quicklip relaxed his tone, "No. Saw thousands in da valley, tho."

The voice eased noticeably, "Come here. But if you try anyting, I will kills ya."

"Ok. I don't need anyting. Just tryin' to figure out why so many creeps and wer all da orcs are."

The two Hotta orcs met Tuff, the apparent leader of the small clan they encountered in the seemingly otherwise desolate town. They saw his lean, muscular physique, sunken eyes, and scarred skin. He was somewhat hunched as he walked, a sign of deformity or damage sustained in battle. They offered handshakes, but were denied reciprocation.

Tuff engaged, "I no trust you. Orcs come fro' all ova to steal our food anda supplies."

Quicklip reassured, "We don't need stuff. I already told you. We need a talk, den we go."

"Go? Go wer? Creeps will kill ya."

"We gots to." Quicklip exclaimed, and continued with the platitude, "We be orcs. Dats wut we do," and laughed. "We meetin' our udder soldias, too."

He quizzed, "You gots soldias?"

Quicklip offered, "Yup, but no army here yet. We just askin' questions to learn 'bout da creeps."

Tuff eased a bit, then looked intently as he asked, "You feel da creeps here?"

Quicklip quizzed, "Feel?"

"Ya. Dems hide in dese buildin's durin' da day. We hunts dem befo' nighttime."

"I tink I do feels dem. I didn't know why I want a fight sumptin'."

Tuff explained, "Yup. Dems know yer here, too. Come. We hunt dem."

Nubbs snapped, "Cool!"

Quicklip obliged, "Sure, we hunt wit' you if you want. But we come to tell you sumptin'."

Tuff asked, "Wut you tell me?"

"We come fro' planet Hotta. Wargod Nuttybomb comin's to save all orcs fro' Darkster."

Tuff pulled a leaflet from a pocket in his overalls. "You come wit' Wargod Nuttybomb?" He showed the leaflet that offered imminent salvation.

Quicklip explained, "He not here yet, but yup."

Tuff paused before he spoke. "I beed waitin' fo' him. We no hunt. Come inside. Der much a talk about."

Nubbs saluted, "I drink to dat."

Tuff smiled before revealing, "I has some mo' shlogger inside. Come; we talk."

"Yes!" Nubbs shouted.

Quicklip said sharply to Tuff, "Don't mind him. Da best part a him ran down his mudder's leg."

Nubbs asked, "Wut?"

"How da hell are you da sperm dat won? Dat's wut."

Not understanding, Nubbs simply said, "Whatevva."

Quicklip gauged the Marshil orcs' ability to survive as he entered their sanctuary. It was little more than a three-story stone building that had the doors and windows barricaded for protection against creeps or orc invaders. His eyes took in the stacks of supplies, mostly food and weapons that cluttered the entire building. He muttered, "Nice place."

Tuff pumped out his chest in pride and exclaimed, "Tanks. We beed here fo' six months. It longa time to stock up anda figure out creep movements."

Nubbs hastened, "Wer da shlogger tho?"

Several orcs smiled as they recognized how lucky they were to have stockpiled the rare pleasantry that quenched their thirsts and took them away from their problems. Tuff instructed, "I show you dis place first."

Quicklip and Nubbs were surprised to find an indoor well that tapped fresh water from the ground below. Strange plants were growing along the walls in a courtyard that hid inside the building itself. The leaves were pulled daily, dried, and smoked. Their affects were similar to shlogger, but not as rare a commodity as it replenished itself while shlogger wasn't renewable, at least not under the current conditions. It was explained that some orcs ventured out to bring back small amounts of crops that could be distilled into shlogger, but very few crops survived Darkster's spells. A deep, expansive basement, with underground corridors, led out in each direction for miles, all lined with survival goodies. Quicklip complimented, "You gots a good setup here."

Tuff replied, "Tanks. Some a yer Hotta orcs helped."

"Der Hotta orcs here?"

"Yup. Two a dem. Dems real smart, too; smarta den lots a orcs here. Udders dies fro' creeps, tho. Dems just didn't know to fight durin' da day."

Quicklip was puzzled. "When did Hotta orcs come here?"

"Durin' da war wit' yer planet. Dems wus hostages, I tink. Not my hostages, but Darkster a hostages."

"Anda wer is Darkster? How many creeps?" Quicklip questioned as he fired into the mass of moaning bodies.

Tuff woefully decreed, "Way too many. All da deads have comes to life."

"All?"

"Yup, all," Tuff confirmed. "Da whole planet be cursed by Darkster."

Quicklip and Nubbs looked at each other in disbelief. They had never heard of such a thing. Orcs were brutal warriors – dimwits who survived by taking action, even if not the smartest one. If the orcs on Hotta were somewhat more intelligent than those on other worlds, they were still orcs and occasionally

59

reverted back to brute force. Spells and curses were something in fairy tales, much like the creeps that found their way into childhood lore.

Tuff stated, "Left Marshil afta makin's millions a creeps. First, him started to get most da orcs outta here, but I guess he tought dat if we died, der wus just mo' creeps to fight against Hotta troops."

"But even millions a creeps don't seem dat bad. Dems just walkin' around stupid in da valley."

"No! No! Dems wus not rampagin'. Dems wus lost in da valley and no orcs to eat. When dems on da move, it worser dan anyting! Anda dems prolly not soldiers, just town orcs."

Quicklip apologized, "Ok, ok. Sorry. I tought dems wus all lika dat. How many orcs left on Marshil?"

Tuff calmed himself and answered, "Dunno. So many killed by creeps. Den, dems became creeps. It used a be dat towns be evvywhere and many orcs live in da cities. But now, creeps live in da cities at day and kill at night."

"How did Darkster maka curse on all da plants anda da weather too?"

"Dunno. Der was a great ground shake and lava come up fro' unda da ground. Dat wus befo' da creeps come. Creeps killed lotta da plants, tho. Dems lika aimless livestock. Just trample evvyting when dems rampagin'."

It became clear to Quicklip that Tuff didn't know the possible science behind a nuclear winter. Even if Darkster caused the ground to quake and volcanic activity to erupt, how likely was it that creeps killed all the vegetation? It was probably gases and dust thrown into the atmosphere from volcanic activity that blocked out light from Marshil's parent star. It would only take months for most of the plant life to die off and temperatures to plummet. The creeps were a whole other matter.

Then, Quicklip had another moment of clarity. Creeps were nothing more than dead bodies in a trance of sorts. They were prone to decay at a faster pace under hot and wet conditions. Their demise could have been slowed by cooling the climate, so they didn't rot as quickly. Marshil was now cool and arid; these were ideal conditions to inhibit decay. But how did Darkster manage that? Maybe it was just coincidence, but maybe not.

Quicklip thanked Tuff for the tour and wished him well before leaving with Nubbs. He hoped he gathered enough information so Nuttybomb could devise a plan to capture Marshil and move against Darkster. He finally asked the most important question, "Wer be Darkster?"

***

Darkster awoke from a deep state of mind in which he communicated with his god. He yawned, and then stretched, feeling fresh in mind and spirit. The exhilaration of speaking one-to-one with the evil entity intensified his resolve to end Nuttybomb's life and pursue his destiny of ruling the star cluster.

He had become quite powerful since his last encounter with Nuttybomb and the Hotta orcs three years before. While he brought an entire planet to its knees, raised an army from the abyss, and brought his father back from the dead, Nuttybomb's old guard had deteriorated skills and Nuttybomb was dying. He wasn't aware of these facts though. As far as he knew,

Nuttybomb was a potent adversary, capable of putting up a good fight.

He thought about the past battle with his enemy, seeking to reveal weaknesses he may have overlooked at that time. His mind kept returning to hatred and evil. He remembered partially severing Uhra's spine and leaving her for dead. He wondered what became of her. He wished her a slow death or maybe a life of suffering, anything to rip Nuttybomb's heart from his chest.

Soon, his mind wandered to his training. His father taught him to harness power by praying to the dark god of Iblis, as well as how to fight in hand-to-hand combat. He never attained the level of mastery that his father had with weapons, but he felt he didn't need to. His infatuation with dark magic gave him power that no sword ever could! Darkster smiled as memories flooded his mind.

***

The two orcs traveled for several hours as they headed to a spot where they were to meet other soldiers, but when they arrived, they were alone.

Nubbs asked, "Wer are dems?"

Quicklip looked around and replied, "Dunno. Still got some time tho. Da ship be here soon."

"I gots some mo' shlogger fro' Tuff. Want some?"

"No, tanks. I tryin' to tink."

Nubbs insulted, "You tink too much. Relax."

A perturbed Quicklip shot back, "Ya, anda you don't tink 'nuff. Yer brain lika sponge all wet wit' shlogger. If der millions a creeps anda dems really as bad as Tuff says, dens we gonna have a bad fight."

"You still gots a family back home. I don't. I tink about one drink at a time. All I gots is right here. I fight when it happen. You keep tinkin' and I keep drinkin'."

"Shutta up and looka dat way. Someone comin."

They strained their eyes to see into the distance against the sand that pelted them. It appeared to them that some type of animal was approaching. No, it was a monster. They laughed when they agreed it was both.

Ucktock yelled as he closed in on Quicklip and Nubs, "Hiya." He was unaware that the way he lumbered toward them while holding up Muddy gave the appearance of one strange figure instead of two. "Wut so funny?"

Nubbs deflected, "Nuttin'. Want some shlogger?"

"Absatively!"

Nubbs held his tongue out at Quicklip in defiance. "See? Somebody want my shlogger."

Quicklip sprang, "Ya, anda dat all dems want fro' you."

Nubbs shrugged off Quicklip's sharp response with, "I drink to dat."

The orcs talked about their encounters with creeps and other orcs. They discussed the curse on Marshil and how many creeps roamed about. Ucktock didn't need to embellish about his and Muddy's ordeal with the undead that nearly killed them. Muddy's wounds were significant enough to drive the point home.

Within an hour, three more Hotta scouts crawled into camp. They had been badly mauled by creeps and were lucky to have survived at all. Their stories added to the mix of tales told before the ship came to bring them back home.

In all, only seven of twenty scouts were picked up at the specified location. Of those, only three weren't wounded. Those who were hurt received immediate medical attention aboard the ship as it climbed into space; a docking ship awaiting their arrival. Other scout ships began to report similar losses back to Nuttybomb.

***

"Sir, der are Hotta orcs on Marshil."

Darkster's cold, piercing eyes leered beneath his hood at the orc who brought him information about his enemies. He breathed, "How many?" in a cold, raspy, monotone voice.

The orc shivered as he responded, "Not 'nuff information yet, Sir. But not many. Maybe hundred?"

"A hundred dat you know 'bout?" Darkster quizzed his unsuspecting fool, toying with words to catch the dumb underling in a state of confusion. He hoped for clarity and information that would help him defeat Nuttybomb, but all the same, he was sadistically driven to play like a cat with a mouse.

The orc thought for a moment before elaborating, "Yessir. Der may be some mo', but no big armies." He prayed to his gods that he answered correctly, for dozens of orcs had been slain by Darkster for spitting out the wrong words.

"Wut 'bout Nuttybomb?"

The underling asked as he provided a leaflet that was dropped on Marshil and recovered, "You mean Wargod Nuttybomb?"

Darkster sprang forward and ripped the paper from the orc's trembling hand. He hollered in a shrill voice, madness revealing itself, "wargod? He no wargod!" He surveyed the leaflet before stating, "Get outta my site befo' I kill you."

The orc ran away.

Darkster spat under his breath, "Too bad I need dat damn orc fo' his math. He only one who know wut hundred is. Now, wut to do 'bout Nuttybomb? He stupid fo' advertising dat he comin'. I be ready fo him."

Four
Warchief

Doc Cutstick warned, "It not good. Yer pictures lit up lika da stars. You gots slugs anda shrapnel evvywhere."

Nuttybomb asked, "So? Now wut?"

"So, you still gots a feva and you gots blood in yer one lung. It looka lika yer heart be bleedin', too. I gotta go in anda fix it anda remove lots a da metal. All a dat and maybe mo', too. You had lots a broken bones that looka mostly healed. They should be fine."

Uhra wasn't pleased with the findings, but at least there was a diagnosis and treatment that could fix her stubborn husband. She wanted to be sure. "Den, he be betta?"

Cutstick admitted, "Dunno. I nevva seen so much stuff in a body. You might even gots poison stuff fro' da humans or sumptin' you picked up fro' anudder world. Just 'cause we orcs don't really get sick on Hotta, don't mean dat we can't evva. Da heart anda lung be a must. Hope dat does it, but dunno."

Nutty complained, "I ain't got time fo' all a dis, Doc. I got wars to fight against Darkster, Humans, and Spidanoids too."

Cutstick was direct, "Nuttybomb, you might not have much time, period. You no fight if you a dead."

Uhra gasped. Nutty looked into her eyes, feeling worried about his health for the first time. He didn't want to leave her. What good was defending her from the problems throughout the star systems if he wasn't there physically to comfort her and to be with her?

Nutty knew Cutstick was the best at what he did. He nurtured Uhra back to full health and she was able to walk, a miracle considering how badly she was hurt. The doc had saved thousands of lives, including Biggabomb, Nutty's own father by performing lung transplants. Guthrak and Gunza recovered under his care, too, as did Quicklip. Nutty wanted to question the doc, but he understood that the doc knew his business. All he could muster was, "When you fix me?"

Doc Cutstick didn't hesitate, "Now. Right now, if you can."

"I gots to give orders anda make someone else leader while you fix me. I need a lil time."

Uhra cut in, "Just maka Biggabomb leader again."

Nutty frowned, "Him not da same since da last war. His lungs not too goods anda da gas messed up his brain."

"What 'bout Guthrak?"

"No, him great fighta, but he not know tactics and logistics."

Uhra was scrambling. "Basha?"

"No, him fightin' Spidanoids on Plenna."

"Ok, so... Booma, den."

Nuttybomb couldn't think of anyone who was well-rounded enough to fill his shoes. He wasn't sure of himself as the best leader at times, but he was much better than anyone else. "C'mon Uhra, him's Booma. Hims doesn't know da stuff needed. Anda he on a ship above Plenna."

Uhra felt like she was beating her head against the wall. "Well, it gotta be somebody, even Quicklip."

"I ain't heard fro' him. He on Marshil. I dunno wut to do. I really dunno wut to do, Uhra."

She clamored, "It don't a matta. Doc, maka it tomorrow. We figure it out by den."

Nuttybomb didn't argue. He knew the score...and it was one he was losing. He took Uhra by the arm and escorted her out of the doc's medical area. They talked as they walked home.

Nutty said, "Maybe Moonoak could handle some stuff. No, he dunno war. Nubbs can't."

Uhra offered, "Ucktock?"

"No. Plus, he on Marshil too."

"You ok?" Uhra asked.

"Yup. I feel bad dat I didn't know a fix my own body. Tought I wus doin' ok."

Uhra asked, "Wut we gonna do 'bout da kids?"

"Dems too small to be leader." Nutty laughed.

Uhra exclaimed, "Younut!"

***

Headhunta said, "We needs a change yer name."

Cracka stated, "But I want my name. No change it."

The impatient father smacked his son across the face and growled, "You gots no say. You new name be Darkster."

The boy rubbed his face and hung his head. He slowly uttered, "Fine."

"Now, pick up yer sword," Headhunta commanded angrily.

"But I wanna use da whip."

Headhunta warned the boy again, "Don't defy me or yer gonna get worser dan a slap. Anda I already tolds you dat da whip be too hard a start wit'."

Darkster picked up the heavy sword and held it in front of his body like he'd been instructed to do.

His father moved swiftly and graciously, uncharacteristically for an orc. He made repeated slashes and thrusts, evading Darkster's sword and scoring imitated hits. He yelled, "Dammit, boy! You even tryin's?"

The boy stood there, not knowing if he should answer with the truth or what his father wanted to hear. He probably could have tried harder, but between being forced to change his name and use a weapon he didn't want to, he wasn't giving his best effort. Instead, he shouted, "Shutta up!"

Headhunta wasn't the slightest bit upset by his son's words. On the contrary, he said, "It 'bout time you get mad, you lil, stupid orc," to provoke him.

Darkster swung the sword that was a bit too heavy for his size to handle effectively. Every swing and miss, followed by a sneer from his dad, angered him further.

His unyielding father spat, "You gotta do betta dan dat." He laughed hardily.

The boy dropped his sword and snapped his fingers. Headhunta's left shoulder pad burst into flames.

Headhunta jumped back and fought off the flames with his right hand, patting them until he was left with only smoke encircling his head. He smiled and said, "Why you lil bastid, you didn't tells me you could do dat. I impressed."

Darkster sneered. "Der udder stuff I can do, too."

"Well, letta us use what you can do wit' a sword anda you will be very powerful," the surprised, yet delighted father said.

The boy ceased to feel anger. Acceptance from a gifted warrior, who happened to be his father, gave him a bit of happiness. The feelings of hate and greed continued. He used his father's words as fuel to burn the fire in his soul, especially the part about being very powerful. This was the moment when the sadistic child became a determined monster. All things before and after were laid out in a destiny he chose. He was now Darkster.

***

Moonoak was greeted with a broad smile, a handshake, and a pat on the back. He was just as happy to see Nuttybomb, as was the reverse. "Hello, my old friend. Good a see you," the elder shaman addressed.

Nuttybomb guided his mentor into a room that would be considered a parlor- somewhat formal, but also comfortable. He poured some shlogger for his guest and began, "Good a see you, too. How you beed?"

"I beed good. Anda you?"

"Eh, ok. Got some pictures to take wit' da doc in da mornin'. Dunno, prolly fo' nuttin'. Got a cough and a feva."

Moonoak was sincerely concerned. Not only was Nuttybomb his friend, but the ruler of several orc worlds, and possibly, the chosen one. The books written by Grim told of one who would unite all orcs and catapult them into a golden age. Nutty had certainly done that on his homeworld of Hotta and several other worlds in different star systems. But he would have to do the same on dozens more if the writings were true. "You looka sick. May da gods shine upon you."

"Tanks, but 'nuff 'bout me. Let's talk 'bout Darkster," Nutty suggested.

"Ok?"

Nutty queried, "What you learn while I gone?"

Moonoak informed his chief in a way that invited mutual dialogue. "What I know is dat Headhunta, Darkster's dad, came from good bloodline lika you. I don't know much 'bout Darkster's mom, tho, but I workin' on it."

"Headhunta got powers, too?"

"Yup. Well, I tink so. I tink he goed down a path a stealth. Him walk wit' da shadows and he play tricks on yer mind so you don't see him."

Nuttybomb agreed. "Dat maka sense. He wus known to hide anda kill away from da udder guards. He killed whole units by himself. He even went up to da enemy in space anda killed der leader anda all a da guards. Amazin' really dat he wus nevva seen by anyone with da place bein' so busy."

"Exactly. Gunza and Guthrak prolly agree wit' his way a killin's lika dat."

Nutty eagerly pressed, "Ok, what else?"

"I able to find were Headhunta lived longa time ago, back when he fight unda Boss Dagga anda Ole Man Boppa. Darkster wus lil and be named Cracka back den."

"I rememba."

Moonoak continued, "Cracka wus a bad kid. He wus always alone. Headhunta be gone fo' war alots and da mom dead or gone lots, too. Der lots a different stories. Dis what I know. Back to you. Whutcha gonna do?" Moonoak asked Nutty.

"I gotta get fixed."

"Good. I agree. Now wut 'bout Marshil and who in charge?"

Nutty rubbed his forehead, as if somehow the answer would come to him the harder he did. "Dunno. Maybe Marshil not worth takin'?"

"So, don't taka it den."

"But almost have to so we can get close to Darkster. Plus, all da creeps be sufferin' forevva. We gots to."

Moonoak tried to alleviate Nutty's stress. He agreed with his friend to calm him. Besides, it was a technique he used to get him to work out problems on his own. He knew Nuttybomb was much more intelligent than he was. He simply allowed the process to play out. "Ok, so we invade Marshil."

Nutty begged, "But how we fight creeps? Anda how we get dems back to rest?"

"You fight dems lika anyting else. Dunno how to get millions a creeps to rest tho."

"I need you and da elders to do it...to get dems to rest after we fight dems."

Moonoak scoffed, "Millions! You want me and ten udders to get millions back to peace?"

Nutty admitted, "Yup. I dunno how."

"Me either."

Nutty rubbed his chest to somehow alleviate some of the pain he felt. "Gots to try. Do all a dems at da same time. Lika Darkster did a curse."

Moonoak explained, "No. Da soul a very personal ting. Gots to help each creep one at a time. Darkster

72

made a big promise to all dat he would offer dems paradise. It different to give dems real paradise."

Nutty explained, "Just do da best you can. I trust a you. I still dunno who to maka leader while doc works on me." With Booma, General Basha, a million troops, and a large fleet in the Cypra system, as well as contingents on and around other worlds, Nuttybomb's forces were spread thin. Perhaps he wouldn't be able to invade Marshil after all, but he couldn't give up.

Moonoak advised, "Gunza is yer best option as leader while yer laid up."

Nutty complained, "No, he not an option. Uhra will kills me if I send her dad."

"You want me anda elders to do a miracle on millions a creeps, but you won't do wut you must?"

Nutty rubbed his forehead as he sought after a solution that evaded him. He still reasoned, "But he not da same since da fight with Darkster and Headhunta."

"None a us da same, Nutty. We all weaker now. But him da best option. You knows it." Moonoak shook his head in a "yes" motion like an experienced salesman, leading his customer to make an unnecessary purchase.

"Tings wus so much easier when I wus a kid gettin' beat up all a da time."

Moonoak jabbed, "Looka it dis way. It not changed. Uhra gonna beat you up."

Nutty agreed, "Yup, she is. Hey, one mo' ting."
"Ok?"

"I can't meditate. I mean, I not able to talk to da place wer I get information."

Moonoak prodded, "How long dis be a problem?"

"Maybe six months," Nutty admitted.

"You beed sick. It prolly get betta. Don't worry."

Nutty added, "Der mo' tho."

"Ok?" The shaman waited.

"Been havin' trouble readin' minds anda doin' special stuff. Da last time wus a human. I not able to do since."

Moonoak coaxed Nutty with, "No worry too much. Lika I said, you beed sick. Doc fix you and you prolly get betta." At least, that's what he said. He was concerned that Nuttybomb may have lost the ability to do amazing things that no other orc dreamed of doing. What if his ailments affected his brain permanently? Facing off against Darkster would be futile then.

The two spoke for another hour until Uhra entered the room with a familiar orc.

Nutty stood up and raced across the room to greet his father-in-law. "Gunza, how are you?"

Gunza replied, "I good."

Uhra asked, "Dad, you come to say good luck to Nutty befo' doc works on him?"

Gunza shook his head. "No. I say good luck to him, but he asked me to come, so I here."

Uhra was surprised. "Oh. Nutty?" She folded her arms and began to tap her foot to a rhythm that only she knew.

Nutty grimaced. Then, he chortled before spitting out, "Gunza, I need you to be warchief."

Uhra insisted, "No, Nutty. No way!"

"Sorry, Uhra. It yer dad's choice."

She turned to her father and pleaded, "No, Dad. You not young anymo'."

Gunza exhaled, "Ain't dat da truth. It be ok, Uhra."

"No, it not be ok. Looka how bad Nutty been hurt wit' all da fightin'. You gonna do da same ting?"

Gunza turned to Nuttybomb. "Fo' how long?"

Nutty admitted, "Dunno. I hope doc fix me quick."

"Who I gots as guards?"

"Quicklip, Nubbs, Arc, anda Gobbygoo."

Gunza asked, "Who da hell be Gobbygoo?"

Nutty explained, "We gots him fro' Cypra. Trust me. He goods."

"Wit' a name lika Gobbygoo, he betta be."

"Da udder guards ok wit' you?"

Gunza wasn't so sure. "Arc? Dat kid a freak."

"Maybe, but he do stuff dat I can't. I talk to him. He listen to you. Dems good?"

"Against Darkster and Headhunta? No. Can I get Guthrak?"

Nutty obliged, "Ya, if you tink he can still fight."

Gunza smiled. "Him wus born a fight." He stopped smiling when he saw Uhra's twisted features and angry eyes staring him down. He addressed Uhra, "Look. It be ok, lika I said. You be here wit' Nuttybomb. Yer mom died a longa time ago. Udder dan you, I gots no one. I just gettin' old and sittin' in my chair. It no fun."

"But Dad…," Uhra pleaded.

"But nuttin'. It time fo' me to finish da fight wit' Headhunta. Lemme do wut I gots a do."

***

Biggabomb bellowed, "Food shoulda beed done a hour ago."

"Well, maybe if you got yer big, fat, oogly ass outta da chair anda helped, it be done," Muga retorted. Unlike years before, she countered her husband's insults with playful banter of her own. What seemed mean to others was normalcy to them.

"Well, maybe if you not eat all da food anda have a make mo', it be done." He enthusiastically gave a broad smile, showing some missing teeth.

Guests began to arrive. Three knocks were followed by, "Come in," echoed from the orc of the house. Gunza opened the door and walked inside, his large frame fully occupying the doorway as he entered. He had filled out over the last few years since his last battle; he hadn't been nearly as active as he was during the home battles on Hotta a few years before.

Guthrak came to the Bomb residence next, complete with his legendary knife-in-jaw decoration he was known for. The exposed handle sported the customary hanging feathers and jewelry, meant to accentuate the blade that he won in battle; it showed others not to mess with him. He simply greeted, "Hey, Chief," to Biggabomb and nodded to Gunza. He wasn't as heavy as Gunza. In fact, he remained bulky, muscular from working in his machine shop daily.

Biggabomb welcomed his old friend and elite guard before saying, "Muga, my old friends are here."

Muga walked into the front room where Biggabomb sat lazily and threw insults for fun. "Wut dat horrible smell?"

Biggabomb joked, "Dat yer cookin'." He laughed hardily.

Guthrak lifted an arm and sniffed his pit to see if the offensive odor came from him. He snorted in satisfaction and sat down on a crate near Biggabomb. He shook his head in discomfort and spat, "It yer feet, Chief. Dems stink!"

Muga cawed, "Maybe if him wash dems once in a while."

Guthrak and Gunza laughed.

Biggabomb responded, "I tink you dipped dems in yer food. Dat wut dems smell like." He reluctantly removed his aching body from his chair and left the room to engage in a quick bath. He breathed heavily as his lungs struggled to take in adequate amounts of air. He asked, "Muga, wer da wash rags?"

"Wer dems always beed."

He shouted, "Nevva mind. I found dems. Wait, wer my robe?"

Muga shook her head in disgust, "Wer you put it."

"Nevva mind. I found it. Hey, wer da bucket fo' water?"

Muga snapped, "Gods dammit, you ovagrown potato. It in da bathroom in da tub!"

Biggabomb quietly laughed to himself and jeered, "Nevva mind. I found it."

Under her breath, Muga cursed, "Him not so attractives no mo'. Him not da warchief no mo'. Him not even smell good. I need a dump his big, stinky ass."

Within minutes, Biggabomb met Muga in the back room and asked, "I smell ok?"

"Fo' bein a big turd, ya."

He opened his arms and wrapped them around her, giving an ample squeeze to show his undying love for her. She reached up and melted in his arms, something she never grew tired of.

Hearing the commotion between the two, Guthrak remarked, "Dems must really hates each other."

Gunza corrected, "Nope. It foreplay," and laughed.

Nutty and Uhra came into the house without knocking first. Nutty always felt at home in the place he grew up and was comfortable enough to enter without announcing his arrival. Guthrak stood up to greet his current warchief as a display of respect. Gunza nodded to his son-in-law and hugged Uhra as she came to the center of the room.

As if on cue, Moonoak knocked at the door and was invited in. The males set up a table by stacking crates and putting boards on top. Crates were pulled around the table as seating and they got as comfortable as they could while they waited to eat.

The other guards were soon there, too, and the stories began to fly.

Guthrak started the tall tales conversation with a question, "I evva tell you how I gots dis knife in my jaw?"

"No," a few of the younger guards replied.

Guthrak asked surprised, "No? Well…"

He scratched his genitals and began, "Evvyone tink it happened in battle, but a no. I was workin' in my a workshop, cause dats wut you do in a workshop, anda dese three Wivvaflow orcs come in. Now, I'd seed 'em befo' in different bars anda I knew dems wus trouble. But I got a business, so I ask, 'Whatcha need?'

"Da one guy says, 'A heater coil.'

"So, I says, 'I ain't got no heater coils.'

"Same guy says, 'Wut kinda workshop ain't got heater coils?'

"So, I says, 'Dis kinda workshop, you igorant Wivvaflow asshole!' Dunno, it wus hot dat day or sumptin'. I just wusn't in a good mood."

Quicklip asked, "You evva in a good mood?"

Guthrak replied with a twisted smile, "Not so much. Guess you gotta catch me just right. Anyway, dunno why, but dems not lika dat too much."

Chuckles filled the room.

Nubbs sat on a crate with a new cup of shlogger and asked, "So, wut happened?"

Guthrak answered with a question, "Wut happened? Dems tried to beat a my ass. Dats wut happened. So, dems are all swingin' at me anda I stuck behind da counter. I grabbin' anyting I can get a free hand on to hit 'em wit'. I threw a can wit' screws at 'em. My sammich, I tink, too. I said wen I threw dat, 'Don't say I nevva fed you.'"

Believing Guthrak to be a great warrior, and not understanding how the elite guard could possibly lower himself by throwing useless objects in defense, Quicklip asked, "Wut da hell wus wrong wit' you?"

"Wrong wit' me? Nuttin'. Oh, I wus drunk. Ya, real bad hangova. I hit one a dems wit' a pulley, left a big circle mark on his forehead. Lemme see...Oh ya, I smashed one a dems ova da head wit' a toolbox. Shit went evvywhere. Da one orc slipped, anda wen he stoods up, he was bent ova to gets his balance. I shoved a crowbar uppa his ass. Still stuck der, I tink. Dems couldn't get it outta da bone. Anyway, I wus laughin' so hard watchin' him dat one a da udder bastids stabbed me in da face. Dats how I gots dis knife."

Quicklip followed up, "Wut happened with da three orcs?"

Guthrak said, "Nuttin'. Orcs comes in and brokes it up afta dat."

"Wut evva happened to da orc wit da crowbar inna his ass," Quicklip pressed.

"Dunno. I nevva saw him afta dat. I heard he kills himself outta embarrassment. Kinda hard to walk round all bent ova wit' a stick in yer ass." Guthrak laughed, almost violently.

The orcs celebrated with backslaps.

Uhra went to the back room and met Muga with a hug, "Want I help, Mom?"

Muga chuckled, "Wanna pour drinks fo' da war vets?"

"Sure." Uhra grabbed a handful of cups, retrieved a pitcher of shlogger, and served the males that traded war stories around the table. Then, she brought out some biscuits and saw them disappear as soon as she gave them out.

Nutty changed the subject to current affairs and the tasks at hand. He explained the creep situation on Marshil and that Darkster had left after cursing the world. Numbers were thrown around as to the probable orc population there and how to get them on board to fight the creeps.

Furthermore, he announced Gunza as warchief while he received treatment. The warrior was accepted without quarrel and supported without question. Guthrak stated to the new leader, "You still a gonna kiss my ass."

Gunza laughed, not insulted at all by his friend. However, he did have concerns about the population accepting him as warchief and he addressed it. "Nuttybomb, wut 'bout you namin' me warchief while all orcs look up to you and expect you to lead?"

Nutty instructed, "I will announce to all tomorrow dat you warchief. You all know dat we dropped papers on Marshil dat say I wargod. Dat might be problem if I not able to fight anymo', but I sent papers befo' I knew how sick I am. I just say dat I am ovaseeing tings fro' afar. It be ok, I tink."

They all nodded. Biggabomb added, "Sound lika good plan. Wut I apposed a do?"

Nuttybomb respected his father and wanted the old orc to feel important even if in a limited capacity. He asked, "Would you maka plans to defend Hotta if we invaded? I gots so few generals here right now. Darkster not on Marshil anda I not know what da hell he gonna do."

"You gots it. I still gots my old book a tactics. It lil dusty, but still good."

Nutty complimented his father, "I learn fro' you by readin' dat book. We win da war cause you maka plans so good."

Biggabomb wasn't stupid. He understood he was no longer able to do the things he could just a few years before. "Wut 'bout fightin'? I not as good as I used a be?"

"Don't lead battles. It ok to send in troops. You done yer fightin'."

Nutty knew how lucky Biggabomb and the old guards were to live as long as they did. Life expectancy for orcs was around thirty-five and that was for orcs that didn't fight so many wars. The orcs of Hotta had upped that number a bit by developing new technologies and having adequate medical staff and facilities. Even still, few made it to the ripe old age of forty, very few to forty-five, and no orc had ever reached fifty. Biggabomb and Gunza were thirty-six and Guthrak was thirty-four. Yes, they were lucky indeed!

Nutty also kept in mind that the lifespan numbers may have been skewed a bit by the orc's only real disease known as da feva. While it decimated populations by killing nearly half of all children, it still ravaged those that reached adulthood as well. In fact, Uhra's mother succumbed to it when Uhra was young.

"Right?" Biggabomb asked Nutty again, "Right?"

Nutty realized he hadn't heard what his father had said. "Sorry. Wut?"

"I wus talkin' 'bout da time we fought Darkster in da cave."

"Da cave, ya. Wut?" Nuttybomb was sweating profusely. He rubbed his forehead and looked down.

Biggabomb joked, "You don't listen to yer dad no mo'?"

Moonoak intervened, "Nutty, you ok?"

Nutty keeled over and fell from the crate he sat on. He began a series of violent seizures that took everyone by surprise. White and pink foam frothed from his mouth, his jaws locked in a semi-opened position.

Gunza yelled, "Uhra, get doc!"

Uhra entered the room with a half-smile from hearing Muga talking about Biggabomb's inadequacies, but her face turned to horror upon seeing her husband convulsing. She ran out the door and down the street as she screamed, "Doc Cutstick! Doc Cutstick, hurry!"

Five
Under the Knife

Nuttybomb couldn't announce to the orcs on Hotta about his transfer of power to Gunza. Nor was he able to go over a plan and contingencies. His collapse left him unable to do anything but fall into a deep coma.

Gunza's new title was questioned by many without Nutty's verbal blessing. For all the orcs knew, Gunza had killed Nuttybomb and taken command by sheer force. They believed this scenario was unlikely, but orcs tended to believe the least likely things at times, and without Nutty able to confirm that he relinquished power, all sorts of rumors began.

The family knew not to report his condition and Doc Cutstick was instructed to keep quiet, possibly fueling the rumors even more. Nuttybomb's frail state of health might not only bring into question his authority, but open a can of worms regarding his invincibility. The mere existence of perceived immortality kept a power struggle from ever happening. But now, he struggled for life itself while his family tried to cope and take the right steps to fool the public.

Uhra left the medical area to be with her kids while Doc Cutstick fought to stabilize the wargod. Before Cutstick could operate, he needed to ensure that Nuttybomb wouldn't die from anesthesia or any of the procedures. Nutty's weakened body had received far too much trauma on top of the results from poisonous, foreign bodies allowed to remain in his organs, tissues, and bones. There was only so much an orc could endure, even one like Nuttybomb. Cutstick couldn't ensure anything other than the dire straits his patient was in.

He worked into the night, administering fluids, shots of adrenaline, and applying assisted breathing to Nuttybomb. He even used electrical shocks to restart Nuttybomb's heart twice. He informed Uhra as needed, trying not to worry her too much, but allowing her to be prepared for the worst.

Dawn began with blood transfusions, followed by ice baths to bring down Nutty's sky high temperature. The day continued with a number of procedures already conducted with additional drugs prescribed. Nutty remained unconscious.

Gunza checked in several times to see if Nutty had awakened. He hoped to get some direction before he made decisions on his own, but it wasn't to be. So, he consulted with Moonoak and the two devised a plan to invade Marshil.

The problem Gunza realized was he wouldn't be facing a typical army. Creeps didn't move or attack in formations. They didn't keep reserves to the rear and they didn't try to outflank the enemy. On the surface it would seem they were easier to fight against, but there would be no enemy line; the enemy would be everywhere.

Furthermore, Moonoak explained that heavy weapons couldn't be used; no grenades or explosive devices were allowed either. The creeps' bodies needed to be somewhat intact, so they could be sent to the afterlife as individuals; something impossible to do if the bodies were disintegrated. They had to be preserved, even in the heat of battle.

Then, came the task for the shaman to free the bodies of their afflictions and to direct them to salvation. The curse for each stricken orc needed to be removed and final resting granted. If killing millions was difficult, this was nearly impossible.

Gunza opted to speak to the masses before gathering his troops and setting off for Marshil within the week. He had yet to meet with the scouts that were on their way back from the cursed planet, and as such, couldn't strategize until receiving accurate information. He would meet the scouts in a couple months as he neared Marshil and complete his plans for invasion then.

He chose to take most of the capital ships at his disposal; only a small force would remain above Hotta. The vast majority of cruisers, destroyers, and support vessels would accompany his enormous troop barges, providing protection for the vulnerable behemoths. His force would be severely outnumbered by Darkster's fleet, but he hoped his edge in technology would make up for the lopsided number of ships if an engagement took place.

***

Gunza spoke with Booma who was almost an entire light year away. They were able to communicate in real time by using actuators; human-made devices that essentially folded space and created wormholes to connect distant places by a shortened path. The abandoned human actuators were designed to allow deep space travel, but once it was discovered sound waves could be sent, communication was also used.

85

Booma was shocked to hear about Nuttybomb's awful health. It was *his* health that was thought to be more fragile than Nutty's; they both sustained damage to their hearts and lungs. Whereas Booma took a full month just to be able to get around on his own, Nutty was up and about within two weeks. The news was shocking indeed.

But business needed to continue, and it did. Booma informed Gunza that Gobbygoo was in transit back to Hotta, but it would take nearly a month for him to arrive. He got Gunza up to speed with the Spidanoids he was fighting on Cypra and the few run-ins he had with minor human vessels as well. Finally, he offered advice about how to handle an invasion force from deep space unloading on a planet's surface, something he had experience with.

Gunza thanked Booma and commended him on a job well done. He wished him all the glory that the gods might bestow on him and a safe return. Then, he pulled his old, trusty sword from under his bed and played with it. He swung it a few times, but dropped it by accident. He spat, "Dammit!" and tried again. But again, he dropped it as he worked it end over end in a spin. His blade wasn't an extension of himself anymore. Three years of inactivity left him rusty to say the least.

He heard a familiar voice harken, "You gonna open da door or not?"

Gunza put down his weapon and opened the front door for his old battle mate. "Sorry, old friend. I not hear da door. You ready, Guthrak?"

"Yup," confidently came from the ancient warrior. "At least, I tink so." He laughed in admission.

Gunza smiled and replied, "Know whutcha mean. My sword gots mo' dust dan a Wivvaflow whore's brain."

Guthrak acknowledged, "Now I know wut *you* mean."

***

Doc Cutstick, upon communication with Nuttybomb's family, began the treacherous operations he knew were necessary if Nuttybomb had any chance of living. He couldn't stabilize his patient and finally decided that no amount of conservative treatments, especially allowing the virulent infection to prosper any longer, would benefit its moribund host.

Long, white cloths were draped over Nuttybomb, exposing areas to be operated on. Cutstick and his helpers wore an array of mismatched clothing, only discernible as medics by the blue gowns that clung to them. Newly furnished masks were tied to their faces to keep down the possible spread of contaminants through airborne transferal, a revolution in orcdom. Bright lights were moved over the same areas to be operated on and the work began.

The chest was opened, clamps spreading and holding the ribcage apart so vital organs could be accessed more easily. A metal shard was found floating, unattached to anything of importance, and removed without complication. Several bullets were attracted to a mechanical device that held a magnet at its tip. These slugs were also removed without incident.

Two more items were lodged in Nuttybomb's ribs. One was carefully dislodged, but the other was imbedded within the healed bone. Cutstick instructed his helpers to cut out the bullet by removing most of

87

the rib that grew around the massive piece of metal. They did as commanded and put the remaining rib together by use of hardware and screws.

All the while, blood transfusions were pumping Booma's fluids into his brother's weakened body. The virtual blood match was hoped to give Nuttybomb a fighting chance while the dicey procedures took place. Nutty's own blood had been replaced several times over, but the rampant infection and the toxins festering in his body pushed even the purest blood entering his veins to unsafe levels.

Orcs rarely succumbed to anything other than the feva, a disease that was inherently fatal to them. Most died due to blunt trauma, a result of battle or perhaps the mishap when one blew himself up. Otherwise, an infection had to border on a scale of monumental intrusion, rarely ever found in the species.

Doc Cutstick knew he was in uncharted territory. He worked quickly, but methodically. Careful not to tamper with Nuttybomb's heart or lungs until absolutely required, he continued to extract any unwanted intruders.

He found himself making a small incision in Nuttybomb's spleen, and then, his intestine; each time an offensive, organ penetrating foreigner was removed. Stitches here and there closed the sensitive areas before more dire extractions were performed. Cutstick operated with an efficiency that was well thought out and executed. He was clearly Nuttybomb's surgeon for a reason.

Cutstick's helpers used previously taken pictures to find and remove other objects from Nuttybomb's extremities. One arm had to be cut in almost a dozen places and the bones broken and repaired in three locations. The other arm needed less attention, but some areas of cankerous tissue were cut out.

Blood sucking leeches were attached to suspected areas of infection while maggots were poured into open wounds where obvious rot had taken hold. Two toes and part of a finger were found to be too far gone and amputated as a result. Puss was visible throughout Nuttybomb's body as well. Suction was used to clean it as best as it could before more maggots and leeches were placed. The foul stench of decomposition hung in the hot confines of the medical area.

The medics shook their heads in disbelief at the condition of their revered leader. How he survived this long defied all logic. Comments like, "Only a god could survive dis," and, "Him da baddest sonama bitch in da star cluster," were exclaimed in amazement.

Cutstick clamored, "Him not survive yet. Keep workin' and shutta up. Him life in our a hands and da hands of da gods." He ordered more adrenaline to be administered every time Nutty's vitals dropped to even worse levels. He decided to operate on the kidneys before attempting to open up the liver.

The easiest, least invasive tasks had been performed, for all the risk they posed, and the amount of skill required. However, they were by no means easy in the context of the sheer amount of area they encompassed or the time it took to execute them. Even with nicking major arteries and severing important nerves, they were child's play in comparison to what awaited the medical team.

One of Nuttybomb's kidneys had already shut down before Cutstick opened it. He went to work by cutting out dead tissue and grafting what he could from the working kidney. An enormous chunk of metal was carefully cut out of the organ as Cutstick sighed, "Unbelievable." He struggled to sew up the wound around massive scarring and loss of tissue that had caused the kidney to shut down.

Doc Cutstick decided to leave the other kidney alone for the time being. It too was damaged and at risk of failure, but with one already in nonworking condition, he thought it best to bypass it. It was riddled with small debris – probably metal shavings that, were either filtered as byproduct or possibly, deposited as shrapnel. *No matter*, he thought as he moved some intestine to begin work on Nuttybomb's liver.

The team was exhausted. They had been working for over eight hours and were fighting to keep blurry vision at bay. Several worked on Nuttybomb's legs, while others aided Cutstick by closing wounds, removing intrusive objects, changing blood and other fluids, or applying bandages. Only areas that were absolutely clear of infection and debris were closed up. Other areas were investigated further in search of contaminants.

Cutstick had no idea how long he would be operating on his warchief, so he rotated his staff, therefore allowing them rest while fresh bodies replaced them. Even less experienced medical staff were brought in to help those that had become too drowsy to continue. They were watched closely by experienced docs, who only allowed the most rudimentary tasks to be performed. The stakes were simply too high to allow mistakes.

Over the next several hours, Cutstick painstakingly worked to flush Nuttybomb's good kidney while he worked on his liver. Nuttybomb's body responded by crashing again and again. Time would tell if his brain was seriously impaired by his heart stopping repeatedly, but for now, work continued into the night.

***

The carnidawg moved amongst the tangled grasses that concealed her hunger. She prowled ever so slowly, her coat blending into her surroundings. She got within the distance that a single pounce could take down her prey and she sprang.

Arc had been meditating, somewhat unaware of the impending attack that threatened his life. However, he snapped into reality just before death's blow could render him nothing more than a simple meal for the ravenous beast. He sidestepped the rushing leap of the carnidawg and drew his sword.

The enormous cat/dog mixture landed and abruptly turned to strike at its prey. This time, it wasn't downwind – a tactic that hid its presence up until its attack. It was now that Arc smelled the gamy aroma of the awesome predator that chose him as its meal, its tail now flicking excitedly in the sultry air.

Arc was in a defensive stance as he sized up his opponent. He knew all too well that many orcs were no match for adult carnidawgs and only the finest warriors defeated the apex predators. He hoped he was one such warrior; his breathing quickened its pace as nervous anticipation wracked his senses. He muttered, "Yer a big bitch, aren't ya?"

The carnidawg crouched, her menacing teeth bared as she too evaluated the lethality of her prey. She had killed orcs before, although this one somehow eluded her clutches on the first lunge. She watched his hands held over his head, somehow realizing the carnage his weapon could inflict on her. She edged closer to the orc.

The inexperienced, but confident Arc closed his eyes and hummed incoherently under his breath. His eyes danced beneath their lids before he opened them with a new gleam that gave off light around his retinas. He teased, "C'mon, girl. Letta us play." He swallowed hard and deeply inhaled. Then, he waited.

The carnidawg growled and leaped. Its huge paws released six-inch claws, accompanied by nine-inch teeth that filled its ravenous, crushing jaws. Its substantial power reached within two feet of Arc before he acted.

One of Arc's hands dropped from his weapon and discharged a bolt of electrical energy that he absorbed from the very air that surrounded him. He ducked beneath the stunned carnidawg's charging body; it seized up and dropped clumsily behind him.

The beast sprang to its feet and swiped at Arc, but it was met with the slash of his blade. The carnidawg howled in pain as its paw was severed above the wrist. It jumped back in disbelief, but readied itself to kill the orc that stood before her.

Arc challenged, "How dat feel, you ovagrown hairball?"

The cat growled in anger in between twitches that assaulted the torn bones, tendons, muscles, and nerves that Arc had claimed so far. Her senses were wrought with confusion; until now, it was her prey that smelled of blood and cried in agony. But now, it was she who was at a disadvantage in a hunt. She crouched again, but this time in a more fearful, defensive posture. She held her mangled limb from the ground and cried out with a loud roar, a display of her prowess meant to strike fear into her opponent. But Arc knew better.

Arc was an orc, and being an orc, rarely let fear overwhelm his ability to fight, even against insurmountable odds. The difference between him and others (that made him so deadly and rightfully confident) was his unique ability to harness energy from his surroundings; this was unheard of until his being able to wield such a powerful weapon. He had dealt a serious blow to the carnidawg and he knew it, and although compassion missed many of his kind, the respect they felt for such worthy opponents caused them to end any unnecessary suffering. He spat, "Letta us finish dis."

The carnidawg roared before another electrical shock gripped its body. Before it realized the lightning bolt from Arc's hand immobilized her, his lethal blade cut across her throat and buried itself in her skull. Arc's kill was quick and merciful.

He knelt beside her, pet her head, and began a ritual to free her soul. His whispers were communicated from the carnidawg to the gods and back. Arc thanked her for the encounter, and upon the beautiful female's ascent to the afterlife, he removed one of her fangs as a keepsake and went about his business.

The tooth was drilled and added to his already impressive collection of kills that he wore in the form of a necklace. Teeth and claws of various kinds adorned his bare chest and showed others of his aptitude in battle. One of his most prized souvenirs was a massive Spidanoid fang that he had attained on Cypra. Some scorpion claws from his homeworld and additional random tokens from other worlds rounded out his awe-inspiring adornment. Even being several years Nuttybomb's junior, he was indeed a powerful warrior.

Arc's mind attuned to Nuttybomb. He idolized the warchief and respected his accomplishments as well. Like so many others, Arc offered himself without thought to protect his leader at all cost. So many orcs intuitively sensed how important Nuttybomb was to their very existence; the warchief's stirring speeches further excited the masses into a collective frenzy.

Arc's earlier meditation brought him into a focus that gave him insight into Nutty's condition. He couldn't communicate while Nuttybomb was comatose, but he could sense the struggles within his leader's body and mind. Nuttybomb was bordering on death and this weighed heavily on Arc.

So, while the pride of his kill carried him effortlessly to a nearby lake, his heavy heart dragged his mind along with him. It was here that he was to meet Moonoak and a few of the elders. His early arrival gave him time to reenter the trance that was cut short by the carnidawg's attack. Now, he sat quietly and relinquished his thoughts to a clarity that few were able to attain.

His eyes fluttered while his mind left his body. The awareness of souls recently departed filled his senses, colors and smells bombarding him in unparalleled beauty. Their passing was acknowledged before calm washed over him.

Arc was in a state that transported him to Nuttybomb. Communication with his leader was still impossible, although the pain and distress that ravaged the warchief plagued him. He was vaguely aware of Nutty's high temperature and pain, but he was keenly aware of his troubled soul fighting to remain within the physical. Furthermore, while he couldn't pinpoint the cause of Nutty's physical ailments, he knew of the infection that was eating him from within. He sought answers to aid his weakened warlord.

An answer came in the form of Moonoak. The spiritual leader sat alongside Arc and began a series of breathing exercises. He entered into a similar trance as Arc and entered the same realm of consciousness.

Arc smiled as he spoke softly, "Moonoak."

Moonoak replied, "Arc. Young one, you a able to communicate now. Very good. You not a child no mo'."

Arc admitted, "It come anda go. I not always able to calm lika dis."

"You still young anda new to dis. But you gettin' so much betta."

"Anda stronga too." Arc nodded in confirmation.

Moonoak shared his concern with him. "It not 'bout gettin' stronga in fight, it 'bout gettin' stronga in mind anda spirit."

Arc quarreled, "Stronga in fight mean I survive to get stronga in mind anda spirit, tho. Plus, it fun to get strong inna fight."

"True, but nevva foget dat it about mind anda spirit first. Den, you able to fight as a stronga warrior."

"But once I kill all enemies, I can get mind to do anyting witout resistance."

Moonoak shuddered as he sensed the dangerous potential of his underling. Arc was becoming powerful and if his abilities couldn't be controlled, and if he chose to take a path to glory first, he might end up like Darkster. Orcs who put themselves before their species inevitably invited corruption to their souls. Moonoak privately took caution while he urged his student down a path of goodness.

Without Nuttybomb to guide the upstart, Moonoak struggled to diffuse Arc's thoughts of using his powers to kill or maim. The border between being a shaman as opposed to becoming a warlock or evil necromancer was tethered by the thinnest of margins. Although Arc had displayed several noble qualities at times, he also exhibited dark, unexpected traits.

Perhaps continued training would shape his pupil in a positive way, or perhaps reinforcement by using Nuttybomb as an example would help. If Arc truly worshiped Nutty as presumed, maybe Moonoak could reference only his good deeds and drive home the importance of a soul that sought salvation in the afterlife.

Five elders found Moonoak and Arc in states of altered consciousness. They each sat amongst their teacher and fellow students before transcending consciousness themselves. They, too, shuddered upon feeling the uneasiness that surrounded their dangerous cohort.

Arc's eyes opened as he smiled.

***

How ships broke gravity of planets and applied their own gravity was of little thought to most orcs. Only the most intelligent orcs understood the hows and whys that science hid from their less than brilliant counterparts. Years of tinkering led to an explosion of information sharing as Nuttybomb's hometown of Bigtown became the center for discovery and learning.

Yes, Nuttybomb had propelled his species into an era of enlightenment that broke every boundary set before him and his kind. Simple travel became antiquated overnight as confiscated enemy spacecraft were reverse engineered, thrusting the Hotta orcs into space, both literally and figuratively. Confrontations with humans and other species opened up possibilities that until now, were unavailable to isolationist societies. Their technologies were studied and applied to Hotta's own. Nutty's orcs had accomplished in a mere four years what other civilizations needed hundreds or even thousands of years to do.

All of this meant little to Gunza, except that he recognized how special his son-in-law was. He had never known an orc of such quality, and although his submission to a younger orc, let alone his daughter's husband, would have been unthinkable until recently, he accepted it without question. Nuttybomb was everything he ever could have wanted for his daughter and Gunza knew he was lucky.

He watched the main viewscreen, filled with stars against the black backdrop. He briefly thought about his crash course in three-dimensional ship tactics, something he wasn't accustomed to in his long history of land battles. And yes, his mind even bounced back to the gravitational system that allowed his feet to be planted firmly on the deck beneath him. He smiled in pride at such an odd technological breakthrough. He sipped some Java before asking, "Is da scout ship on our sensors yet?"

"No, Sir," was replied.

Gunza took another swig from his cup, but spilled some hot fluid down his chest. He noticed that two of his bridge crew had seen his silly accident because of his growling in dissatisfaction toward himself. Then, he realized their eyes were fixated on his hand that still held the cup. It was shaking uncontrollably and not for the first time. He laughed as a front and lied as an excuse, "Guess I drinked too much shlogger dis mornin'."

While the bridge crew laughed and dismissed what they saw as acceptable, Gunza thought otherwise. He put down the cup and ordered, "I go to my room. Let me know when da scout ship inna range." He left his chair of command and scurried back to his quarters to hide his deficiency.

Once there, he paced and spat curses under his breath. His freakin' hands shook and he limped like an old fool, not to mention that now he found himself carrying on a ridiculous conversation that no one else could hear. He sighed and sat back on an oversized chair that comfortably held his weight.

Gunza thought about a possible confrontation with Darkster and Headhunta. Darkster almost killed his daughter and several of his elite guard while Headhunta did plenty of damage to him and Guthrak. Boy, were they gonna get theirs this time around.

He decided to make his way to the hangar deck as it was the only open area where he could swing his sword freely without hitting anything. Shaking hands or not, some hard training would do him some good. He grabbed his sword and left his room.

He began to daydream as he walked, thoughts still on his enemy.

Six
Doc Can't Save Him

It was discovered that Darkster, formally known as Cracka, who was bidding for leadership by attempting to enter Hotta orcs' minds, was the son of Headhunta. A confrontation was inevitable with the two, even as a war against the Invadas was happening all over the planet.

The cave was full of warriors. Nuttybomb had taken over as warchief from Biggabomb and they were both fighting side by side. Moonoak, Quicklip, Thunda, and Nubbs were there too. Most of them were tied up battling against Darkster and the creeps that were brought out of their graves. Guthrak's nephew wandered into the fight as well, although he was unaware of the circumstances.

It happened all too quick! Darkster's trickery fooled the young Thunda into his clutches. Thunda burst into flames, surprising Guthrak and momentarily drawing his attention away from a possible attack from Headhunta. And when it came, he was too slow to stop Headhunta's blade from severing his jugular vein. As a result, Guthrak's clumsy response was simply a knee-jerk reaction to movement that he caught from his periphery. He barely got his own blade lifted to deflect the lethal strike that crossed below the souvenir blade that he wore in his jaw. He was only fast enough to lose a couple fingers and cause Headhunta's knife to swing in somewhat of a horizontal strike. The original upward swing of the blade would have cut the vein along its full length. However, the minimal deflection caused a clean cut across his brain's vital blood supply. As a result, it could have been worse.

Gunza engaged Headhunta in a heartbeat. His enraged strikes, heavy and powerful, were countered by Headhunta's fluidity. While Gunza had all the anger of his wounded daughter flowing throughout his body, Headhunta had a clear head and a determined spirit on his side.

Before long, the two were using multiple weapons. Gunza used a twenty-inch knife in his right hand and a lean battleax in his left. Headhunta had somehow replaced his knife with two long swords. Two dissimilar styles with practically unparalleled skills were set upon each other. Virtual brothers were now matched as enemies, and each knew how deadly the other was.

Guthrak entered the fight in spurts. However, the best that he could do was to engage Headhunta at the same time Gunza attacked. He staggered forward, swung, then retreated. He was forced to rely on his weaker left hand to swing a weapon since losing some fingers and part of his right hand and thumb. Being predominantly right-handed, and not ambidextrous like Gunza and Headhunta, he struggled to keep pace with them. Each time he stepped back, he held his torn throat with the injured hand that somehow prolonged his life.

In a series of chaotic engagements, Headhunta killed Guthrak's nephew, who thought Headhunta was still friendly. Guthrak roared as he flew across the room at Headhunta. He took a deep cut to his right hip and leg as he broke Headhunta's ribs due to such a violent collision. He smashed Headhunta's face over and over with his forearm. A dazed Headhunta reequipped himself with a knife and used it. As Guthrak's arm came down to crush Headhunta's face for the eleventh time, it was torn by the razor-sharp blade.

Gunza never did capitalize on Guthrak's attack. He was stabbed in the back by Darkster who had just been freed up by Nubbs. Gunza threw a quick backhand that sent Darkster flying twenty feet and picked up where Guthrak left off against Headhunta yet again.

Nutty rushed into combat alongside Gunza against Darkster and Headhunta. Gunza was so badly wounded that he struggled to defend himself. He had finally collapsed from blood loss. All the others were fighting Invadas that entered the cave. Nutty had to face Darkster and Headhunta alone. Gunza couldn't even stand up from all the wounds he had received.

It wasn't long before Gunza lost consciousness. He was told after the fact that Nuttybomb had killed Headhunta and severely wounded Darkster. But the father was somehow brought back to life by his evil son before the two managed to escape. It was later confirmed that they joined the Invadas.

**

The sounds of battle still rang in Gunza's ears, as did the smell of blood. Hell, they even pumped him up. He picked up his pace in excitement as he neared the hangar deck. But as he turned to enter the large, open room, his shoulder slammed into a bulkhead.

He grimaced as the impact stopped him dead in his tracks and staggered him. *How da hell did I do dat?*

102

he asked himself. He shook his arm to regain some feeling as he slowly walked into the hangar.

Gunza passed some small ships until he found an area he could move around in without interference. He took some deep breaths and stretched, moaning as he pulled each heavy leg to his chest. His shoulders were rolled in circular motions, as was his head, to loosen up before swinging his trusty weapon. He pulled his sword and began.

A thrust here and a swing there began his training. He reacquainted himself with the blade he intended to use on Headhunta. Although it was quite heavy, the weapon was balanced so that the weight was back at the handle, making it easy to use. He held it in different poses, nodding his head in affirmation that it was a well-made and balanced weapon.

After several minutes, the old warrior swung his sword in a series of spins. It felt like old times to Gunza, and he was proud of himself for not losing any skill. However, that was short lived as he dropped his sword while attempting to switch it from his right hand to his left. He smiled as he picked it up and tried again, but his happy facial expression was also temporary as he unwittingly threw his sword across the room. It clanged against the hard metal deck before screeching as it slid away from his perplexed look.

***

"Prepare my ship!" Darkster commanded.

"Yessir." The frightened orc scrambled to accommodate his leader as quickly as he could. He certainly didn't want the wrath of the evil orc coming down on him. He departed for *Da Malevolent*, the largest warship in the star system. It had to be the largest to stroke Darkster's ego. A second-rate tug would never suffice!

Darkster peered into the sky, envisioning where Nuttybomb might have been at that particular moment. Perhaps he was on Hotta, clinging to the hope that he might be a significant factor in orcs' history. To Darkster, now smugly confident in his own abilities, he was probably dying somewhere; *the stupid Nuttybomb and his weaknesses were probably exposed by another dopey orc*. He hoped the Hotta leader was on his way to Marshil. Death was something Darkster had in store for the weak leader of Hotta.

He focused on his nemesis until the annoying sounds of birds in flight bothered him. There was a whole flock, screaming in his ears and causing his blood to boil. He clenched his fists and grit his teeth. He snarled as his head twisted unnaturally, his eyes focused on the damned fowl that hindered his thoughts. One by one, they dropped from the sky and fluttered on the ground, their wings flapping wildly.

They were no longer able to sing so beautifully as just moments before. Instead, they simply tossed their bodies around without the ability to control their actions. Their brains were emptied, unable to give vital instructions to the rest of their beings. Never to fly again in this realm, they departed for the next...and Darkster smiled.

The Acheronian butcher summoned three of his warriors while he waited for his ride into space. This time, the orc that received the order, tripped and fell in haste. He looked up at Darkster in fear, praying he either hadn't been noticed or that his clumsiness wasn't a serious offense. He was wrong on both counts.

Darkster telepathically informed the orc that he wasn't worthy of living in this world or any other in the physical plane they inhabited. The stricken orc didn't believe he was worthy of his leader, his own thoughts being replaced by the seductive pull of the stronger mind. So, without the ability to counter Darkster's designs, the orc's body began to fail. Just because he was forced to believe in his own life's worthlessness, his subverted body succumbed to the commands to cease breathing.

Darkster couldn't help the cackle that left his mouth as he watched intently. He thoroughly enjoyed the interplay with his subordinates, whether they did or not. Actually, he found it pleasing to feel their pain because of his unprecedented powers. It astounded him to feel the transition from life to death, especially at his hands. The power he felt was unmatched.

As commanded, and finally carried out by an orc who hadn't died, a few orcs arrived to stand before their leader. They were of various height and age. Although none were over twenty, they were trained well and knew to keep silent. However, that didn't matter.

Their minds were entered- all three- with the ease of sailing with the wind, with the casualness of a mother's love for her baby. Then again, perhaps if a mother's love for her baby existed, the three unfortunate orcs wouldn't have been tortured.

They began to drop to their knees. Two held their throats as they gasped for breath; the other tried to pump air into his lungs by opening his mouths as wide as he could. It didn't matter though. They all ended up on the ground, unable to use the air that was all around them. Darkster told them they couldn't breath , and so, they couldn't.

He was as giddy as a school girl. He danced as he threw his hands into the air, pride and joy overtaking his need to finish off his once reliable troops. He cared not for their lives, their suffering. They were pawns in a larger chess match, used to polish his already impressive pieces. *Besides*, he reasoned, *what difference could several simpletons do that would make any difference in the cosmos?* They were miniscule in the whole scheme of things; unfortunately, they weren't miniscule to themselves or their families.

For two years, Darkster summoned orcs to practice on; thousands stricken prematurely as he performed the dark art of sorcery on their meager existences. In the beginning, as he tampered with their thoughts, he reduced hundreds to vegetables by accident. But now, he easily forced his will upon them, overtaking their own thoughts and replacing them with negative, life-ending reality as his craft was perfected. Being in their minds, he particularly enjoyed the cold chill he gave them. He could feel the emptiness in their hearts, and especially, their souls.

His powers weren't just limited to his accomplishments while his subjects were awake and within view either. Other orcs were tested on while they slept. He entered their dreams and haunted them, sending most of them into deep, irreversible comas. His mind would reach out to nearby houses and send signals as queries. Once their minds answered his request to enter their states of slumber, something they did without ever knowing how or why, their vivid nightmares began; they had no control over their thoughts while they slept.

"Da ship ready, Sir," came from a visibly nervous orc.

Darkster stepped over a twitching body and left the area of unnecessary carnage. He yawned and rubbed his eyes as he waded through twenty-foot statues, made in his likeness, washing him from head to toe with self-adorning gratification. The gleaming bronze embellished his musculature and the hard features of his face as reflections hid the true nature of the cracks sculpted throughout the pathetically enhanced caricatures. He pumped out his chest in pride as he strode by them.

He reached the launch area and asked a subordinate, "How many ships we gots to go to Marshil?"

"Sir, seventy ships gonna launch, sir. We gots ova a thousand in space." The orc pointed to the sky as if to convey the direction of the fleet in case his words weren't clear.

"Good, good." Darkster smiled. "How many troops?"

"A millions troops."

Darkster appeared annoyed. "One million?"

The subordinate gulped, "Yessir."

"Why no mo' dan one million?" he snapped.

"Not 'nuff ships to bring dems."

With gritted teeth and a disgusted sigh, Darkster waved his hand in defiance. "No matta. Three million creeps plus a one million troops anda more meetin' me at Marshil. Nuttybomb is a doomed!"

***

107

A few hundred ships ducked beneath the cold, desolate realm of space and descended into the atmosphere that enveloped them in balls of fire as friction slowed their pace to acceptable cruising speeds. Landings took place, somewhat haphazardly as the huge influx of troops exited their respected crafts before their rides left for the stars and new ones replaced them. Within three hours, all troops were offloaded and ready to fight.

The cool, damp air went unnoticed by The Hotta orcs. Sure, it wasn't hot like most of their homeworld, but they had trained in the arctic regions back home in preparation for this very purpose; it was far colder there. Besides, they were oblivious to most discomforts as they relished the battles that were to come and occupied their minds.

Guthrak, Quicklip, Nubbs; Ucktock, and Arc settled around Gunza, eager to proceed. His orders to them were simple. "We here to kill evvy creep. It just dat easy. Den da Elders will do der ting wit' da creeps. Anda we will recruit evvy Marshil orc to help. Any questions?"

Quicklip spoke up. "Ya. Da last time I here most creeps came out a night time. You gotta plan?"

"Well, yes anda no. Basic plan is to clear da northern hemisphere first. It got more areas dat had cities. Bigga populations means mo' dead orcs dat turned to creeps. Our army prolly biggest it evva gonna be on dis planet right now, so we fight mo' forces now and less later. Dis way if we have less troops later, we still be ok. Plus, I hopes to get mo' Marshil orcs to help us early too."

Guthrak snarled, "Ok, dat a plan. Not so basic. Sounda good to me."

Gunza added, "Ya, but I tink Darkster will prolly come outta hidin' and bring a army wit' him. Dat will change evvyting. I gots ships in space to protect too. Plan only for now."

"Gotcha," Guthrak acknowledged.

Nubbs joined the conversation with, "Gettin' dark. Gonna get busy real soon."

Quicklip agreed, "Not much time. We settin' up camp or movin' out?"

Gunza snapped, "We movin'. Letta us go."

They moved ahead of the troops that stretched along a front that covered several hundred miles. Pockets of orcs in reserve followed a few miles behind the front line to move up and bolster areas that came under heavy attack or to cover holes between troops that might be passed over. Generally, cities and towns were primary targets with villages and minor settlements as secondary considerations. The reserves would mop up and hit sparsely populated areas. Well behind the lines were mobile medical units to deal with the anticipated wounded. Some of the best docs and females with medical knowledge waited in them for casualties.

As the silhouette of an abandoned city came into view amongst the light mist, Guthrak made an observation. Through the darkness he saw thousands of creeps coming from the urban landscape to meet the Hotta orcs. An opposition force was usually met with artillery or tanks. He wondered why his army didn't have them for the battle that was imminent. "Why we gots no tanks?"

Nubbs seconded the inquiry. "Ya, how come?"

Gunza explained, "Can't use 'em against creeps. Gotta make sure der bodies are still intact to save der souls."

Nubbs moaned, "Come on. We gotta fight witout our strongest weapons fo' da creeps' benefit?"

"Yup. Dats wut I sayin's."

A displeased Ucktock gave a piece of his mind. "Dat kinda stupid. Dems creeps is no joke."

Gunza rebutted, "You want yer soul lost forevva? Shutta up anda do yer job!"

Ucktock realized he may have offended his warchief by saying part of the plan was stupid. He backpedaled a bit. "I not mean dat it stupid fo' us to save der souls, howevva we gots to do it. It stupid dat we gots to do it dis way. It nobody fault. It just is wut it is." He ducked and rolled, as was his way.

Gunza's ass hairs settled as he agreed, "I know. It sucks, but dis da way it gots to be. Ok. Here dems come. Looka sharp!"

***

"It too late. I can't save him," came from Doc Cutstick's lips.

The infection had taken its toll, even with medications and surgery to repair what he could, Cutstick threw in the towel. He had fought for hours to somehow bring his patient back from an obvious fate. A last resort amputation was conducted to remove most of the dead leg that had caused so much rot to travel throughout.

The female who assisted him asked, "You sure der nuttin' mo' we can do?"

Cutstick slowly remarked, "He fought hard, but his heart stopped, and I can't get it goin'." He looked down at Muddy before pulling a blanket over the warrior's yellowish-green skin.

"Ok. I report it to da military."

Cutstick washed his face and hands to remove Muddy's blood from his own skin. He tossed a red soaked towel into a bin and proceeded to Nuttybomb's recovery room. As he approached the doorway, he questioned a helper, "Any change?"

"No. Him still very weak and in da coma."

"How his heart?"

The helper explained, "Weak lika evvyting else, but it keep beatin' while you in udder surgery."

Cutstick sighed, "Dat good at least. Get me Uhra so I can tell her wut goin' on."

"Yessir."

The doc pushed open a blanket that hung between him and Nutty, revealing the sickest orc he had ever operated on who hadn't died. He was amazed by the fact that a leg injury, although somewhat severe, resulted in the death of Muddy. Yet Nuttybomb clung to life, albeit vicariously, with a hundred times the damage to his body than what Muddy's had sustained.

Cutstick couldn't explain why the line between life and death was so small and why some survived and others didn't. However, he was thankful that he was able to keep Nuttybomb alive until this point and he was fully aware that he was probably the only orc on Hotta who might have been able to pull his fallen leader back from the brink of death.

His thick fingers pushed ever so slightly into Nutty's eye socket and pulled open a lid, revealing

111

pupils that were unable to respond to stimulus. Cutstick sighed in disgust, knowing full well the signs of a potential miracle just weren't there. For all his efforts to revive his legendary wargod, it may have been too little, too late.

Finally, the dismayed doc hung his head and commented to his assistant, "No mo' I can do today. It late. I goin' home fo da night. Tomorrow we try electric on his heart."

His assistant whispered, "You sure? It only work a few times befo'. Might kills him."

"It our only hope. Him nevva wake up wit'out it."

"You only one who can do it. Get good night sleep, Doc. I see you in da mornin'."

***

Massive forces were gathering beyond sensor range of Gunza's fleet that hung above Marshil. Enemy ships that numbered in the thousands were waiting to begin their assault, first to eliminate Hotta's fleet, and then to begin deploying troops on the planet once space above the atmosphere was devoid of opposition.

Darkster seemed a bit more pleased with these numbers than the meager forces he left with just two days before. His smaller force was now linking up with the much larger, main fleet that awaited his arrival. He couldn't wait to destroy Nuttybomb and his followers. His hands clenched into fists as he thought about every Hotta orc eventually bowing to his will, forcing them to convert their loyalties from his arch nemesis to his egotistical self.

His voice rattled, "Wut?" upon his thoughts being interrupted by his communications officer.

The orc who thought about speaking to Darkster didn't even say anything; he never so much as uttered a word. Yet Darkster heard him and replied. The orc, taken aback by the unlikely response spoke carefully. "Kingskull wanna talk a you."

Darkster rolled his tongue around in his mouth, smiled, and said, "I talk wit' him ova da speaker. Go ahead."

At the flick of a switch, the main viewscreen switched from thousands of space faring vessels to an ugly, scary looking individual, decorated in ironclad armor, piercings, and visible scars. His beady, red eyes squinted to get a better look at this "Darkster" who sat amongst the darkness of his dimly lit bridge.

Darkster addressed the face he saw on the large screen, "Kingskull?"

"Yup. I decided to join you and rid da star cluster a dis Warchief Nuttybomb."

A smile was followed by a snarl as he spat, "Him call himself Wargod Nuttybomb now."

Kingskull displayed his rotting teeth as he smiled broadly. "Well, we see about dat." His long, gold earrings rang as they smacked against his metal shoulder pads.

Darkster questioned, "How long till you get here?"

"I comin' up behind you," the foreign leader stated.

"Good, good. So, I hear dat you rule ova seven worlds?"

Kingskull's face took on the expression of madness. "Nine! Nine worlds!"

Darkster clicked his long fingernails on the arm of his chair. "Hmm. Dat not wut I heard."

"Well you heard wrong! Da Great Skull Clan kills all befo' it! Evvy world fall to Da Great Skull Clan!"

"Even creeps?" Darkster teased.

"Wut?"

"Yer Skull Clan even kill creeps?"

Kingskull didn't fully understand the question. "Creeps just kid stories. How we fight fake stuff?"

Darkster leaned forward as he relished the thought of being so superior to this ugly orc before him. He teased, "Oh? You nevva fight a creep?"

"No. Der no such ting."

Darkster corrected, "You wrong, Kingskull. Anda you will see my army fro' da dead soon."

Kingskull knew of orcs fabricating ridiculous stories or simply embellishing facts to prop themselves up, but what he was hearing was absurd and he said so. "Don't insult me wit' stupid stories. Der be no creeps."

Darkster shook his head and frowned. He scowled, "If you say a so," before dismissing the annoying Kingskull with a simple push of a button on the arm of his chair.

Standing from his raised chair, Darkster gave the order, "It time to attack da weak Hotta orcs ova Marshil. Attack ships first. Den our fightas and bombas wit' support ships. Now! Attack!" He pointed frantically as if to somehow drive the ships that couldn't see nor hear him toward their destination.

The fleet began to rearrange itself as ships left formation and diverged back into the mix. Organizing such a huge number of ships took nearly an hour as the dismayed warlord spat orders in a foul tongue. He wouldn't be denied this first victory that he perceived

114

as just one in a long line of victories to come. No, it was his time, his destiny!

Seven
Bait

Horror filled the souls of orcs that were confronted by creeps for the first time. They never imagined how insanely grotesque and violent they were. And they were fast! Not restricted by certain physical limitations that plagued their lively counterparts, they rushed forward unto their victims, even as their limbs dropped from their lifeless bodies. Sure, those without legs dragged themselves into mayhem and weren't as quick to engage, but strength of muscle nor speed of reflexes seemed to matter. They were just driven from beyond.

Quicklip yelled, "Sunnammabitch!" as he drove his sword through the eye of one creep, then the ribcage of another, only to find them still fighting furiously.

Ucktock snapped, "Gotta cut der heads off!" He sidestepped a creep and swung around to decapitate it. Rot splattered on the back of Quicklip before the creep dropped motionless. He rolled to one side, and then to the other. He stood from a crouch and took the head from a new attacker.

"Quicklip cringed as the putrid smell overtook his assailed senses. He screamed sarcastically, "Ya tink? Dat wut I tryin's to do," as he smeared rot down his back while trying to remove it.

Gunza and his bodyguard were slowly managing to make their way through the onslaught of creeps that engaged them. They noticed parts of their lines halted in their tracks by the sheer number of creeps that rushed them.

Gunza ordered, "Spread out! Our troops aren't doin' goods."

Guthrak hollered, "Wut da hell wrong wit' dems? Dems fightin' lika girls!"

"Der too many creeps fo' dems. Anda look."

"Looka wut?"

Gunza pointed out, "All dem creeps got weapons."

Guthrak and some of the other guards squinted in disbelief. The old elite guard quizzed, "How da hell dem all get swords?"

Just then Quicklip yelled out, "Here dems comes! Dem gots weapons too!"

Reality began to sink in as the Hotta orcs soon found the armed opposition fighting like a well-trained unit. It had become all too clear that they weren't facing a collection of ill equipped, mindless enemies. No, this was a determined army, not just a mass of random creeps.

Still, the guards fought valiantly, and as their prowess thinned the number of creeps around them, they gave aid to the weaker troops that had been struggling.

The first battle lasted around twenty minutes and reports began to reach Gunza. He and his guards were cut and bruised, but generally, they were okay. However, six thousand Hotta troops had lost their lives and another ten thousand sustained serious wounds. His forces couldn't withstand such heavy losses while only fighting creeps. *Dis not good*, Gunza thought.

He moved his troops toward the next cities they would attack and wondered if he should concentrate all his forces against each city instead of splitting them up to attack multiple cities at the same time. He quickly dismissed the idea as foolish. He didn't have months to eradicate Marshil of creeps; in his estimation, he only had a couple weeks at best.

Gunza's estimated timeline was shattered as his forces attacked the next city. It was here, while he was busy taking it on the chin against creeps that he learned of Darkster's fleet closing on his own. "Oh, my gods," he muttered when told of the enormous number of enemy ships approaching his.

He was struck with the probability of losing his entire fleet while his ground forces, worn down by creeps, would have to face the brunt of Darkster's main army. Scouts had estimated Darkster's ground forces to be no less than ten million troops. Gunza had around six hundred thousand to counter. No fleet would mean no way to leave the planet for him and his massively outnumbered troops. Things just became desperate!

***

She pulled back cloth that covered her face, her dithered features still hidden by shadows cast by the hood that covered her head and her identity. Her frail, stooped figure clung to the edges of buildings like ripened fruit pulled to the ground by gravity. Her twisted will drove her toward her inexhaustible task as if by fate.

The witch's gnarly fingers wrapped themselves around a wooden staff that she used, not only to help her broken body traverse the uneven bricks that covered the road, but as a fulcrum in which to cast her

118

evil bidding. Light flickered from a child's skull at the top of the staff and threw ominous colors against her sickly skin. She licked her parched, cracked lips through rotten teeth, drooling on her worn robe below.

The door opened without physical force, revealing its contents to her prying eyes. Muddy boots laid haphazardly in the corner of the room with a few coats hanging above them on designated hooks. It was dark and quiet, calling to her desires.

She carefully stepped over the slight clutter of toys on the wood planked floor as her eyes took in several comforts that her mind began to process. The room showed signs of children, entities she despised, but it also displayed medical garments that hung near the coats; a sign she had located her prey.

A small orc unexpectedly stumbled upon the witch, startling both parties. The child's overactive bladder had caused the boy to leave his bed in search of relieving the bothersome organ. Instead, he found a ghastly sight that had invaded his home. He wiped his eyes to see better, crust and slime encasing his sleepy orbital sockets. He stood there as his bladder emptied itself before the nightmare that lurked a few feet away.

The evil that hid itself quietly to this point raced upon the child. A spell was cast and the little one was reduced to a convulsing vegetable. The shockingly audible infliction caught the attention of other sleeping residents as well. One of them, the oldest member of the household, awoke and raced from his own bed to inspect the phenomenon that drew him like a bug to a light.

Like his child, he fought to clear his eyes of mucus that always seemed to affect those sleeping. He hollered to his wife as he neared the front room, "Mama, get to da chitlins!" His look of despair was easily conveyed and understood by his wife, who obeyed his command. They darted in opposite directions.

The father's stomach quickly churned as he anticipated finding harm to one of his beloved. He didn't know what ungodly sound caused his body to be thrust into overdrive, but his innate sense at his body's physical reaction sent off alarms. His profession made him all too aware of why his heart and lungs pushed his senses to heightened states. Fear was beginning to grip him!

He dropped to his knees in the front room when he saw one of his sons seizing. He tried to assess the situation to discover why the boy was convulsing. The father checked the boy's pulse with one hand as he pulled a coat from a hook. Then he wrapped the garment into somewhat of a ball and placed it under the shuddering head of his son to lessen damage to the brain.

Meanwhile, he still guessed as to why his previously strong, healthy son was now ill and pondered about the screams that woke him and his wife. Perhaps it was his son who screamed before succumbing to convulsions, but it sure sounded like the voice and language weren't those of his boy. They weren't what one would consider cries for help or words slurred by something physical. No, they sounded distinctly foreign.

Upon checking his son's eyes and mouth, and further ruling out reaction to a poisonous bite, the father stood up. He had now concluded that something else was among him and his afflicted heir. He slowly closed his eyes and rubbed the back of his neck where hair stood up on end. A cold shiver raced from the base of his buttock up to his head. He turned to face something he somehow knew was there, but didn't know why.

"Why did you hurt my boy?" gulped the father. The darkness only partially revealed a figure in its midst and the horrors it hid, yet somehow embraced, which only enhanced the fears it elicited in the father. His voice cracked as he pleaded again, "Who a you? What did you a do?"

The response wasn't what was sought. "You a doc, right?"

"Yes, but wut wrong wit' da boy?"

The witch played with the father. "Den you helpa him, no?"

The frustrated and desperate father cried out, "Not if I not know wut wrong wit' him."

"You a Doc Cutstick?"

"Yes, but so wut?"

The next response gave perilous indications for both father and son. "Even his dad, da great Doc can't stoppa my spell fro' mushin' his brains. Anda he can't stop his own brains fro' mushin'. Da great doc can't save him! Goma vey, Goma vee!!!"

Doc Cutstick fell to his back in pain. Blood gushed from his nose and the veins in his forehead bulged. He finally understood the screams that he tried to decipher earlier, but now it was too late. His hands reached for his head to keep it from exploding, but they never gave comfort as the muscles in his arms tensed and constricted, constraining them from

121

reaching their destination. All he could muster was the scream, "Mama, get outta da house!"

A helplessness engulfed him as he laid next to his son. The two shook violently, banging body parts against each other until their breathing finally ceased. By then, the witch was long gone from the Cutstick residence.

**

"It not a retreat," Gunza explained.

Guthrak spat, "We runnin' lika dawgs wit' our tails 'tween our legs."

"Look, old friend, we got some army back on Hotta, ships too. I can get some mo' fro' da utter worlds too. We just make our stand der."

"Ok, but I don't likes it."

Gunza understood. He and Guthrak had been through a lifetime of challenges, many of which seemed insurmountable. And yet, here they were. In the past, they usually repositioned themselves to take advantage of an enemy's weakness, eventually fighting through to victory. Full retreat was unconscionable. But since they left their homeworld and ventured into space, the old tactics didn't apply the same way. Their ships above were their lifeline, their resupply, and their only chance to reposition. This cold, dead world was their bad position, and their ships, the better position.

Gunza began to explain, but Quicklip interrupted, "Is it true? Doc Cutstick beed killed?"

Gunza acknowledged, "Ya, it true." He closed the gate to a truck and sent it on its way.

"Wut 'bout Wargod Nuttybomb?" Ucktock pried.

Gunza sighed, "Dunno. Him real bad fro' wut I hear. But he still fightin'."

Guthrak taunted, "Him's da only one still fightin'. We runnin'."

Gunza snarled, "Dat 'nuff talkin'. We gotta go. Now!"

The Hotta orcs began the arduous task of breaking down equipment, medical tents, and reloading everything onto the ships that were called down to the surface. Having to fight off several attacks from creeps as they prepared to flee only hampered their efforts. They were beating the creeps that were assailing them. Why were they retreating?

The air was thick with the feeling of defeat. Far too many orcs seldom understood that fighting under better circumstances might have given them better odds to win. Even those that understood, didn't necessarily agree with retreating and living to fight another day. They were orcs, and being orcs, they fought their hardest, regardless of it meaning certain death. Even their recent rise to civility and decency didn't change their inherent traits. Tens of thousands of years of evolution made them this way. Pretty cities and petty luxuries would never change that.

Gunza was reminded of this fact when he boarded his ship. He overheard grumblings of disenchanted soldiers who had boarded before him. He looked over to see Guthrak's look of "*I told you* so". He growled, "Screwa dems. "

***

Kingskull was much older than his smug ally, and much more experienced. Fifteen years of war obliged him with knowledge of tactics – something the upstart

Darkster knew very little about. Moreover, the gains from his victories subjugated six worlds beneath his leadership. These worlds were conquered, as much by fear, as from the destruction of their defenses.

His brutality subdued the masses beneath his rule, a tyrannical force with no bounds, an entity unto itself. His term, "Follow me or die," swallowed up followers from every corner of two star-systems, granting him more power in which to wield. He was cunning as well. Intelligence dictated choices to promote or remove by whatever means, as opposed to his counterpart's impulsive and sadistic snap judgements. Furthermore, he played politics to bring enemies to his doorstep, always offering a position beneath him, or death as an option. Even his brother fled his wrath.

His disbelief in Darkster's creeps was valid. He had never seen, nor heard of such things in reality, despite fifteen years of death and destruction surrounding him. He reasoned over and over to the contrary of such a ridiculous possibility. Besides, he was here to explore and test all clans in this star system for weaknesses, waiting for the opportunity to add to his already mighty empire. The embellishment of a crazed leader was something he dealt with several times. Darkster was just one more.

Regardless of the lunatic's claims, Kingskull was smart enough to evaluate everything he saw and heard. It would just be a matter of time before he found out if Darkster was to be taken seriously on multiple levels. A chink in the younger orc's armor would render him another one of the conquered, whereas a well-armed and protected force could be used as a potent ally.

It was this so-called wargod he was after anyway. Nuttybomb had a reputation as strong as Darkster's, maybe even stronger. He had fought against Humans, developed technologies at a staggering pace, and saved a people from certain eradication. Minimally, Kingskull would use one of the newfound clans to his advantage. Maximally, both.

His thoughts were interrupted by, "Ships comin's to space fro' da planet."

Kingskull ordered, "Follow dems. Maka sure dems is da Nuttybomb ships."

The subordinate explained, "Looka likes dems are. Dems go ova der, Darkster ships ova here." He pointed his thick nub of a finger to the stars, showing the different positions of forces. Soon the finger was back in his nose where it served a better purpose.

"Yes!" the ruler of seven worlds exclaimed. He continued, "Follow dat group der comin's fro' da planet. Hurry!" He stood from his ship's throne, his full stature and elevated stage casting shadows on his underlings to his rear.

A weapons officer inadvertently ducked as the shadow quickly enveloped him. He stated, "Big guns ready,"

Kingskull ordered from his own flagship, *Da King's Slayer*, "Get Darkster fo' me."

Within a minute, Darkster's voice hailed, "Wut is it, Kingskull? I busy huntin' Nuttybomb ships."

Kingskull snarled, "I see you. I gets der first, I tink."

A high pitched and irritated response of, "We'll see," came back.

"Der won't be much left fo' you to kills," taunted Kingskull.

Darkster spat, "Don't gets to close a dems. My ships mighta miss dems anda hits you."

Now, the mighty Kingskull smiled. He was already getting under this Darkster's skin. A warning was what he expected from another orc leader. Pride and stupidity ran rampant throughout green skins. Apparently, Darkster wasn't too different. Kingskull would continue to bait the inexperienced leader to gauge his actions and reactions going forward. Momentarily, he was satisfied. He calmly stated, "My ships got bigga guns den yers. I no needs a getta too close."

Silence.

***

The old orc told a story. Then, he told another. They were pretty much the same story with different places and times, but essentially, they were nearly identical. He was always the hero, fighting his way through a mass of enemies, against all odds to find victory.

He pumped out his chest and raised his arms as certain events seemed more important to him, bravado ringing from the great words he spewed. His mouth crafted unbelievable truths, mostly lost on ears that couldn't comprehend. His adventures had become the stuff of legend, his accomplishments as the underdawg, inevitably shining through.

Joy and Crazybomb clapped at their grandpa, prompting more tales to be spun at a moment's notice. And before each rendition, they sat down, fixated on the next journey to come.

He began, "One time…I wus fightin against the Barbary Clan."

Uhra interrupted with, "Dad, really?"

Biggabomb replied, "Wut? Dis is impotent. Da kids should know dis stuff."

"You did goods in all da wars, but please," she implored.

"But dems likes it."

Uhra explained, "But Nutty's not doin' good anda no mo' war talk. Please."

Biggabomb agreed, "Ok, ok. You right. Sorry, kids. It time fo' bed anyway."

The kids cried out, "Oh."

He teased, "I know, I know, but yer mean ole Mama won't lemme tells no mo'."

Uhra tapped her foot and gritted her teeth. "You don't know mean."

The old orc chuckled, "Maybe not. I gotta go, kids, befo' yer Mama kills me. G'nite." Biggabomb patted each kid on the head and turned to Uhra. He said, "Nutty gonna be ok. Him's a tough kid."

"Ya, him's tough, but him's notta kid no mo'. Hims body is so beat up."

Biggabomb grunted, "I know da feelin'."

Uhra leaned into him and said, "Tanks, Dad. G'nite."

"G'nite, kiddo." Biggabomb lumbered out of the kid's room and down the hall to his place to sleep. His tales would have to wait for another day.

The marble walls gave the room a palatial feel, as did the guards outside, offering protection to royalty. Thin, silky materials draped from the high ceilings and down three of the walls added to the grand aura.

To Biggabomb, it was simply a room; just a room to sleep, to rip his dirty toenails off, to belch, fart, and anything else that gave him comfort. The large bed felt empty, though, without his wife, Muga, who was at their house in their shared bed. However, it didn't matter too much as he had known a life of battle, sleeping in trenches or out in the open, exposed to all elements the gods could throw at him. Missing Muga wasn't what he wanted, but it was nothing compared to war.

His eyes closed. Being at Nuttybomb's house with its amenities and décor gave him complacency he seldom experienced before. Even though he was tasked with providing additional protection to Uhra and her kids, slumber crept over him. With the windows and doors all closed and locked, a sense of security assured him of safety.

He awoke, only for a moment, looked around the room as he laid, and drifted back to sleep. But soon, he awoke again, this time aware that he wasn't in a state of sleep. It occurred to him that tossing and turning wasn't his way, especially since his lungs had healed enough for him to sleep straight through the night. He didn't see or hear anything, but something was amiss.

Biggabomb sat up, wearily wiped his eyes, and stretched as he yawned. As he stood, he pulled the material at the back of his pants from his crack, scratched the right side of his buttocks, and made his way into the hallway. A noticeable draft coming from the kids' rooms alarmed his senses.

His gait quickened as he advanced down the long corridor. He opened a door and saw his granddaughter,

Joy, pointing to his immediate left. A breeze from the open window she faced swayed the drapes.

His grandson, Crazybomb, whimpered, "No," as he, too, pointed in the same general direction.

Biggabomb's eyes surveyed the room as he stood at the entrance. The children were only ten feet away, certainly close enough for him to reach if necessary. The window, obviously open, was around six feet to his left, the drapes blowing eerily close to him. In the darkness, he cautiously stepped around to his right, checking the corners as he made his way around the perimeter of the room. This only took a few seconds, and soon, he had circled the kids and come to the far side of the open window.

He slowly pulled the drapes back to one side, looked back at the kids one more time, and peered out into the courtyard below. His eyes widened upon finding two bodies lying on the grounds beyond the window. These were the guards he had put his faith in to provide protection for his son's family. Now, they provided nothing but concern.

The hair on the old boss's neck rose, a chill working from the base of his spine to his head. He sidestepped from the window toward the kids as carefully as he could. If there was an intruder, he may have already left. If not, the grizzled old veteran would position himself to shield his grandkids.

The other side of the drapes moved away from the window, much too fast to have been caused by the wind. Biggabomb was startled by the movement that his eye picked up in its periphery. What fell upon him wasn't a shadow he would have anticipated, for it didn't match the directions cast from the bit of light emitted through the open window. Instead, as his head spun instinctively, his eyes gained full view of the horror that evolved.

From the murky shadows sprang an old friend, and now, enemy. Headhunta's sword ripped into Biggabomb's stomach and intestines. Biggabomb's senses immediately heightened, his ears never homing in on his attacker; only registering the splashing of his own innards on the rapier and floor, and his own moaning from agonizing pain.

Biggabomb threw his right elbow, knocking Headhunta back into the wall. The attacker staggered back, remaining upright as his rear found the support his feet needed to regain traction. He shook his head to clear some cobwebs and attacked again. With guts emptied, the hunched warrior took another slash across his face and chest.

Uhra rushed in to see her father-in-law being butchered, just feet away from her children. She screamed, not just in panic, but in a hasty attempt to draw Headhunta away from Biggabomb and the kids.

The floor was now covered in a slick layer of Biggabomb's liquids. Uhra slipped in blood and fell between Headhunta and her kids. Her head slammed against the stone floor, stunning her for what seemed like an eternity.

Headhunta turned, not so stealthily as before, and sprang toward Uhra. But Biggabomb, not quite finished yet, managed to get his hand around Headhunta's free arm.

Years of battle prepared Biggabomb for this very moment. He would die in a matter of minutes, but his only purpose was to slay the enemy before him. He had seen Headhunta fight countless times; he knew his actions; his next moves. He counted on the attacker's need to eliminate the strongest opponent before finishing off the woman and children. He tugged on the arm he held so precariously.

Headhunta swung around and thrust his sword into Biggabomb. The old orc was as ready as he could be and threw his free arm up, catching the blade as it found flesh and bone.

Biggabomb cried out. The sword pierced through the thick, hard bone of his forearm and halted just inches from his chest. He punched Headhunta with the fury of a true warrior, crushing his jawbone, and sending him to the floor. His weight carried him forward and down upon his assailant, his legs wrapping around his foe to secure leverage.

Headhunta's head cracked against the hard floor, causing temporary loss of vision and the vital ability to defend himself in that split second. He felt crushing blow after crushing blow to his face.

The two struggled for position for over a minute, Biggabomb's weak, but heavy body on top. Once he had control with his legs, preventing Headhunta from escaping his grip, Biggabomb used Headhunta's own weapon against him. His full weight came down, the protruding sword in his arm as the means to sever arteries in the enemy's neck.

There was nothing Headhunta could do. Weakened by concussive force, as well as age, and Biggabomb's blood keeping him from gripping anything effectively, he eventually succumbed to the force being applied. He gurgled and spat blood as the weapon easily slid through outer layers of tissue. His feet kicked violently, but to no avail, as it passed through his airway and met his spine. He sputtered, "Good job, Boss," before the blade completed its destiny with the granite floor behind his head.

Uhra crawled to Biggabomb, avoiding the head that rolled passed her. She cried, "Dad? Dad?"

Biggabomb didn't respond. He received death's blow two minutes earlier when his torso was scattered around the room. His brain finally allowed transition into the next realm upon his final victory over his once beloved guard. His untold tales would never reach the ears of his grandkids, nor anyone for that matter, ever again.

Uhra laid beside him, hugging his chest and back, running her hand over his forehead. "You did good, Dad. You saved us. Tanks. I wuvs you." She shook uncontrollably, her sobs just short of wailing. Her breath was short and quick. She didn't know how she would tell Nutty and Muga- that was, if Nutty survived.

Nuttybomb's guards came from everywhere! They took up positions all around the room and parts of the house. Uhra was questioned as to her and her children's safety.

She vaguely replied, her attention still on Biggabomb. She got to her feet, thought of something silly, and looked into his blank eyes. She smiled as the last tear ran down her face as she said, "Looks lika Muga's cookin' didn't kill you afta all."

Eight
Full Retreat!!!

Anguish bent Darkster and crumpled him to his knees, not directly from his own pain, but from that of his late father. In the moment his direct ancestor perished, his connected soul felt life leave his own body. He was cold and empty, more so now as evil provoked him to inflict suffering at an even greater scale than previously.

He rose to his feet and growled. Assumption gave him cause to think that Nuttybomb was responsible for his monumental loss, for who else was capable? The so-called wargod had felled Headhunta once before. Darkster's impatience to rid the star cluster of the bastard was becoming maddening.

Each step he took brought him closer to anticipated gratification – each breath, the necessary life to end another's. Driven to ease his agony until he could slay his enemy, consolatory actions were sought.

Darkster marched, spitting obscenities. All the while, his eyes aimlessly fixated somewhere beyond. All orcs he encountered, bowed and offered niceties, mumbling random words in simple nonsense out of nervous anxiety.

He entered the detention area.

A large, dark green orc met him. "May I helps you, Sir?"

Darkster commanded, "Open da closest cell."

"I tought we wus savin's dem to kill on da planet and turn into creeps," the guard said cautiously.

"Dems will turn to creeps later. But dems will die now. Hurry or you will be a creep, too."

The guard grabbed his keys and opened the designated cell as quickly as he was able. He stepped back and allowed the hobbled, but crazy orc to rush out from inside. The orc charged toward Darkster, hoping to destroy him with his bare hands.

Darkster freed his whip and uncoiled it, sparks flickering along its fiery length. The sound and smell of electrical discharge filled the air. When the weapon was unleashed, the sound of sparks was replaced by the snapping of something breaking the sound barrier.

The lights dimmed. The charging prisoner was met with unfurled fury in the form of a deep cutting cable and the energy of everything around him. He was knocked to the ground, his body writhing with each pulse that worked its way through and around him.

The guard was to be the prisoner's next best hope at escape. The newly freed captive turned to attack him, instead of the powerful leader. But as he stood and pivoted, Darkster's intentions found him between his shoulder blades. More agony shot through him, sending him to the floor once again. He wasn't so quick to get to his feet this time. Most of his strength had been sapped by the cumulative waves of energy. His heart throbbed and was beating unevenly. His head, feeling like it would explode wasn't too far from it. His heated blood expanded his arteries, veins, and tissue, not the least of which stressed his organs.

Darkster's mood generally dictated his actions. He could use his mind powers, a sword, or the whip he liked so much. It simply came down to his palate at the time. He growled, his gnarly teeth grinding as he spat through them. "Stand up and die lika orc," he instructed.

But the prisoner couldn't stand. Like a boxer, concussed multiple times, he was virtually helpless to get up and go another round. He leaned forward and allowed piles of blood to exit his nose as his body began to shut down. He looked up, grimacing, and said, "You a stupid gurl."

The insult didn't bother Darkster. He understood the orc's last attempt to inflict whatever desecration he could. Perhaps the prisoner hoped a final whipping would mercifully bring his anguish to an end. Either way, Darkster stepped over the prisoner as he was watched the whole time.

Darkster spat, "Open da next one."

***

Muga was devastated by the loss of her husband. Biggabomb was all she knew since she was twelve. They were friends first, and later, equal partners. Biggabomb may have boasted and thrown around innocent insults about her cooking to impress his friends, but she knew he loved her unconditionally. Her mocking his body's foul-smelling odors was never more than banter; counter insults that were never to be taken seriously.

Uhra's kind words were nothing more than that in Muga's state of grief. Her daughter-in-law attempted to somehow ease her pain, but how could she? She couldn't bring Biggabomb back from the realm beyond the physical one they struggled in. No help was needed around the house. How could she possibly help?

The thing that seemed to bother Muga the most was that he died at home, so to speak. He wasn't off in some far away land, actively participating in battles. He hadn't been shot at thousands of times, leaving her a continent away to worry while she watched over a handful of children. No, that part of their lives had passed, replaced by what should have been their golden years. His lungs were replaced, as was an arm. He had received multiple surgeries for one of his eyes, had countless bullets removed from what seemed like every part of his body, and repairs made to several key organs. He made it through the wars only to be killed in an environment considered far less dangerous. It just didn't seem right.

Orcs lined up as far as the eye could see. Some had fought side by side under the Great Biggabomb. Others just came to show their respects for the fallen warrior. A few were intelligent enough to honor Muga for her time served as wife to the great leader and mother to his children, and all it entailed. Plus, she was the mother of Wargod Nuttybomb, the greatest ruler they had ever heard of. The turmoil she felt as he fought for his life must have been overwhelming in such a wearisome time.

One by one, they passed. They left every kind of keepsake to accompany his soul to the afterlife. Guns, knives, swords, boarcakes, shoes, pieces of body armor, and shlogger were given as tribute. Even a child gave his orc soldiers that had been whittled from wood by his grandpa.

Maybe Biggabomb saw these gestures from wherever he was now. Maybe not. Maybe the consolation of what couldn't heal him was the fact that the orcs' gifts healed themselves.

The whole thing *was* uplifting to Muga. It wasn't their words necessarily, just like it wasn't Uhra's words that helped her. It was that so many loved him, missed him; that he had touched so many lives; that her suffering along with him wasn't in vein.

Muga and Biggabomb's other kids weren't around to participate in the unplanned event. Nuttybomb was ill and fighting for his life. Booma was in a different star system dealing with Humans and Spidanoids. Pretty was gods knows where after her ordeal with the humans. Runzda and Kago were on their way from the other side of the world and would arrive soon, but had not as of yet.

Additionally, several million soldiers were scattered throughout the star cluster in a myriad of theaters. They would miss any chance to show tribute or console themselves as vast distances separated and the ugliness of war pushed on before anything else. The great Biggabomb's passing would be a thing in passing, unremarkable to those tasked to carry on in his shadow.

In the end, it was just that; the end of him.

***

An enormous amount of equipment and material was abandoned on Marshil as Gunza's Hotta orcs left the surface of the planet and began their trip into space. While capital ships and most heavy support vessels remained in orbit around Marshil, transports and smaller supply ships were those required to leave the atmosphere as quickly as possible. They approached the main fleet as Darkster's closed and started firing.

Darkster spread his fleet to encircle Gunza's fleet and to keep Kingskull's from reaching them first. The extra time to do this allowed Gunza's troops to reach their primary ships and begin their own maneuvers.

Kingskull didn't think kindly of being blocked by Darkster and stated so. "Why da hell would you stops me fro' killin' yer enemy?"

Darkster jeered, "Don't matta who kill dems. You too slow."

"I know my ships be fasta den yers anda mo' powerful too," Kingskull jabbed.

"You don't even know 'bout creeps." Darkster, still distressed over losing his father, felt no need to mince words. In fact, upsetting others did him some good.

Kingskull spat, "Wut I *do* know is I travel a *year* to helps you. You needs a learn some gratitude."

Darkster growled, "Gratitude fo' da weak."

"Maybe, but rude tings one do fo' da dead," the elder orc inferred.

"Dat a two-way street, my long-travelled orc."

Rubbing his chin, Kingskull said, "One way or anudder, I come to kill."

Darkster smiled. "Anda you will. You will." His flagship shuddered as its main guns opened up at long range. The bridge illuminated red from each pulse that emerged from the massive cannons.

Brom informed his leader, "Dems outnumbered bad, but it hard fo' us to only hit dems wit' circle arounds 'em."

"I undastand, but I wants dems all dead anda Kingskull a watch my glory. Dis ship be strong, so I not too worry 'bout damage fro' our own ships."

"What 'bout all our udder ships?" Brom questioned.

Darkster sighed and rolled his eyes, "No worry 'bout dems. As longa as we wins, who cares? But maka sure you don't hit any our ships." He took a bite of some boarcakes he had his personal cook prepare just for this occasion. He would sit back and give commands while watching the destruction unfold before his very eyes. He smacked, chewing with his mouth open, and dropping saliva saturated morsels around him.

He squinted to see the movements of the enemy ships, not knowing who was aboard each. He was still unaware of Nuttybomb's health and Gunza being his replacement.

Gunza asked his targeting officer, "Wut dose ships back der?" referring to Kingskull's fleet as it approached just behind Darkster's.

The officer replied, "Dunno. Different kinda ships dan da close ones." He was knocked to the floor from an enemy salvo.

Another crewman was thrown from his post, too; flames burned his face, neck, and hands. He crawled back to his chair as if nothing had happened. He began pushing buttons and stated, "Damage on da port side into deck seven anda eight."

The lights flickered and settled as a red hue over Gunza's bridge, revealing backup power had engaged. Warning lights blinked throughout, accompanied by the steady beep of alarms.

Gunza ordered from his raised chair, "Head dat way and return fire in dat direction," pointing to starboard. He hailed his fleet and continued, "Dis be

Gunza. Fuel ships stay here, but get mosta crews to cruisers and battleships. All udder ships follow me anda fire in direction my ship is firin'. Destroyas clear da way. Mine layers follow us. Drop mines all ova so enemies hit dems. All fightas and bombas launch. Attack da biggest ship dems gots." He watched intently as things began to unfold.

Gunza's fleet, being outnumbered by Darkster's by a three-to-one ratio, was taking damage as it reorganized. However, with fighters and bombers tying up some of Darkster's fleet, especially what Gunza assumed was his flagship, incoming fire lessened over time.

For the most part, the fleet headed in a homeward direction. Destroyers targeted everything within a fifteen-degree area, obliterating a dozen enemy ships and opening a small hole for Gunza's ships to attempt an escape. The capital ships fired upon any sizeable foes along the way, concentrating their firepower to maximize destruction. This knocked out some of Darkster's potent guns as the fleet advanced toward their point of escape.

Darkster couldn't tell what was happening from the confines of his bridge so he could adjust his plan. Fighters and bombers swarmed his ship like angered killer bees, blocking his view of the battle beyond his view screen. He screamed, "Gets rid a those fightas," angrily, waving a closed fist in the air. He growled when his plate of boarcakes fell on the floor.

Brom reported, "We takin's some damage, but not too bad. Mosta damage to front and on main guns."

"Keeps firin' where we wus into Nuttybomb's fleet. Anda keeps movin' forward. I want him dead!"

140

"Yessir," came from his subordinate.

Darkster's flagship moved and fired blindly through the maelstrom provided by Gunza's fighters and bombers. It destroyed one Hotta cruiser and left one disabled within two minutes by sheer luck on its current path into the fray.

Darkster ordered his fleet to close in on the enemy and to follow them if any ships found a way to escape. He was unaware of his ships firing passed the enemy and into each other on opposite sides of the noose he tried to tighten. Damage reports were vague, and none told of what ships caused disrepair. So, he continued onward.

The Hotta orcs' encounters with the humans helped them to improve their ships. As a result, Gunza's capital ships were making headway, and they fared pretty well. Smaller ships were taking a pounding, though, as their armor couldn't completely protect them. Around thirty ships were already destroyed or disabled. Many of their escape pods launched and found their way to the relative safety of larger vessels. However, many were also destroyed or sent astray, never to been seen again.

Da Rampage, Gunza's capital ship, swung to its port side to provide some cover for the exposed, and therefore, weakened side of his fleet. Several others were ordered to follow her in order to bolster her efforts. Their combined firepower began to inflict minor damage to enemies on that side and drew most of the attention away from the lightly armored ships. Now, the heavier capital ships formed somewhat of a protective shield for the smaller ships within.

Gunza clenched his fist in triumph as he saw the enemy battleship, *Gripper*, shredded by his battleship and the battleship, *Bend Ova*.

A few of his other vessels sacrificed themselves as they impaled much larger enemy ships. The crews from the smaller vessels boarded their opposition's impaled metal hulks and began the task of subduing their crews. Passageway by passageway was cleared quickly before the enemy knew they were being invaded, and in a short time, the command centers fell. The invaded ships were now used to help fire against Darkster's other ships.

Dozens of Darkster's ships, confused by perceived attacks from their own fleet, fired back. In err, many fired upon each other, further escalating the confusion and causing more friendly fire to ensue.

Gunza's targeting officer reported, "Sir, we lost a fuel ship."

"We have plenty a fuel to get home. Dids it destroy anything around it?

The officer looked at his screen, called up some information, and said, "Hard a tell all damage. It looka like it kill two a our ships and maybe ten a da enemy ships."

In fact, it had wrecked over thirty enemy ships. Half of those were dead in the water. The others were still underway, but hampered by fires and considerable structural compromise as the fuel ship lit up everything around it.

So far, Gunza's plans were effective in keeping damage to his ships to a minimum and causing as much carnage to the enemy as possible. He took a minute to update his tactics, giving orders to specific ships. He quietly exhaled, waiting for outcomes to reach him.

Fighters and bombers began to pull away from *Da Malevolent*. Their new targets were Darkster's fuel ships. If they could keep his fleet from refueling they wouldn't be able to get to Hotta. Furthermore, Gunza hoped that inflicting collateral damage to other ships would improve his odds.

The swarm of tiny ships engaged destroyers that were protecting the fuel ships. Several friendly fighters and most bombers were lost, but so were the destroyers and every fuel ship. Other ships came to offer protection, but they were struck by a chain event that altered the battle. Over two hundred enemy ships were destroyed or crippled as fuel ship after fuel ship detonated, sending flaming projectiles into the surrounding space and every nearby craft.

Darkster, elated with a clear view of the battle ahead, now targeted Gunza's ships. Two cruisers were blown to bits by *Da Malevolent's* powerful main guns. The battleship, *Down Yer Throat*, was struck twice by the monster, leaving her aft aflame as she drifted to starboard helplessly.

Darkster jumped from his chair, joyfully waving his arms above him like a child.

His hands lowered, and his expression changed however, when he heard, "Sir, our fuel ships a all gone."

He angrily asked, "Wut?" as if his ears hadn't heard the awful words they did.

Brom walked over and stood before his leader to shield any more officers from being killed by the maniacal and testy orc. "Sir, dat wer da fightas and bombas goed."

Darkster screamed, "Dammit!" spitting all over his chin and chest. Realizing he wouldn't be able to pursue a fleeing enemy to Hotta, he went on, "We needs to end dis now. No mo' circle around Nuttybomb. All ships follow and attack!"

Kingskull addressed his desperate ally, "Darkster, wus dems yer fuel ships?" He smiled from the comfort of his seat.

Darkster spat in response, "Not now, Kingskull."

"Don't worry. I'll get da wargod." He hooted hardily over the comm system, clutching his gut as he spewed obnoxious laughter.

"Not if you dead first," Darkster mumbled to himself.

Gunza wondered who Kingskull was. The leader seemed to be an equal to Darkster, although Gunza couldn't fathom how that might be; Darkster would never allow anyone to tell him what to do. Tales of his ruthlessness against anyone who even questioned him were well known.

Regardless, there was a way out of losing every ship in the fleet, and Gunza took advantage of every opportunity to expose every weakness in his enemy for survival's sake. The last of his own fuel ships had exploded, taking out another ninety or so pursuers. The numbers still weren't good, but preferable to those at the beginning of the engagement.

Darkster didn't feel the same way. He was beginning to understand just how much damage his fleet had sustained. Even if he killed Nuttybomb in the battle above Marshil, invasion of Hotta would have to be postponed, or possibly even cancelled. At the very least, he had to destroy Nuttybomb and his remaining ships.

An enormous explosion rocked *Da Malevolent*. Darkster was thrown from his chair and into a console in the back of the bridge. His head peaked from behind the cracked console, smashed by his body upon impact. He blinked several times and got to his feet. "Wut happened?" he questioned in disbelief as he rubbed his aching head.

Brom crawled to his own console and called up some data. "We hit sumptin'."

"We drive into a ship?"

"No. Dat too much esplosion fo' a ship. Busides, we can ram almosta anyting."

Darkster was impatient. He hobbled back to his chair and asked, "Den wut?"

Brom's facial expression showed confusion. He replied, "Dunno. But our udder ships hit stuff too."

Darkster walked a bit further as he tried to understand what had happened. The two stood together and watched dozens of ships' bows appear to simply explode.

Brom shrugged his shoulders and stated, "Dunno."

Kingskull jeered, "Looka lika da wargod rippin' yer fleet to pieces." Before Darkster could respond with an insult, the jeering ally quizzed, "Wut da hell wus dat?"

From Darkster's view point, he saw Kingskull's fleet gain on, and slightly surpass his own in pursuit of the fleeing ships. Kingskull's ships started encountering the same kind of explosions from unknown sources.

Kingskull ordered, "Stop da fleet! Stop da fleet! All ships stop!"

Darkster and Brom stared at each other until Brom ordered over the fleetwide channel, "All ships stop! Stop now! All ships stop!"

"Wut you tink yer doin's?" Darkster snapped.

Brom answered, "We musta hit bombs. Dems dropped bombs behind dems, I tink."

Darkster understood. Brom had stepped up once again. Unfortunately, he also understood that large ships didn't stop on a dime. It took many miles for a large, heavy warship to come to a halt, even in the vacuum of space. He hailed Kingskull.

"Wut you want?"

Darkster, angry with destruction to his fleet, but loving the carnage he watched, said, "Looka lika you run into bombs."

"It looka dat way. You did too."

Gunza's voice was heard by all. "Dems are called mines. A gift fo' both a you."

Darkster growled, "Dis not ova yet. I still gots hundreds a ships on yer sides. You still gotta get passed dem all."

"I will," was confidently replied.

Darkster asked in an irritated voice, "Who are you?"

"I be Gunza, Warchief a da fleet."

"I amemba you. My dad, Headhunta cut you to pieces. Where be da so-called wargod?"

146

Gunza thought for a few seconds and said, "I rememba Headhunta, too. I still alives, tho. And Nuttybomb...He be evvywhere."

Darkster snarled, "Him gonna be wen I gets done wit' him. Anda I kills you too!"

"Sum udder time, perhaps," Gunza teased. "I have mo' a yer ships to kills. See you again soon."

Darkster ordered all ships near him to reverse course. Upon hearing the orders, Kingskull did the same with his entire fleet.

The Hotta ships, better built than Darkster's, made easy work of the several hundred that still assaulted them. Very few remaining Hotta ships were lost. Additionally, Gunza towed every battered ship he could while his repair ships went to work on getting them up and running again.

Darkster's fleet had been reduced to around seven hundred functional ships, Kingskull's to fifteen hundred. Gunza's two hundred remaining ships became dots, silhouetted against the black canvas of stars. They soon faded into the distance as they headed home.

Nine
Witches, Warlocks, and Destiny

"Dunno. Him just not wake up," the new doctor said as he removed bandages from Nuttybomb's chest. He went on, "Stitches looka good anda I see no infection. But him won't wake up."

The nurse pulled a thermometer from Nutty's rear and stated, "Him's still got a feva."

"Dunno if dat fro' still infection or sumptin' else, maybe poison." The doc tossed bloody wrappings into the nearby trash. He turned on the light atop his head, a piece of equipment typically used by miners. He looked in Nutty's mouth, ears, and nose. For good measure, as if some diagnosis would miraculously come to him, he pulled back Nutty's eyelids and shined the light in them.

The nurse asked, "Nuttin'?"

The doc confirmed, "Nope. Nuttin'."

"Der nuttin' mo' you can do tonight, Doc. If you wanna head home, I looka afta him."

Removing the light and pulling the mask from his face, the doc responded, "Dat sounda good. I be here all day tomorrow. If anyting change, wake me. I sleep in one a da back rooms tonight."

The nurse grabbed some extra blankets and put them away in a closet just outside Nuttybomb's room. She returned and sat in a chair facing him. She kicked off an old, worn shoe, rubbed her aching foot and exclaimed, "It up to you now, Chief. Dunno wut else we can do."

***

Guthrak snapped, "Der, we escaped. Now wut?"

Gunza replied, "Now, we head home anda hope Darkster don't know 'nuff to slingshot around Marshil to get fasta anda catch us."

"Weren't we apposed to slingshot?" Guthrak asked.

Gunza sighed, "We were, but no time." He turned to Moonoak and quietly asked, "We gots 'nuff speed to get home?"

Moonoak rested his chin in his hand. He glanced back and stated unhappily, "Yes anda no."

Guthrak quizzed, "Wut dat mean?"

All eyes from the guards and clergy were glued to Moonoak. Some of their ears found better opportunity as several heads turned slightly to hear better. Moonoak sought to find words of comfort.

Gunza questioned, "Well?"

Moonoak reluctantly returned, "Well, we were apposed to be on Marshil fo' four mo' months. But we left early. Anda we no slingshot." He sighed as he made eye contact with Gunza.

Gunza knowingly stated in the form of a half-question, "So, Hotta move too fast around star fo' us to get home on dis path?"

Moonoak nodded in agreement. "Ya. Around five mo' months till Hotta come back round da udder side."

Guthrak hollered, "Dat just great! Just great! We run lika scaredy dawgs anda we not even make it back to our udder fleet." He snapped his fingers against the knife that stuck though his jaw, leaving a distinct ping.

"Relax," Gunza ordered. He continued, "We will figure out where to go fo a while. We alive, ain't we?"

Quicklip interrupted, "I ain't no scaredy dawg."

Guthrak barked, "Well, it don't matta. We looka scareds."

Gunza spat, "I don't give a shit wut we looka like. I in charge to save all a us, our orcs on da planets too. I do whatevva I have to. We not scareds. We smart."

"Ya? We destroyed our fuel ships. Wus dat smart? Wer da hell we gonna go now?" Guthrak spat on the floor.

Moonoak added, "We hads to. Dems wus comin's wit' mo' ships. We be outnumbered ten-to-one. We lucky to still be alive to fight anudder day."

"Well, I hate runnin' to die anudder day here in space. Letta us land and fight lika orcs!" He pumped his fist in the air.

"I hate a say it, but betta dyin' in space so we don't get turned into creeps."

Quicklip snarled, "Hey. Dat's a good way to looka at it."

Gunza had heard enough. "No mo' fightin' ova dis. Now we gots to tink 'bout wer to go anda fight again. Anyone?"

Guthrak smirked. "Wer would I hide if I wus a scaredy dawg?"

Ucktock said, "We can't go to any planets 'cause dems too far lika home, or dems back wer Darkster ships are."

Quicklip asked sarcastically, "You tink a dat all by yerself?"

Unaware and unphased, Ucktock replied, "Ya." Then, he thought of something. "Moonoak, we can't go to planets. But wut 'bout dat ole broken moon? It just rocks now."

Moonoak perked up and raised his voice in excitement, "Da asteroids."

"Yup."

"Lemme check," the shaman said as he ran some figures in the computer. He muttered to himself, "Da moon part would be passin' in a few days. Prolly asteroids in front and behind it by a couple weeks maybe."

Guthrak, bearer of bad tidings offered, "Wut 'bout food and water? We got lika four hundred thousand orcs to feed. You tink a dat?"

Gunza defended, "Ya, I know. I tought of it. It not good. We can support 'bout half dat."

Moonoak cut in with, "We can make it to asteroids, I tink."

"Dat good 'nuff fo me," Gunza exclaimed. "But we all won't live. Lika half a us gotta go back to Marshil."

Guthrak snapped, "Me. I go."

"I figured you a say dat, ole friend. Listen…I gotta take capital ships to defend Hotta."

Guthrak agreed, "A course."

Arc stood up and spouted, "I go a Marshil too. Creeps be cool."

Gunza asked, "Cool?"

"Ya," came from the enthusiastic sorcerer. "I lika wen I cut der heads off."

Gunza stood and confronted Arc. "Creeps are our dead brudders. Der nuttin' cool 'bout cuttin' our brudders heads off."

Arc explained, "Dems not my brudders. Busides, I lika killin's stuff."

Gunza glanced at Moonoak who nodded in a shared concern for the youth. He was powerful and dangerous now; he may have been on the verge of evil like Darkster. He would be watched very carefully going forward.

"We load troops on udder ships anda you takes dem. Head out lika you goin' to da human actuary ting. Den, swing back. Anda only send one ship at a time. Too many will get Darkster's attention. Got it?"

"Got it. Wer should we land, tho? Too many creeps wer we just came fro'."

Nubbs answered for his leader, "I know wer to land. Orcs got a base der. Anda shlogger too. I show Guthrak and udders wer to go."

Quicklip jeered, "You tink a anyting dat not shlogger?"

A returned smile and, "Not really," came from Nubbs.

Moonoak added, "I send some shamans, too, fo' savin' souls."

Gunza said, "Dat a solid plan, all. Letta us do it. I justa hope Darkster don't catch us first."

Quicklip asked, "Did anyone else notice dat da udder ships wus gainin' on us befo' dems hit our mines?"

***

A chill was in the air, a highly unlikely occurrence during the late summertime on Hotta. Usually hot and humid, and accompanied by afternoon thunderstorms, the drop in temperature was odd in its timing. Even so, the guards stood at their posts.

"You see da size a da boobs on da new nurse? Ha ha ha," the first guard said in laughter.

The other asked, "Which wun?"

"Da left boob," He shook his head in disbelief, but continued, "Da nurse wit' da big boobs, you stupid head."

"I tought you meant one boob wus bigga dan da udder," the other orc admitted. He giggled, not at his stupidity, but at the thought of different sized breasts fighting for space beneath a shirt.

The first guard added, "Der two new nurses. Dems friends, or sistas, or sumptin'."

"You know dems?"

"No. I tink I heard der names. Hottie and umm..." He paused as he thought. He lit up when he remembered. "Sweetie," he stated firmly.

The second guard asked, "Which wun gots da big boobs?"

The first guard's smile vanished. "Dunno." He rubbed his arm at the feeling of goosebumps, an unfamiliar sensation to him. "It get cold real fast?"

"Ya. I tink so. Gots a chill up my back." He shivered before pulling a hood up over his exposed neck. "You hear dat?"

"Prolly da bushes in da wind," the first guard offered.

"Der is no wind."

***

She had worked her way between fences, hiding behind hedges as she travelled. Ever so quietly, sometimes waiting an hour or more, just to move a few feet. She squirmed along property borders, keeping to sheds and vehicles, never being out in the open. She became the shadows that hid her.

One had already died by her hand earlier that day, her potent potions strangling the unaware father who

153

stumbled too close to her liking. Making little noise and succumbing to her poison quickly, he was of little trouble, as it turned out. He was left beneath some metal sheathing, not to be found, until his eventual rotting smell would give away his whereabouts.

It was her third day in Bigtown, capital city on Hotta. Rumors of Nuttybomb's poor health found their way to her prying ears as she had huddled beneath an open window. Spying was second nature to the witch.

But that was yesterday. It was in that same area of town she had scavenged up some mudbread that someone left out to cool. This morning brought some freshly picked, but slightly over-ripe apples. Sustenance came in any forms necessary.

Now, in the center of town, she was close to her final destination. She crouched behind some bushes and looked through openings in the foliage. As she lowered herself, her robe got caught and pulled on a branch.

She heard two guards having a conversation.

"Ya. I tink so. Gots a chill up my back." He shivered before pulling a hood up over his exposed neck. "You hear dat?"

"Prolly da bushes in da wind," the first guard offered.

"Der is no wind."

She reached inside her robe and slowly removed a potion. It was raised to the gods with accompanying words, whispered in some foreign tongue.

The first guard walked to the hedges as he said, "It's over here."

The second guard followed closely, turning his head slightly to pick up details.

154

Before they could discover the source of the ghoulish sounds, the old woman burst through the greenery and splattered both guards with her deadly concoction. Initially, they struggled, but soon fell quietly, their bodies dragged behind the bushes.

The witch avoided the walkway and back door the guards were defending. Instead, she backtracked to a window she had passed just minutes before. However, it was locked, temporarily keeping her at bay. She was an orc though, even a bit old and decrepit; strength to pry a bolted window open wouldn't elude her. No, it was the excessive noise revealing her that she contemplated.

She carefully pried downward on the bottom sill with a crowbar, producing a counter force upward on the lower window. A dozen or more restrained prods heated up the pressured bolt, each push and pull eventually cracking its softened steel. The pop was still significant, although better than had the metal remained solid. It was worked just enough to breakdown its strength into a working malleable content.

She settled behind shrubbery, giving time for potential explorers to find the new entrance, and just as she suspected, she witnessed a light emerge in the room. The muted sound of footsteps led to a nurse looking out the window. As far as the witch could tell from her concealed observation, the nurse was none the wiser. She watched the befuddled nurse leave the window and extinguish the light. Moreover, she determined the nurse left upon the corridor light being blocked by the closing of the room's door. She waited five minutes before moving.

Her gnarly fingers lifted the bottom window, her reflexes being tested as she caught the broken bolt with her left hand while pushing up with her right. Her eyes darted around crazily. She propped the window open, and climbed in.

With a newly acquired vile in hand, she went to the door, cracked it, and peered into the corridor. Down the hall, two orcs disappeared behind an adjoining hallway. With their voices trailing off into nothingness, the confident bitch entered the well-lit passageway.

From room to room she went, searching for Nuttybomb or any information leading her to him. So far, she had no luck- other than proceeding farther into the medical building's central areas. She reasoned, as long as she wasn't detected, Nuttybomb would eventually be found through process of elimination.

Back in the corridor, she stopped outside another room, this one showing light around the perimeter of the door; it wasn't a dark room like the others had been so far. She placed her green, crusty ear to the door after brushing some hair away to listen inside.

"Chief," the nurse said. "C'mon, you gotta wake up. Please, wake up."

The witch listened carefully for other voices, footsteps; anything that might reveal the number of orcs inside the room.

The nurse exclaimed, "Dammit, it cold in here. Dat bastid, Orcbok betta not have changed da settin's on da AC."

The door was barely cracked, but before entering carefully as she always did, she relented, darting back to the room she had just left.

"Doc! Doc!" the nurse screamed.

The doc scrambled to Nuttybomb's room. "Wut? Wut?" he yelled.

"I tink him's wakin's up."

That's all the witch needed to hear. If there was so much excitement about Nuttybomb stirring, she assumed he must have been in very ill. She would easily subdue a doctor and a nurse, but a healthy Nuttybomb could be very dangerous. She decided to carry out her plans to eradicate her biggest threat.

Her mouth contacted the gods, her words fermenting the potions into ungodly lethality. With the corridor traversed, the door was thrown open, and liquid sprayed the room.

The doc, inflicted with debilitating offerings, was forced to the floor as his muscles and neurological entities confounded him. His arm somehow locked around one of the witch's legs as she sprang toward the nurse.

The nurse screamed, "Help! Help!" grabbing everything from cotton to needles and throwing them haphazardly in the witch's direction.

Nuttybomb rolled off his bed and onto the floor, the cold tiled floor catching his face, chest, and arms. He slowly moved to his side and sat up, just out of distance of the witch's next potion, for he was partially blocked by the bed which upturned between him and the crazed woman. He slowly kicked his way backward against the wall.

The nurse, out of other options, jumped onto the witch. Her attack sent a potion into the corridor, where it splattered harmlessly. She desperately grabbed at the crazed woman's hands, keeping them from finding more potions from somewhere on her decrepit body.

The witch lurched forward, her disgusting mouth adhering to the nurse's face, her mangled teeth puncturing deep into tissue. With a free hand, she grabbed another potion and attempted another spell. She released her bite and pushed the injured nurse to the floor. Her words began the ritualistic rant, but were stopped short of completion.

Nuttybomb rushed his body against hers. The potion dropped somewhere behind the witch, still toxic, but not as potent as its intended ferocity. Smoke from the spilled vile filled the air, choking the three orcs who fought for their lives.

The stunned nurse held a hand over blood that was spewing from the open wound below her left eye. She stumbled forward and dropped her body on top of the witch and grabbed one of the bitch's free arms. Manipulating it until the elbow was forced to separate, a loud pop was accompanied by a shrill scream.

"I killa you, you Bitch!" The witch screamed. She kicked frantically, trying to remove Nuttybomb's massive weight from her body. Her free hand dug into his eye, her mouth ripping into his face. But she could not get any potions that were tucked in her robe, now stuck between her and Nuttybomb, contained by his weight.

Nuttybomb was so weak. He scarcely had the strength to move his arms. But somehow, he pulled her hand from his eye with both of his hands. His sickened body reared up and dropped back down, cracking some of her ribs.

She shrieked again in pain, wildly biting into his face again. Now *he* howled in pain.

The nurse tried to dislodge the witch's mouth from Nuttybomb's face, but wasn't able. Instead, she rushed to her feet and jumped to the side where the witch's hand was being confined. She slipped in fluids on the hard floor, knocking herself out when she fell.

Nuttybomb struggled mightily. His weakened state robbed him of the ability to fight an enemy the way he knew how. What's more, consciousness was foreign as he struggled to survive in a hazy state of hallucination. His thoughts were disconnected, muddied, not only by his physical deficiencies, but also from the potion that nearly missed him. Smoke permeated the air, gagging him as he fought to breathe in clean air.

He rose up again, powerless to remove the witch's voracious mouth from his cheek. This time, he slammed his face down, smashing hers against his, and opening the back of her head beneath his crushing mass.

His face was free. He gazed upon her misshapen head, her face with a deep gouge that separated her nose and mouth from her eyes. He lined up his forehead with her nose, raised himself, and dropped again. He stopped once her twitching body ceased to move.

The witch was dead.

***

If the death of his father was devastating to Darkster, the loss of his mother buried his soul even deeper than it had been. He screamed in his quarters, smashing the bulkheads with his fists. He spat words

159

of damnation, aimed at every Hotta orc, but particularly, Nuttybomb.

He slumped to the floor and prayed to his god, seeking vengeance, opening evil anew, and swearing to never waver in his quest to enact sinful atrocities against an entire people until genocide rendered them nothing more than wandering creeps. They would be damned for eternity, granted false salvation by this bringer of the apocalypse.

There would be no more mistakes like leaving too many of his ships vulnerable to attack; no more miscalculations. His past impulses were learned from, taking into account his own actions, and squarely placing blame on his own shoulders. What eighteen years of life's experiences couldn't teach him, the death of his mother did; patience and perseverance.

His destiny was now cast. He had tortured and killed throughout his life, the treachery of his slaughters building to unequaled barbarism. He began raising the dead several years before, promising them salvation, only to vanquish their souls, using them as mere fodder to attack his enemies. He found the power to devastate an entire world, the sleeping forced to an existence of roaming aimlessly, restlessly, never quenching an endless thirst, never feeding an insatiable hunger; their helpless souls bound to a walking hell, relegated to a perpetual presence of suffering.

Yes, the god looked favorably upon his devotee. And now, Goliath was prepared to unleash his devastating power upon the unluckiest of souls, for this servant was obedient, this servant was willing to sacrifice all in the demon's name, and this servant was evil beyond any before.

"Kingskull," Darkster summoned.

"Wut is it?"

Darkster's tone was subtly different, measured. "I take you up on yer offer to use yer ships to refuel, if you still offer."

Kingskull liked the younger orc seeking help. "Sure, no problem. By da way, I figure der nuttin' fro' keeping Nuttybomb usin' dese mines evvywhere."

"I figure if we go long way round, will take longer, but we no run into any," Darkster stated.

Kingskull complimented, "Good tinkin'. I lika dat idea." In the depths of his mind, he still had mistrust for Darkster. He would continue to observe his ally's words and actions very carefully.

Darkster's wicked brain automatically caused him to distrust everyone. He had his eye on Kingskull and his larger, threatening fleet as well.

Both fleets took time to refuel. They came to an agreement on the path to Hotta with Marshil as a possible contingency. Scouts were sent ahead and in varying degrees of the same, general direction. Others were sent to Marshil.

***

"Younut," Uhra sighed, wrapping her arms around her husband. She closed her eyes tight, like the grip around his chest as she buried her head into the crevice between Nuttybomb's head and shoulder.

"I ok," he said, his hands grasping her shoulders as he gazed into her loving eyes. "Sorry I wasn't der to help wit' da kids and my dad wen Headhunta came."

Uhra took a step back and chose her words. "It ok. You wus sick. You da leader, anyway. If not here in hospital, you prolly woulda beed fightin's sumwhere

161

else. Anda sorry 'bout yer dad." She didn't want to say how sick she was of missing him; of not having a man around; of how close she came to him not being around forever.

"Tanks." Nutty sat up as Uhra propped up some pillows behind him.

An orderly knocked before entering the room. He rolled in a small table on wheels with an electrical device on it and left it against a wall opposite Nuttybomb. He happily said, "Here ya go."

Nutty asked, "Wut da hell is dat?"

Uhra turned to her husband and questioned, "You ain't seen one?"

He shook his head, "No."

The orderly plugged in the device and turned it on.

A screen came to life with humans gathered around. The words were very much like those that orcs spoke. From the device was heard, "Rabbit Harrison, anything else you would like to say?"

Nutty leaned forward, his eyes fixed on the screen.

Uhra asked, "Dat Rabbit Harrison da one you fought?"

"Ya." He wasn't able to add more dialogue as he was preoccupied.

Following some more chatter, "Not guilty of all charges," came from the built-in speaker.

Nutty questioned, "Wut is dis ting?"

Uhra smiled. "It called TV. It a human ting dat yer orcs bring back fro' Plenna or Cypra, dunno. But dis Rabbit Harrison wus in trouble again?"

Nutty thought for a few seconds. He blinked his eyes and stated, "Dis happen lika year ago, maybe two.

I tink it taka dat long for da stuff to get all da way to us. So, I tink dis old news." He scratched his head.

Uhra said, "You can learn lots fro' dems humans. Dems smart. Well summa dems. Sum maka me laugh."

Nuttybomb was unaware of the variety of shows that humans broadcast. He didn't know the species to be funny. Other than the banter that accompanied his fight against Rabbit Harrison, his limited interactions were predicated upon a shared need to combat a mutual enemy. He also knew that orcs might get the wrong idea about humans from TV. He would monitor the broadcasts to verify whether to illegalize them or not.

A nurse knocked and came in. She did some nursing things and began to look at Nutty's vitals.

Uhra asked, "How hims doin'?"

The nurse wrote a note in Nuttybomb's chart and said, "Him's ok, sorta."

"Sorta?" Uhra leaned forward and tipped her head.

"Hims wus real sick," the nurse explained. She elaborated, "Still weak. Still gots some poisons in him. Feva down some. If numbas get a lil betta, he can go home to rest." She shuffled some papers.

Uhra's eyes lit up. "Be goods to have ya home fo' a bit, my big, strong Warchief." She batted her eyelashes.

The nurse hid a smile as she caught Uhra's accentuated actions.

Nutty rolled his eyes. "I gots wars to fight."

Uhra snarled, "Anda wars still be der till you get betta." Her eyes became a bit harsher.

"You here anyting 'bout Marshil?"

"Marshil?" Uhra spat as her hands folded across her chest. "You don't ask 'bout yer kids?"

The nurse made a muttered, "Yikes," and left the room.

Nutty said nervously, "No, it just dat I know dems ok wit' you. Dat's all."

"Really?" Uhra prodded.

"I sorry. So much a catch up on. I waked up in a fight. I nevva tought life would be lika dis."

Ten
Don't Honey Me

One by one, under the cover of divergent paths and suitably timed departures, ships under Guthrak's command left the asteroid belt and headed for Marshil. The incredibly vast areas traveled gave little chance of detection.

However, several vessels *were* encountered by Darkster's scouts and subsequently reported to him. Ultimately, appropriate measures on both sides led to only a few vessels from each faction being detected or destroyed. Henceforth, surmised Hotta ship activity was scant enough to not draw considerable attention from Darkster.

Regardless, he was a changed orc; his newfound diligence propelled him to leave no stone unturned, no matter how unlikely a positive encounter might have resulted. This also meant that he wouldn't commit a bulk of his resources for an apparently impractical gamble. He was more careful than ever.

Still, he directed more scouts to Marshil and the space between there and himself, hoping to unlock any hint of the Hotta orcs' movements. Most of his fleet would continue toward Hotta in pursuit of the fleet that somehow escaped destruction.

Darkster viewed a monitor from his seat and asked, "Brom, what dat area der?"

Brom submissively approached and glanced at the screen. "Dat da broken pieces of an old moon. It too small and gots no atmosphere to live on."

"Can ships hide in dem rocks?"

165

"Dunno. I never beed der myself. But der beed orc pirates dat used a try anda hide ships near da moon."

Darkster quizzed, "You tink Nuttybomb ships would try a hide der?"

"Der lots a rocks. Maybe some bigga 'nuff to hide around," Brom explained.

"Could three hundred ships hide der?" Darkster questioned, his eyes squinting.

Brom answered, "No. I don't tink so. Not dat many big rocks. Could hide some ships," shrugging his shoulders.

Darkster ordered, "Ok. Let's get some scouts to dat moon and da rocks arounds it."

"Yessir," was immediately replied.

"Kingskull," Darkster hailed.

"Wut?"

Darkster said, "I gots reasons to tink dat Nuttybomb be hidin' around a broken moon."

Kingskull spat on the floor of his bridge and asked, "Wut reasons?"

"I pretty sure his ships can't get all da way home right now. It might be a good place a hide."

"Him call himself a wargod. Him gonna hide? Unlikely," the older leader alleged.

Darkster agreed with concern, "Maybe so, but he did run fro' us in da battle. Him's very smart. Might even be a trap."

Kingskull laughed, "I lika da sound a dat. Now *dat* sound lika wargod."

Darkster cautioned, "Hims ships might not be der at all."

"Wutcha propose?" Kingskull now passed as he conversed.

"I tink you ships be fasta dan mine," Darkster conceded. He went on, "Maybe you go to da broken moon anda get him. But I take my ships back to Marshil, in case him's go back der somehow."

Kingskull laughed even harder, "You aspect me to believe you would let me kill yer enemy while you go to a vacant planet? You musta tink I stupid." He couldn't fathom the younger orc even uttering an inferiority in any way.

Darkster explained, "Whether I tink you stupid or no, don't matta. We needs Nuttybomb dead if we are to take ova Hotta. It wut needs a be done."

"Hims scares you," Kingskull jabbed.

Darkster calmly stated, "No. Him just killed my mudder and father, both very dangerous. Dat maka him *very* dangerous."

"How hims do dat?"

"Dunno," Darkster admitted. "But hims did it while all da way out here in space while dems wus on his planet. Hims must be very powaful now."

Kingskull stopped in his tracks and smiled, "All da betta wen I kills him!"

***

Uhra came through the front doors and made a right down the corridor leading to Nuttybomb's room. Long ago, she stopped taking notice of the green tiled walls that lined the belly of the medical building. The floor tiles were larger and light gray. These, too, weren't of any significance.

What was of importance, was how she appeared to her love. She fixed her hair to "pretty up" before seeing her healing husband. She stopped at a cracked

167

mirror that hung outside the nurses' room to check herself.

She puffed up her hair and applied some lip cover, puckering as she applied the red coat around her mouth. She wasn't paying much attention to a conversation that was occurring in the nurses' room until something caught her attention.

"I don't care, Sweetie. I would do stuffin's wit' Nuttybomb again," a voice said.

Sweetie giggled, "Him happy stick looka lika puppy dawg now. Hottie, you wuvs hims puppy dawg."

"Uh huh," Hottie sighed.

They both laughed devilishly.

Uhra blinked her eyes and shook her head. Was she hearing this correctly? These were the same Hottie and Sweetie that Nuttybomb's mother mentioned a couple years before. She wasn't sure what she had heard. The words were clear and loud enough, but for some reason, she couldn't make sense of them.

Hottie stated, "It worked real good. Anda I don't care wut it looked like. I tink it kinda looks hot."

"You would," Sweetie poked.

"We can taka turns, honey. I don't mind. Der plenty a Nuttybomb's puppy dawg happy stick to stuffin's you too."

Uhra dropped her lip cover and hair brush.

The giggling inside the room suddenly quieted. No conversation could be heard. The silence was deafening!

Uhra walked across the hall and knocked on the nurses' room door. No one answered. So, she knocked again. There was still no response. She tried to open the door by turning the door knob, but it was locked from the inside.

Uhra spat through her gritted teeth, "Hottie and Sweetie, opens da door befo' I break it."

Upon the lock being turned, the knob slowly spun, and the door slowly opened. Sweetie stood in the doorway with her eyes widened and a hand over her mouth.

Uhra pushed passed her, closed the door, and locked it.

***

Gunza sent out fighters as scouts to locate and chart Darkster's forces. They took a myriad of paths, zigzagging to obscure their points of origin in case they were discovered.

One such fighter came across Kingskull's fleet as it got within two days of the broken moon. The pilot, unable to escape destruction, sent a coded message to Gunza on the fleet's whereabouts.

"Moonoak," Gunza addressed. "Darkster is gettin' too close. We needs to go. Wer can we gets to?"

Moonoak exhaled sharply. "Dunno. Only Marshil be close 'nuff to get to I tink."

"Gods dammit!" the cornered leader cursed. He thought for a few seconds and asked, "Can we make it to Tempest?"

Moonoak appeared confused. "Da enemy home world?"

Gunza confirmed, "Ya. I know it far, but Darkster would nevva aspect us to go der."

"Ya, it too far," Moonoak said, shaking his head in rejection.

"Dunno wut to do. I not a warchief. I nevva learn dis stuff. I used a fight, not plan."

Moonoak hated saying it, but say it, he did, "Now, Marshil da only place we can gets too befo' da enemy get us."

Gunza walked to a window and looked out passed the asteroids and the destroyed moon. He crossed his arms and stared – he stared into a vast nothingness; a nothingness like his vacant mind. He couldn't see his enemies, but he knew they were close; too close for his liking.

Ucktock commented, "Maybe tink lika human. Dems smart as a hell."

"How do I do dat?" Gunza asked in a ridiculous, childish voice. He turned and waited for some unknown wisdom that was granted to Ucktock.

Unable to recognize how stupid his comment came off, and how he was mocked, he continued, "Well, if I beed human, I would sneak around."

"Wut da hell you tink we beed doin's?"

"Ya, no. I know."

Gunza shook his head and hung it over his chest. "Go ahead, Ucktock. Wutcha mean, sneak around?"

Ucktock said, "Well, dems gonna know we be here. So, we gots to go. Letta us go back to Marshil a different way. We left Marshil to go home. Don't ya tink dems tink we here or on our way home?" He held his arms out, hands up to somehow plead his case.

Moonoak added, "Maybe our fightas led dems in dis direction. Maybe we needs to go way outta da way to confuse Darkster 'bouts wer we be."

"Maybe," Gunza said. He called the guards to a table with a built-in monitor. He began drawing out planet locations, the broken moon, and known fleet locations. He elaborated on a plan he was devising. "Dis Marshil. If we go way out dis way and come back round, maybe Darkster no see us. I tink we needs to send some ships in opposite direction and have dems look like scouts. Da scouts draw dems further away."

Moonoak concurred, "Dat a good plan." He nodded in affirmation of Gunza's design.

Ucktock chuckled. "See? Now you tink lika human." He patted Gunza on the back with a hardy slap.

"Do humans sacrifice themselves to save der brudders?" Gunza asked shamefully.

Ucktock understood the question. "Prolly. It da smart ting to do."

***

Guthrak oversaw the current mission on Marshil. Quicklip, Nubbs, and Arc were his guards; a half dozen Moonoak followers were his shamans. While Quicklip met Tuff and informed him of the military's imminent arrival, Guthrak and the others returned to their landing spot from just days before. They gathered all equipment and food that had been left behind in their hasty retreat, and as before, they retreated again; this time before the massive creep army reached them.

Soon, they caught up with Tuff and Quicklip.

Guthrak exchanged pleasantries with Tuff before asking, "How many soldias you gots?"

Tuff answered sheepishly, "Round two hundreds. How many you gots?"

"Round four hundred thousand," Gunza proudly stated.

Tuff added, "I knows der round a thousand mo' passed da valley."

Guthrak turned to Quicklip. "Dat da valley wer creeps be?"

Quicklip shrugged and deferred to Tuff.

Tuff exclaimed, "If it gots creeps in it, den ya. Dat's da one."

Guthrak quizzed, "How many creeps?"

"Too many fo' my orcs a fight."

"Well, I tink we should kill as many as we can befo' mo' show up, especially if Darkster shows befo' Nuttybomb gets here." Guthrak watched his troops unloading and setting up equipment.

Tuff's eyes darted around. He said, "Darkster comin's back here?"

"He might. Der be a game a cat anda mouse wit' him. Maybe he come...maybe he no come. Dunno. But we can kill creeps and save der souls until den. Lessa dems we gots to fight later."

"We only gots a few hours to kill creeps befo' it get dark. Afta dat, we best a stay hidden inside."

Guthrak flicked the jewelry hanging from his ornamental jaw piece. "Mo' hidin'. Just great."

The newly landed troops gathered and cleared the valley of creeps without much trouble. Most returned to the ships as safe havens during the night, while others worked out supply trades with Tuff in his bunkers.

The following day brought the same ghastly chill in the air that seemed to visit every day on the cursed world. Regardless of discomfort, Guthrak's troops worked diligently to clear the nearest city of vanquished souls. Unfortunately, dozens of creeps

172

remained in the destroyed metropolis by nightfall. The army fell back to their strongholds until the next morning's chill beckoned them.

Pilots from scout ships reported back locations of creeps within half a day's travel, so the army could engage them and return to their ships once again. The day saw the cleansing of over one hundred thousand souls, a quarter of which were raised soldiers within Darkster's ranks.

While Guthrak's pilots scouted for creeps, Darkster's pilots scouted for Guthrak's forces. Both found what they were searching for.

***

Darkster read report after report. He interrogated his pilots, pulling every bit of information from their simple minds as would be allowed. Reconnaissance photos gave him fairly reliable information about what ships Guthrak had on the surface, as well as how many troops.

What he didn't have, was the location of Nuttybomb's capital ships; they eluded him so far. He paced in his quarters, working out contingencies in his head, based on numerical probabilities.

And so was the ambiguity of his dilemma; probable victory on the surface, but possibly exposing his fleet in orbit. He so desired bringing finality to his enemy as soon as possible, but he was unwilling to compromise his fragile advantage, for disadvantage was easily possible.

He decided to contact his ally. "Kingskull…"

"Wut is it?"

"My scouts found ground forces anda transport ships on Marshil, but no capital ships."

Kingskull said, "I comin' near to da broken moon. So far, no capital ships. Maybe Nuttybomb took all da fuel fro' da transports anda headed home."

Darkster acknowledged, "Possible, I guess."

"Hims scout ships keep comin' fro' dat direction."

"Don't be so sure," Darkster warned. "Him's very crafty. Busides, do you know da planet orbits in dis system?"

Kingskull snarled, "I know how long fo' Hotta to swing back round dis way. I ain't decided if I go afta it or wait fo' it to come back round. Gonna check da broken moon first."

Darkster posed the intellectual question, "Do you tink it possible dat Nuttybomb justa makes you waste yer time? Maybe him's hidin' out here somewhere, waitin' fo' you to go all da way to his planet?"

"I tink you put too much smarts in dis Nuttybomb. I smart 'nuff to know all tricks. I beed in so many wars...I knows lots."

"Ok. You knows lots," Darkster poked.

Kingskull angrily retorted when being tested, "I do!"

"Just lika you know 'bout creeps?"

"I hear nuttin' but rumors 'bout you and creeps. I hear lies 'bout you goin' into orcs heads wen dems dreams. Dat you use magic to make yer whip some kinda super energy. Dat you can cause fires, makes orcs tink dems on fire, all kinda stupids stuff. I already tells you wut I know 'bout creeps. Dems kids stories I learned wen I wus lil."

Darkster growled, "Well, now dat you bigga, I teach you growed up stuff."

174

Kingskull remarked in sarcasm, "Perhaps if you live longa 'nuff, we meet face to face anda you can learn some stuff, too."

"I doubt it," Darkster teased.

"I doubt you live longa 'nuff to," Kingskull countered. He laughed in a deep, boisterous hoot.

Darkster yearned to kill Kingskull now, almost as much as he was driven to kill Nuttybomb. But Kingskull would have to wait for his demise. Full out provocation was summarily dismissed as it would lead to facing Kingskull's more powerful fleet. The crazed orc gave pause, restraining his impulsive urge to insult his so-called ally.

Kingskull prodded, "Wut? No threats, Darkster?"

With an eyebrow raised, Darkster calmly replied, "No threat needed. Dems just words."

Wanting to keep the upper hand, and thinking he would find Nuttybomb first, Kingskull also wanted to diffuse the tension that was arising between the two as they argued. He bit his lip and said, "Fair 'nuff. I let you know wen I find Nuttybomb ships."

***

"Boss?' an awkward orc said as he lowered his head in reverence.

Nuttybomb opened his eyes, focused, and said, "Ah, Gobbygoo."

Gobbygoo stood in a somewhat hunched, unassuming posture with arms hanging at his sides. He was pretty big, although not nearly as large as Nuttybomb. He was a bit slender, too, but visibly muscular, even by orc standards. He avoided eye contact with his wargod.

"I glad you here now," Nuttybomb stated.

The orc restrained from scratching an itch on the side of his nose. He simply stood there. His nose twitched, and his eyes watered, but he would not scratch.

Nutty asked, "Sumptin' wrong?"

Gobbygoo shrugged his shoulders.

"You gots nuttin' to say?" Nuttybomb pressed. He sat up in his bed.

"Dunno," came quietly from Gobbygoo's mouth.

Nutty smiled. He encouraged conversation by asking open-ended questions. "Wut can you tell me 'bout fightin' against Spidanoids?"

Gobbygoo shrugged his shoulders again.

"So much for open-ended questions," Nuttybomb muttered to himself. He thought a compliment might put his newest elite guard at ease. "I hear you a great fighta."

"Dunno." His posture remained unchanged.

Nutty said, "Letta us try dis again. I needs you to talk so I can learn about you. Dat will help me to know how you fight, tink, do stuff."

Gobbygoo gazed up. "K."

Nuttybomb smiled. "Ok. Tell me 'bout yerself."

This time, the awkward orc shrugged and said, "Dunno wut a say."

"How 'bout wer you come fro'?" Nutty urged.

"I just comes fro' Plenna. Dat wer you saw me wit' Booma," Gobbygoo explained.

"No, I know dat. I mean, I heard you came fro' a different planet first...a long time ago."

Gobbygoo looked around. "Oh. Ya."

Nutty was becoming frustrated, although he tried to restrain his temper. He talked slowly and deliberately, annunciating each word as he asked, "Wut planet you come fro' befo' you live on Plenna?"

"It wus called Da Green Planet."

"How far away was it?" Nutty questioned his underling.

Gobbygoo simply answered, "Far."

"How long it takes you to get fro' Da Green Planet to Plenna?"

"Longa time," Gobbygoo answered, struggling to get the words out.

"How long is longa time?"

"I tink five year. Maybe ten."

Nutty quizzed, "But yer not sure?"

Gobbygoo shrugged his shoulders once again.

Gobbygoo's inability or unwillingness to speak was nothing new to Nuttybomb. Many orcs struggled with language, but none of Nutty's other guards had that issue. They were all pretty bright, as well as being superb fighters.

Nutty thought about each of his guards, one by one.

Gunza, Uhra's father, was smart, strong, loyal, and a fierce fighter. Age had crept up on him, but he still had solid qualities. He was a fairly easy choice as Nutty's stand in.

Guthrak, around the same age, was a monster, sharing many of the same qualities, although somewhat more agitated in general. He looked the part of a grizzled warrior, and probably chose physical fighting over words, but could speak fluidly. Nutty's mind momentarily harkened back to Guthrak saving his life from some stupid biker kids. He smiled to himself.

Moonoak wasn't much of a fighter. He was certainly the most intellectual of the guards, preferring spirituality and healing over battle.

Nutty smiled again as he thought about Quicklip's sarcastic sense of humor. Memories of the guard throwing insults at Thunda reminded him of his untimely wit. His use of words was sometimes poetic and insulting; a rare quality indeed.

Nutty relished the very thoughts of thinking. Three years of war had restricted his mind, tirelessly wearing it down, and removing the joy of creativity, replacing it with an old, beaten brain. He hadn't thought freely since the times he took daily walks with Uhra.

His thoughts returned to his guards.

Nubbs, although tipsy at times, was fun loving, a good fighter, and laid back. The thought of him offering the enemy some shlogger and gaining notoriety for the outlandish deed left an indelible mark.

Ucktock was still a bit of an unknown quantity. He probably wasn't as smart as some of the other guards, but he had common sense. His thoughts usually came through as disconnected or random, but Nutty found him to be wise beyond his lacking verbiage skills.

Arc spoke well. He was a bit of a hot head. He was young. He did things that surprised Nutty. He was dangerous.

Nutty's mind found his description of Arc puzzling. Arc's attributes and traits weren't unlike the others. But in Nutty's assessment, Arc wasn't one of his most trusted guards. In that little voice that guided Nutty - told him right from wrong - the very conscience that answered his own questions – it spoke to him in short, choppy answers, that Arc was different.

His happy thoughts left him upon the assessment of Arc. Yes, there was his brother, Booma. There was King Basha, too. But spoiled was the freedom to explore his mind in this instant; the opportunity to be unbound by his imprisoned leadership; proper protocol demanded.

Why he forgot that Gobbygoo was standing before him, was elusive as well. It was just as well; the orc would stand there all day and never question his wargod.

Nuttybomb crawled out of a fog and returned to reality. "So, Gobbygoo…Did you come to Plenna alone?"

"Yessir," Gobbygoo answered respectfully.

Their conversation was interrupted by loud bangs and females screaming. They listened for a couple minutes, but then, it was over.

A nurse poked her head into Nutty's room.

Nuttybomb asked, "Wut da hell wus dat?"

The nurse gazed at her feet and quietly replied, "Yer wife is here."

Nutty propped up his pillow and said, "Great." He softly fluffed it with a light punch or two.

"Well, she was prettying up for ya, wen…"

"She always looks good," he stated proudly with a broad smile. As he looked up and said, "Hi, Honey," his jaw dropped.

Uhra staggered in with her hair standing up on end. Lip coating was smeared all over her face. Her outfit was torn to pieces and she had one broken shoe on. She growled, "Don't 'Honey' me!"

179

Eleven
Waiting Game

Guthrak drove his ground forces through the endless torrent of creeps. Most of the stricken were unarmed; still dangerous, but not nearly as formidable as Darkster's equipped mass of horror. Guthrak correctly assumed that these were the city's general population.

With his army divided into seven different-sized fighting forces, the restoration from unrest to peace was achieved at a faster pace than the day before. Things seemed to be going according to plan.

Arc's eyes rolled back, turning white, then glowing yellow as he gazed at the heavens. His mind pulled energy from the sky and ground around him, his hands changing into propellants of lightning. White blue energy and heat danced around his eyes, hiding any ocular familiarity. He leaned forward, unleashing a maelstrom of current from his extended arms.

Two hundred creeps were stripped of mutilated flesh, clothing, and virtually everything else, leaving their bones to drop upon the dusty coating beneath their feet. With their souls hovering nearby, shamans worked quickly to absolve them of all misgivings, and to grant the opportunity to pass into a peaceful afterlife.

Guthrak measured Arc's actions and took note. The young orc was now decimating several hundred opponents simultaneously with less time needed to regain strength between attacks. The old, grizzled veteran had never seen anything akin to this complete, widespread destruction.

"Slow down, Arc. You gotta give da shamans time to do der job," Guthrak instructed between waves of advancing creeps.

"Well, dems betta hurry up. I can go fasta dan dis."

Quicklip interrupted, "We all betta hurry up. Just got word dat der be ships comin' to Marshil by our transports."

Guthrak growled. He ordered, "Keep fightin'. I gots to handle dis."

Arc taunted, "You can go. I kills mo' dan you anyway."

"Careful, Kid," Guthrak spat. He turned and headed to his command post.

Quicklip tugged Arc by an arm and asked, "You stupid or sumptin'?"

"Get yer hand offa me." Arc ordered, then warned, "Guthrak don't worry me and neither do you. I mo' powaful dan both a you."

Guthrak overheard and glared back as he walked away.

"Ya? Do Nuttybomb worry you? 'Cause he will not be happy if you say shit to Guthrak," Quicklip cautioned.

"Nuttybomb won't do nuttin'."

Quicklip questioned, "Oh no? I wouldn't want a be da one who he get mad at."

Arc snarled, "Whatevva. I just practicing fo' Darkster." He watched as a very agitated Gunza marched back to meet him face to face.

Gunza huffed and puffed, growls from deep down in his belly coming out through his nose. He pulled the battleax that hung from his back and threatened, "Letta us get dis ova wit', kid. Ready a die?"

"Me, die?" Arc jeered. "Looka lika you lose in fights befo'. Dat why you got a blade stuck in yer face." He laughed hardily.

Guthrak threw a crushing right blow that sent Arc to the ground. "I no lose to a stupid kid lika you though. Get up so I finish you."

Arc's legs were weak. His misshapen head, due to a smashed cheekbone, wobbled on his neck.

"I coulda killed you, ya lil bastid," Guthrak explained. "Get up and fight me or go fight da creeps. But either way, get to yer feet, now!"

Arc stood wearily. He blinked his eyes and shook his head.

Quicklip took his arm and dragged him toward the creeps. "C'mon. Letta us fight da enemy, not each other."

"Gods dammit," Arc cursed as he spat a mouthful of blood on the ground. He should have anticipated the old orc knocking his block off. Hell, if he was in charge, he probably would have done the same thing. He couldn't fault Guthrak. Actually, he kind of admired the old war-dawg. But every dawg had its day, and this was Guthrak's. Arc swore to himself that next time would be different.

Guthrak yelled, "Finish dis last wave. We gotta move back to base." He muttered under his breath between swings of his ax, "Fuckin' Darkster. Fuckin' kid. Fuckin' creeps. Dems can all fuck off."

Enough troops remained to the rear to fell any advancing creeps from doing severe harm to Guthrak's retreating forces. Furthermore, they protected shamans who needed to trail the main force and cleanse souls. They followed the main force all the way back to their ships.

Guthrak was furious. The latest report told of his ships in space coming under attack from Darkster's fleet. Unable to outgun or outrun the enemy, they would soon be destroyed.

Four hundred thousand troops were to be stuck on this dead world. With no way to escape the surface, they would be left to fight an overwhelmingly superior number of armed creeps, food and water shortages, and quite possibly, Darkster's main army with the tyrannical leader himself at its head.

Guthrak scoffed, "Arc, you might just get yer wish to fight Darkster."

Arc smiled.

***

Nuttybomb was seen in public for the first time in months. He seldom evaded cheers and whistles from bystanders, striding tall and straight, hiding his pain and ongoing medical issues.

But behind closed doors, he doubled over, losing his breath. Several minutes of shaking and heavy breathing saw him rebound to a crumpled mess. The unprecedented ruin to his body meant no prognosis; no timeframe for complete recovery, if ever at all. He just grinned and bared it in the open, always trying to uphold the spirits of his followers' watchful eyes by appearing like the wargod he claimed to be.

He straightened and entered the design area of a factory. The smell of oil and soot were sharp on his nostrils. The odors reminded him of Guthrak's old machine shop- dirty, but useful in its purpose.

He was met by a short, fat orc. The orc wore a long overcoat with all kinds of tools hanging out of a multitude of pockets. As he spoke, his eyebrow, which hung on his forehead from temple to temple, seemed to dance in correlation with the importance of his words. He said, "Wargod Nuttybomb, it almost finish, I tink. Maybe two mo' days."

Nuttybomb complimented, "Very good. You done well here."

"Tanks. Da actuator bigga dan da human ones. No way fo' us to maka all da same parts small like ders."

"Understood," Nuttybomb said, nodding his head as he looked at blueprints. He looked up and asked, "It already in space?"

The orc replied, "Yessir. Bein' brought passed da moon now."

Nuttybomb ran some numbers in his head. Gathering a fleet and an army would take a week, give or take. The actuator would be completed by then. It would take two days to get past the moon, jump to the actuator near Marshil, then two more days to get to the planet. He could be on Marshil in less than two weeks.

What physical shape would he be in though? Could he lead his orcs into battle? He certainly couldn't face Darkster in his current condition. If his enemy had the power to subvert an entire planet to his will, killing millions, and condemning their souls, what chance did Nuttybomb have of victory? Hell, even healthy he was probably outmatched.

Nuttybomb excused himself by simply stating, "Dat is all." He sat, his hulking body being oversized for the small chair. The legs spread outward as his full weight came to a full rest. He took some deep breaths and looked up.

There was a TV hanging on the wall. It showed a human soap opera, laced with partners cheating on each other.

His mind went to Uhra. He had never seen her as angry as she was back in the medical facility. She accused him of doing stuffin's with two nurses. He didn't even know Sweetie and Hottie *were* nurses. Plus, he hadn't had any sexual contact with them since they were all kids, at least that's what he believed. His memory wasn't what it was before since the recent surgeries. He had holes in his past that he couldn't seem to remember. But he was pretty sure he wouldn't have stuffed either of them.

Now, he coped in a perpetual fog, and as such, explained to Uhra that he was pretty sure he didn't do any stuffin's with the girls, but he couldn't remember stuff. So, he couldn't definitively deny it. He was honest, but that didn't count for much.

Well, that left the door open for all kinds of possibilities. Uhra asked, "How long did they stuffin's?" and, "Were der udder gurls?" Nutty simply didn't know.

He said that maybe the girls were lying, but that didn't carry any weight against their conversation amongst themselves. Why would they lie to each other about doin' stuffin's? Apparently, they were both present during the multiple sexual acts. Something happened, but what and how?

Uhra hadn't listened to the nurses much; she mostly beat the shit out of them. They took their comeuppance, never swinging back for fear of death.

The worst they did was try to hold her, attempting to limit damage to themselves. That left her dress torn, a broken shoe missing, her hair touching the ceiling, and some smeared makeup. They looked far worse!

Nutty had been thrown out of their house. A 'cheater' wasn't welcome in Uhra's home. It didn't matter that her home was essentially *his* home, earned by the hundreds of wounds he sustained in defense of his people. Part of his disgruntled mind felt that she had no right to the place he gave her, although he would never contest it. He loved her dearly and she was the mother of his children.

He wanted to talk with the nurses firsthand and get their side of things, but didn't dare risk any further interaction with them. He hoped time would rectify things; he certainly wasn't able to in his current condition.

***

Guthrak's side crashed up against a troop ship, jagged metal cutting into his flesh. Although his sidearm was no match for an enemy fighter, he stepped away from cover and fired in the direction of the fast-moving craft. He was unable to score a hit as the fighter veered up and away at breakneck speed.

Two more fighters strafed a clearing to his left, cutting down his troops as they ran for cover. They sent dust and smoke into the air, remnants of the ground, now cratered by their attacks.

Quicklip dodged a hail of bullets. He jumped over crates and landed on his knees behind Guthrak. He screamed, "I tink Darkster found us." His smile was met by Guthrak's growl.

186

Another fighter dipped below the clouds and dove toward the orcs on the ground. Arc crawled from behind debris and stood in the path of incoming fire. His eyes changed, and his hands ignited. Lightning shot from his hands and enveloped the descending ship. First, an engine popped; then, a wing blew off, sending the crippled fighter careening to the ground in a fiery ball of ruin.

Quicklip heckled, "Guthrak, good ting you no kills him befo'."

Guthrak turned, smiled, and ran to Arc. He patted the youth on the back and exclaimed, "I glad you on our side."

Arc turned slowly. His eyes peered through the damage around him, unphased by the terrible sounds of engines whirring and gunfire cracking. His head came to rest as he stared past Guthrak.

"Wut is it?" Guthrak questioned.

Arc muttered, "Darkster landin' on da planet now. Him's here."

Guthrak asked, "Dat way?"

Arc nodded in confirmation, his eyes blank.

"How far?"

"Dunno," was said quietly. Arc closed his eyes and thought as hard as he could, but was unable to gather any information through telepathy.

To get their attention through the clamoring roar of fighters and the carnage they wrought, Quicklip yelled, "We ain't got much in guns to kill fightas."

Guthrak instructed, "Ok, Arc, just taka out dese fightas da best you can." He turned his attention back to Quicklip, "Da fightas can't kills us all. We just

187

pinned down. Prolly a give Darkster time to organize his troops."

"Whutcha wanna do?"

Guthrak picked at the large blade stuck in his jaw. He flicked the dangling jewelry and feathers as he thought. "We can't gets back to Hotta. Might as well destroy our ships here, too. Crash 'em into his troops. Might buy us some time."

Quicklip responded, "I get right on it." He raced inside the nearest ship, losing his footing as bullets ripped through the ramp that led him up into the vessel. A wall caught him before he fell to the metal deck.

Upon reaching the bridge, he gave orders for all ships to lift off and to sacrifice themselves against the enemy. They were to crash into Darkster's landing craft, or even his troops on the ground if no ships were able to be taken out.

The ships were ordered to travel in a general direction. Further instructions included the safety of their crews. They were to abandon ship at the last possible moment, so their abilities on the ground weren't lost.

Sixty ships in all left the ground, spraying swaths of dust into clouds to their rears. Others, unable to fly from enemy fighter damage, were left as cover from incoming fire and possible creep invasions.

Arc destroyed two more fighters without receiving any wounds, but he was exhausted. Furthermore, he still had damage to his cheekbone and skull.

Guthrak, satisfied with the young orc, and realizing the lull in enemy activity, approached Arc. He said, "Good job. Letta us fix yer face, kid."

188

The chip on Arc's shoulder lightened a bit. His grudge for his immediate superior was there, but took a backseat to his need for medical attention. He jeered, "We still gonna fight eachudder wen dis all ova wit'?"

"Kid, I no need any mo' enemies. I beed fightin' my whole life. Afta Darkster, I tink I needs a hang it up." He paused, scratched his chin and continued, "I shouldn't a hit you, but you wus outta line."

Arc knew the chain of command. He didn't like it, but it was there for a reason; the very reason Guthrak punched him; to keep order within the ranks. He rubbed his face and questioned, "How bad it look?"

"It an improvement." He chuckled. "How da knife in my jaw look?"

"Badass!"

***

Gunza understood. He only needed to keep his remaining fleet safe for two weeks. That was a tall order though as he was aware of two enemy fleets in the area and tons of scouts, too. If he survived, he would meet up with Nuttybomb at the nearest actuator.

The excitement of no longer needing to hide, combined with his want to step down as warchief, gave him the necessary drive to continue dodging his hunters. He headed deeper into space, away from all known landmarks.

Space was enormous and dark. A day's travel time would put him out of visual proximity from his foes. But he would go deeper into space, almost by a week's time, stretching the search area by a thousand-fold. He would hide in the vast darkness until such time required his return.

Even with reports coming in about Darkster's forces landing on Marshil, Gunza kept to his orders. Everything he was, his very entity, needed to go to Marshil to help his comrade in arms, Guthrak, and his troops. But he knew the survival of his planet depended on reinforcements – reinforcements that would come from Hotta in the form of Nuttybomb's reserves.

Gunza heard about the altercation between Guthrak and Arc. He laughed aloud in his quarters as he thought about Guthrak, for if anyone would keep the kid in line, it would be his old, fearless friend.

Gunza struggled to come up with how many years he and Guthrak had fought side by side. He guessed they battled under Warchief Dagga for five years and Ole Man Boppa for seven. He guessed ten years fighting under Biggabomb and three under Nuttybomb.

He whispered to himself, "Is dat right? How old I be I now? Thirty? Thirty-five? Forty? No, not forty, I don't tink. I tink I wus fifteen when I beed guard with Guthrak." He shrugged his shoulders.

So, he settled on a figure between twenty and twenty-five years of knowing his old friend. "Dat a longa time. Sorry ole friend."

A knock came at his door.

Gunza stated, "Come in."

Moonoak slowly entered. He lowered his hood and walked over to Gunza. He said, "You seem a troubled."

"Ya. Nuttin' you can do 'bout it though."

"True," the senior shaman agreed. He reluctantly reported, "Mo' Darkster ships headin' to Marshil."

Gunza sighed. He shook his head in disgust and raised his hands with palms up in a show of defeat. "How many?"

Moonoak's eyes gazed at the floor. He quietly said, "Maybe a thousand."

"Oh, my gods! Dems gonna die fo' sure now."

"You don't know dat," Moonoak encouraged. He continued in a positive tone, "Guthrak one helluva fighta, and Arc der too."

Gunza stated, "Guthrak not a kid no mo'. Who am I kiddin'? I not a kid no mo' neither. We gonna do da best we can, but dis is against Darkster. Looka wut he did to da whole planet."

Moonoak hesitantly added, "Der mo', too."

"Ok, maka my day," Gunza sarcastically spat.

"You know I sense tings, right?"

"Ya."

Moonoak sighed, exhaling a deep breath of seemingly tainted air. He said, "Darkster different dan wen we fought him."

"I know. He messed up all a Marshil," Gunza added.

"No, not justa dat. Him's contacted da gods, da evil god mostly."

Gunza asked, "And?"

Moonoak tried to express what he felt, but it was difficult. He made hand gestures, conveying his struggle, and emphasizing his thoughts. "Him in a different way a tinking. I try to esplain…Me anda Nuttybomb don't really talk a da gods. We pray to dem, but we no here dem talk back. We tap into a energy dat tell us stuff. It fro' da gods I tink, but it not dems."

191

"Ok? And?"

"Darkster mind can talk wit' dems. Dunno how. Dunno wut it mean, but it so powaful, I can't esplain. It scare me." The troubled shaman rubbed his chest.

Gunza quizzed, "Anda you know dis just fro' yer feelin's?"

"Yes," Moonoak replied. "I can feel it through our a minds.

"Wut 'bout yer feelins 'bout Nuttybomb?"

Moonoak admitted, "I can't feel Nuttybomb. I assume him's ok."

Gunza questioned, "Well, I gots a feelin' dat dis da last fight fo' a lot a us."

"Can't jump to conclusions. Maybe Nuttybomb just too far away fo' me to reach his mind."

***

Nuttybomb walked around with one shoe on, searching for the other. He backtracked, going over his path the last fifteen minutes, attempting to locate the missing cover for his foot. He thought it not too uncommon, considering he was in a new place of living.

After fifteen minutes, he gave up. Unable to accomplish the simple task, he sat down to finish his sandwich. However, one bite told him it was dry; he'd forgotten to put condiments on it.

He slowly pushed his beaten body up from the crate and hobbled to the icebox in his little room. He grabbed a jar and emptied the last of the runny contents onto his plate. As he shut the icebox door, he did a doubletake. He reopened the door to see his shoe, sitting out of place on the top shelf. Had he left his shoe there?

Nutty smacked his forehead, removed the shoe, and went back to the crate. He took some deep breaths and sat gingerly. He moaned when tasked with bending forward and lifting his foot to put the shoe on. He giggled at how cold it felt as it slipped onto the bottom of his foot. At least he had both feet covered.

He looked around for his now-missing sandwich. The table was empty, as was the floor around him. He glanced around, only to find it on top of the icebox. Some more deep breaths and he was up and across the room.

Before finishing the sandwich, he saw himself in a mirror. The lighting was bad, as were his eyes, causing him to squint. He took two steps closer, so he could view himself better.

Before him, was an old, tired, battered male. Much of his muscle mass was gone, replaced with scarred, pale skin. He looked back at himself, somewhat saddened by his appearance. He was alone as well, standing in the dark, touching various wounds, his right hand finally resting on his heart.

That was broken, too, not just from battle and surgeries, but from what happened between him and Uhra. He needed her. He needed her for his wellbeing, for him to get stronger, if that was possible. But most of all, he needed her to know how much he missed her; how much he longed for her; how sorry he was that he wasn't able to remember what happened.

He tried to connect with her mind. This way, he could communicate with her and exchange his feelings. Unfortunately, he couldn't link with her. One last look in the mirror and he left.

Nutty found himself the recipient of more cheers along his travels. He stopped at the crossroads and Guthrak's old shop.

"Ah, Wargod," came from an officer.

"Hi."

The officer asked, "Wut can I do for ya?"

Nutty looked around, confused. "Umm, dunno."

"Oh, ok." He chortled. "I wus told you needed to organize troops. I tought dat why you wus here."

Nutty played off his memory issues by saying, "Oh, it's you I needs to talk wit' fo' troops? Ok. Ya. How many can we get fro' new recruits?"

The officer answered, not picking up on Nuttybomb's deception, "We gots seventy-thousand here anda forty thousand mo' on udder continent. Dems all just keepin' peace lika you wanted."

"Ok. Gets dem together. It beed so longa since I put evvybody in command. Who I see 'bout spaceship crews?" Nuttybomb asked.

"Umm, dat would be...Stickyfingas I tink," the officer guessed.

Nuttybomb thanked the officer and went about his business. He stopped across the street at the medical facility to get an update on his condition.

The head nurse asked, "Yer vision gots worse?"

"Yup." He said, sticking out his bottom lip as he nodded.

"Lemme look in yer eyes," she instructed. She shined a hand-held light and moved it across Nutty's line of sight. She squinted and did it a second time.

He asked, "Anyting?"

She responded with a question. "Anda you gots a hard time rememberin's stuff?"

194

"Ya." He forgot to mention his current inability to use telepathy, not that he should have. His use of mind control was well-documented, and placed his abilities well above most orcs. Even if he wanted to, it was best not to share such a devastating loss.

The head nurse suggested, "We should taka pictures of yer head. Sumptin' not right."

"Wut?"

She quizzed, "Sumptin' wrong wit' yer hearin', too?"

Nutty smiled and said, "No, just wen I stands up too fast."

"Do you hear ringin' sounds?"

Nutty replied, "Ya," surprised that she thought he might.

"C'mon. Come wit' me."

Nutty hobbled slowly down the hallway and into a room where he was instructed to lie down. His head was strapped to the table to inhibit his movement. A large, half-circle of a machine came down around him and covered him from his waste up. Over the next thirty minutes, it photographed his brain, beeping, hissing, and popping in its duty to reveal all.

The head nurse removed the machine and straps from Nuttybomb. Then, she brought him into an adjacent room where he sat and waited for her. She went to a computer and sat at it, analyzing the pictures that appeared on its screen.

She grimaced and stated, "Nuttybomb, you gots swellin' in yer brain."

Nutty questioned, "So, wut dat mean?"

She pointed to the screen and began, "It mean dat dis part a yer brain getting too big. It put pressure on yer eyes and udder parts a da brain."

All things considered, he laughed. "No, I know wut swellin' means," he said. "What it mean fo' me to heal?"

The nurse apologized, "Oh, sorry. I didn't know if it affect wut you know or don't know. Ok, so, I tink mosta it just be fluid. I can drill into yer head anda sucks it out."

Nutty questioned, "So, no problem?"

She scrunched up her face and said, "Huge problem. Might cause mo' damage. Da area is lika in da middle a yer brain. I hope it be ok, but dunno fo' sure."

"Wut if we leave it?"

The nurse admitted, "Dunno. Might get worse. If it no gets worse, fluid prolly absorb back into yer body. But it a big risk either way."

Nutty asked, "How long dat take to absorb?"

"Dunno. If it not get worse, maybe weeks, months?"

The decision was made. Without Uhra's input, Nutty instructed, "Do it."

The head nurse asked hesitantly, "Wut 'bout yer wife?"

Nutty replied nonchalantly, "She no talkin' to me. Just get somebody a call her."

Nuttybomb was prepped and readied for the procedure. Local anesthetics were given, along with some deeper injections to help with pain. It was agreed not to administer general anesthesia because of the mass of chemicals his brain, liver, and kidneys had already been exposed to.

While extraction of fluid commenced, Uhra was contacted. She picked up the phone and said, "Hello."

Sweetie replied, "Hello. Dis is Sweetie ova at da medical facility."

Uhra angrily questioned, "Wut da hell do you want?"

Twelve
Kosmokrateros

He watched his ships being rammed from afar, obliterating some of his troops and supplies. He heard the frantic screams of his officers as they reported to him with their last words. Without the smallest care for his orcs, the minimal loss to his total numbers angered him.

Darkster paced on the bridge of his super ship, hoping to avoid heading to the planet himself; at least, for a while. Brom was leading his formidable forces on the surface of Marshil, provided he survived the barrage of kamikaze Hotta ships.

Brom said via ship-to-ship broadcast, "All ships landed. No mo' enemy ships hittin' us."

"Excellent," Darkster said in his croaky voice. He continued, "Proceed as planned. Be sure to hold up in da ships tonight."

"Yessir."

Darkster stopped pacing long enough to read a collection of reports that confirmed enemy troop sizes and locations. He told himself, "Good, good. Wit' a million mo' troops comin', der will be no stoppin' me. Anda wit' night almost to da Hotta orcs, dems will be asleeps. Time to have some fun."

He left the bridge and headed for his quarters. His mind began to remove any unwanted clutter, a practice he had learned from his father before meditating. By the time he reached his destination, he was calm.

The quarters he arrived at, were by far, grander than anything on any other orc ship, both in scale and comfort. With his ship being the largest, it was only fitting that he required the biggest accommodations as well. He didn't only sleep there; he ate, trained, and even communicated with the gods in the expansive space.

He looked through the massive windows, deep into space, and beyond. He snapped his fingers, dimming the lights and igniting various candles for illumination. He cleared his mind of all other thoughts and began...

"Lord a da underworld, hear me. Lord a da underworld, hear me. I call to you as yer subservient follower."

The fires blew out, the stars faded. Darkster felt a cold chill that started at the bottom of his spine and ran up to the base of his skull. He swayed uncontrollably, his eyes closed, his heart beginning to pound.

The hate Goliath cast upon him consumed his soul; deception of love and worth was traded to the orc in exchange for control of his afterlife; it was no longer his possession, anyway; it was forsaken a long time ago when Darkster began his path to darkness by conducting ungodly tortures and killings. However, this sealed the deal. His soul wasn't just lost, set off course by his sadistic actions, it was gained as a unique prize by the lord of the underworld, seized as a consolation prize. Only nine times, since the birth of the cosmos, had anyone so evil been allowed such a rare opportunity.

Darkster had beckoned the lord's wrath, and the deity transferred the orc's sacrificed soul for the pittance of temporary supremacy. Yes, supremacy was his in this world, servitude required in the next. A voice told the disturbed orc, "Kosmokrateros will soon be unleashed, and you will be known as Demon Lord!"

Darkster sat quietly, accepting evil in its most uncomplicated form, ruthless and complete. He drifted into a trance- a forced semi-sleep- and began the process.

***

Guthrak asked, "How many?"

Quicklip replied, "A lot. Five thousand."

"And dems all in comas?"

"Yup," Quicklip answered, nodding his head in disgust.

Guthrak spat, "We lost five thousand troops ova night to dreams fro' freakin' Darkster? Dat great, Dat just fuckin' great!" He turned and instructed, "It is wut it is. Letta us go."

The two walked down the ramp and met atop a ridge that overlooked their army. Nubbs and Arc came to the ridge as well. The group of shamans and mages followed.

A sea of orcs, dressed in uniform blue-gray, amassed below. They had standard-issue hand-cannons and swords, contrasting the gun metal and silver weapons they held with the attire they wore. A few thousand wore heavier armor over their clothes. The armor was reserved for the front-line troops, who bore the brunt of hand-to-hand combat. Cannons were hooked to the same blue-gray color trucks, giving a sense of unity across the army. No armored vehicles were present on Marshil.

The raucous troops fell silent in anticipation of what was to be said. Guthrak didn't have the gift of tongue that Nuttybomb did; far from it. But he had

200

been around soldiers most of his life, and knew morale was low because of Darkster's magic.

"Wargod Nuttybomb! Wargod Nuttybomb! Wargod Nuttybomb!" Guthrak screamed, whipping his troops into a frenzy.

Four hundred thousand troops chanted in unison, delays in the words echoed by the farthest orcs, nearly a mile away. They marched forward, the name of their leader becoming their battle cry. And why not? Their devotion was unquestionable. Nuttybomb was more a god than the invisible deities they prayed to, for his physical presence cemented the reality of his existence, his actions earning legendary status.

Guthrak had tapped into the collective psyche of his troops, and now, they would bring the fight to Darkster. Being outnumbered more than two-to-one meant little to the well-trained, battle-hardened Hotta army. Especially now, with a wargod at their backs. They hoped to catch the enemy unawares.

The large guns rolled into position and opened fire. Guthrak and his guards led the charge into a mass of unprepared enemy troops. Even though Darkster had the advantage of viewing the battle from space, orders were slow in organizing his million-troop army.

With artillery weakening the front lines, Guthrak's elites slashed through the opposition early in the engagement. However, Arc's dual role of taking out fighters, as well as providing extra punch on the ground, saw him overwhelmed. Darkster's forces began to reorganize and fill holes exposed in their broken lines.

Artillery still pounded away, weakening key positions and drawing attention away from Guthrak's advancing troops on the right flank. The Hotta orcs swung around and hit the fragile side of the exposed enemy, seventy thousand, wargod-driven orcs driving deep into their foes.

But Darkster's forces wouldn't break. Repeatedly, they adjusted to Guthrak's attacks and began counter attacks of their own.

Quicklip yelled as he stabbed an opposing orc's chest, "You stupid!" He slashed another's face and screamed, "Anda you ugly!"

Guthrak screamed, "Maybe you kill mo' if you don't insult everyone you attack. Give you mo' energy."

"Energy nuttin'! Dems all stupid and ugly. Dems should know wut dems really are befo' dems die." He clubbed an orc over the head with the butt of his weapon and hollered, "Yo' momma don't even luvs you."

Nubbs, fighting alongside his loud-mouthed comrade, fought quietly until an errant bullet found his flask of shlogger. He poked his finger through it to confirm the loss of his favorite ale and sighed. He growled in anger and began yelling, "You face looka lika da ass of a steampig!" He felled an enemy and yelled again as his blade entered another, "I shit in yer eyes, you piece a carnidawg butt hole!"

Quicklip finished an insult of his own when he asked, "Feels good, don't it?"

"Yup," Nubbs confirmed.

"But only yell a couple words. Dis way you properly curse each one and you don't gotta slow down killin's."

Nubbs frantically explained, "But dems killed my shlogger."

Quicklip hollered, "Bastid! You killed his shlogger!" His sword came down between an enemy's eyes.

Arc argued, "Shutta up! It hard a fight wit' you two yellin's stupid stuff!"

Quicklip defensively questioned the orc who was endowed with skills, "Stupid? It not fun to kills fo' all a us lika it fun fo' you. Dis maka it easier fo' me."

"You an orc? Act lika one," Arc spat.

Guthrak ordered, "Dat 'nuff. Shutta up! All a you!"

The battle continued for most of the day with Twenty-three thousand Hotta orcs dead or wounded. Darkster's casualties totaled over one hundred thousand.

Upon receiving reports that Darkster had more forces coming, including fighters and bombers, Guthrak withdrew his forces to the crashed ships that marked the landscape to his rear. Refuge was found among the hulking heaps, used to keep creeps at bay, as well as to bottleneck Darkster's forces. Hotta orcs hunkered down for a long, arduous fight.

Guthrak mumbled, "All dese damn battles da same; slash anda hack, slash anda hack."

Quicklip smirked and said, "Well, Arc changes tings up a bit."

"Ya, I guess," Guthrak agreed, then continued, "Dat kid worries me."

"I know wutcha mean." Quicklip sat on the floor and shoved some boarcakes into his mouth.

Nubbs joined him on the cold, metal deck of the ship. "You worried 'bout Arc?" Nubbs asked and followed with a swig of shlogger.

Guthrak replied, "Ya. I feel sumptin' around him. Reminds me a Headhunta; just creepy."

"I no feel nuttin'," Nubbs stated. He lifted a mug and added, "I drink all da time to stay numb."

Quicklip teased, "No, you drink a 'cause you like da feelin' a bein' drunk all da time."

"Dat too," Nubbs concurred, and followed with a loud belch.

Guthrak said, "Anyway, Nuttybomb comin's next week. He can keep an eye on da kid."

Quicklip added, "If da rumors be true, Darkster will be here, too, wit' mo' troops. Gunza said him supa-strong now. We just gots to fight fo' a week or so till Nuttybomb come to kill Darkster."

Guthrak stated, "Darkster gonna get his ass beat when Nuttybomb get here!"

***

"I can't see," Nuttybomb said, running his hands over his face.

The head nurse explained, "Give it some time. I tink I maybe hit some nerves."

"How much time?"

She replied, "Dunno. Maybe quick, I hope."

Nuttybomb asked in an undignified tone, "You hope?"

"Ya. Letta us just hope it not permanent."

Uhra entered the room. She put down a bag on a nearby table and teased, "Can't get 'nuff a dis place?" trying to hide her anger.

204

Nutty's head turned in her general direction. With eyes crossed, he simply sighed, "Uhra."

Uhra did a double take. She asked, "Wut wrong wit' yer eyes?"

He shrugged his shoulders and reluctantly admitted, "Can't see."

"Can't see?" Uhra questioned, her tone and volume higher than before.

The head nurse said, "Gots to give it time. I took fluid fro' his brain." She moved around, always checking vitals, writing something down, folding blankets, and doing things nurses did.

"Ok, sure. Mo' problems wit' his brain." Uhra crossed her arms, turned and walked to the window. She was angry with Nuttybomb for the cheating thing, although she wasn't sure what actually transpired. Furthermore, the fact that he allowed himself to be wounded without medical attention umpteen times, infuriated her. His lack of care for himself carried over to the family; he had little kids back home. Now, he was blind?

Nutty said, "Don't worry. It prolly be fine."

"Nutty, it already not fine. In three years, you beed home lika two weeks. Anda dis time around, you almosta died. Anda you still sick."

Nutty attempting to remove Uhra's concern, explained, "Well, all da surgeries done now. I just gots to wait fo' my eyes to work. Den, I can go to Marshil anda finish dis war."

"Go to...I can't do dis anymo'. No, I can't do dis." Uhra looked at the ceiling with tears in her eyes.

"Wutcha talkin' 'bout? Can't do wut?"

205

Uhra pointed to the head nurse and ordered, "You, out fo' a minute."

The nurse brought a half-folded blanket into the hallway and kept walking, distancing herself from Nutty's room, and the hostility inside.

Uhra started, "Look, Nutty...I still not ok wit' yer two nurse friends."

He cut in with, "I already explained..."

"Shutta up anda listen. You in no shape to fight Darkster or anyone else. You looka so weak. Anda even if der no future fo' us, you still gots kids."

Nutty pleaded, "Don't say dat."

"Shutta up! You not a wargod, you not a warchief, you not even a soldier. You just a ordinary orc wit' a beat-up body anda broken brain. You can't saves us. Dat outta yer hands now."

"No! Guthrak can't face Darkster alone. Kingskull fro' anudder star system gonna attack us, too. I da last one can help."

Uhra stated, "Listen, if you da last one, dan we already lost."

Nutty slouched and stared off aimlessly, "Uhra, if I no try, dan you, me, and our kids...will all die...and be tortured forevva. I gots a try."

"I hopes you feel betta, Nutty. Bye." She turned away; and then, she was gone.

Nutty exclaimed, "I wuvs you, Uhra," but she wasn't there to respond.

After the coast was clear, the head nurse returned. "How da eyes?" she asked.

"Same," came from a sad and dejected Nuttybomb.

"Any ringin' in da ears?"

Nutty tipped his head and yawned, as if to unclog a pressure difference between his ears, eustachian tubes, and sinuses, but that wasn't necessary: his ears were fine. "Nope," he firmly stated.

The head nurse said, "Good," and began unwrapping the bandages around Nutty's head. She used the same hand-held light form the day before and tested his vision. "How 'bout now? See anyting?"

"Ya," Nutty replied in subdued excitement. He continued, "It fuzzy, but I see da light."

"Anda how yer head feel?"

"I gots a headache."

She chuckled, "You oughta. Just put a long stick in yer brain." She pushed on different spots of his skull. "Dis hurt?"

"No."

"Dis hurt?"

"Uh-uh."

"How 'bout here?"

Nutty gave a clear, "Nope."

"How 'bout bein's dizzy?"

"Ya, I still a lil dizzy," Nutty admitted.

With her help, Nutty sat up and hung his head forward. She asked, "Mo' dizzy?"

"Nope."

"You feel mo' foggy or funny bendin' down lika dis?"

Nutty said, "No, pretty good."

The head nurse was somewhat relieved. "Dat good. I tink you be ok in a few days. Hope eyes gets betta befo' dat, but maybe not."

"I hopes so. Still got a war a fight."

***

207

Dozens of creeps managed to pick off as many Hotta orcs within Guthrak's ranks. Because most orcs were awake, those numbers were far better than the five thousand lost to Darkster's mind control the night before while they slept.

Nubbs managed, "I so freakin' tireds."

Quicklip agreed, "Me, too. Dis gets old, fast."

Guthrak said, "Take mo' drugs. Gotta stay awake. If you fall into coma, we can't get you out."

"Drugs and shlogger don't mix," Nubbs quarreled.

Quicklip snapped, "So, get yer head outta yer ass anda yer drink outta yer mouth. How stupid are you?"

"Not stupid 'nuff to stay here and listen to yer stupid shit." Nubbs got up and walked off.

Guthrak's communication box beeped. He answered, "Wut is it?"

A voice said, "Darkster army tried getting through our hatches again."

"And?"

"We stopped 'em, but I don't know how long befo' dems ovarun us."

Guthrak ordered, "You hold dat position anda fight till da last orc. Undastood?"

"Yessir."

Quicklip mentioned, "Hey Chief, dems startin' mo' attacks on mo' a our positions now. We can't stay here forevva."

"I know, I know. At least we slow 'em down and kills many mo' a dems dan dems kills us."

"Ya, but fo' how long? We sittin' ducks wen da fightas and bombas come. Arc can't take 'em all down. Anda dis, too...He can't even gets outside passed 'em to fight," Quicklip elaborated.

Guthrak stated, "Arc can clear out 'nuff enemies so we can get outta da ship. But we will get one chance. We gotta tink how to exit all ships together. If we mix wit' Darkster troops, fightas and bombas be useless."

"So, we needs to fight our way fro' ship to ship. We get to closest ones first."

"Ya, dat's my tought," the makeshift-warchief said.

Quicklip tipped his head up with an ear to the sky. "You hear dat? I tink we spokes too soon."

"Spread da word!" Guthrak jumped to his feet and darted to the ramp. He picked up Arc as he hustled.

Arc yelled, "Put me down, you big goon!"

Guthrak laughed, "Sorry, kid. It time."

Lightning shot from the opening of the ship, cascading down and outward, electrocuting all enemy orcs within one-hundred feet. As with virtually every other attack, Guthrak and his guards led a charge into their adversaries.

Nubbs was a little slow to catch up, but catch up he did. And boy, did he! The anger from being required to take medications over shlogger to keep him awake, enraged the alcoholic. He fought with a fury he rarely displayed.

Lack of shlogger aside, most Hotta orcs fought ferociously; a result of the highly-stimulating pills inciting them to kill swiftly. They weren't as efficient as they should have been, but they were more alert and quicker than their opponents.

Furthermore, Hotta orcs were larger than their outer star system counterparts. Their strength was greater, and the evolution of their brains gave them better problem-solving skills. Additionally, they had been in constant war over the last three years. Being faster, stronger, and smarter, gave the experienced and battle-tested army a marked advantage.

Enemy attack craft dived down, screaming as they released their payloads. However, that was short lived. Friendly fire was taking a toll on their own troops at a similar rate to the Hotta orcs.

Guthrak's forces worked from ship to ship, adding more troops to the fray. His big guns opened fire into the darkness somewhere into the center of his enemies, keeping the bulk of Darkster's forces from gaining on the Hotta orcs as they made their way to the nearest city.

The nearest city, named Kockrel, was no longer a place where orcs lived and worked. Very few buildings still stood, and those that did, were infested with creeps. It was decided to get the remaining three hundred thousand plus Hotta orcs into the subway tunnels beneath the destroyed metropolis.

The challenges of killing the enemy while fleeing, were compounded by the need to fight inside their lines; separation of the retreating force would allow fighters and bombers to kill with impunity.

"Dis takin's too long," Guthrak shouted.

Quicklip said, "Lots a ships bringin' down mo' troops back der, too."

Guthrak cursed, "Gods dammit! Letta us go. Gotta fights straight through 'em."

The desperate army worked from the enemy's flank, right into the center of its bewildered troops. It was unfathomable for the smaller force to rush into an encirclement. Yet, it did.

Quicklip lost most of his upper left arm to a close-range hand cannon. His insults fell silent, replaced with loud groans, emitted with every step.

Nubbs wasn't much better. Hobbled by slash wounds to both legs, his cumbersome movements kept him defending, rather than attacking.

Arc released every bit of hate and anger he had, opening huge gaps in the frenzy before him. Exhaustion was less of a problem than several days before as pills hyped him up and kept him fresh.

With Quicklip and Nubbs feeling the effects of their wounds, Guthrak bore the brunt of the deadly blows that surrounded the guards. Repeatedly, he evaded the final thrust that would end his life.

The crumbled spires of the city were in view, set to the left of a mountain range. Guthrak and Arc cleared a path as best they could, through the seemingly endless group of bodies, all the way to the edge of the rocky outcrop. Keeping most enemy troops away from that spot, they pulled their own troops along, filling in the holes of the dead with their own orcs.

Advancing while retreating, an oxymoron if ever there was one, gave Guthrak's forces a fighting chance. There were pockets of troops killed or captured as they didn't keep up with his main force, but overall, most were closing in on Kockrel. The morning sun slowly rose on the horizon.

Guthrak kept the mountains to his back, advancing sideways toward the city. His thin line of soldiers wasn't easily picked off by attack craft, rocky overhangs kept them relatively safe. Moreover, there was no discernable distance between both armies. The ships would have been firing into their own troops too.

The city's gates were crossed, and with them, an opening that the enemy ships waited for. Fighters rained down fire from the skies as they dove. Hotta orcs raced for cover...

But not before leaving hundreds of mines in their wake. Explosion after explosion tore into Darkster's closest troops. As many enemy troops were lost to mines as Hotta orcs were lost to fighters.

Smoke grenades were set off to hide Guthrak's army's descent. They poured into the city's tunnels, eliminating hundreds of creeps. They filled nearly every nook and cranny, many dropping to the floor in exhaustion and pain. No number of pills would eliminate their fatigue now.

Blood was everywhere; the blue-gray uniforms were drenched in red and brown, giving no hint of original color. Open wounds poured onto the floors of the orc-made caverns. Bandages were applied, limbs too severely disfigured were removed. Makeshift cots were set up, giving minimal comfort to those most needing it.

Guthrak came upon Quicklip, who was crouched against a wall. "Lemme see dat wound."

Quicklip stood up.

"Show me," Guthrak ordered.

"I can't raise it," Quicklip said with a painful expression.

Guthrak grabbed his arm and looked at it. He turned it and looked into Quicklip's eyes. He sympathetically said, "I tink we gotta take da arm."

Quicklip responded, "Fuck me."

Guthrak smiled, attempting to lighten the mood. He said sarcastically, "No tanks. I'll just take da arm."

Arc stumbled by and noticed the wound. "Damn! Dat bad."

Quicklip snarled, "Ya, tanks. I know."

Guthrak rushed, "Don't go nowhere. I get a doc." He pushed passed other wounded soldiers and disappeared.

Nubbs came as quick as he could, but his legs weren't in the best shape. He offered, "I gots you some shlogger."

"Tanks," Quicklip said graciously. "But I gonna need a helluva lots mo' dan shlogger fo' dis pain."

"Ova here, Doc," Guthrak yelled.

A doc stumbled over Nubbs extended leg and into Quicklip's painful arm.

"Wut da fuck, Doc? Dat's one way to take my arm, I guess!" Quicklip screamed.

The doc instructed, "Clear da area." He pointed to Nubbs and said, "You, outta da way. I fix you next." He went back to Quicklip, this time spending time testing the damaged arm's reflexes and mobility.

Quicklip sniped, "Gods dammit, Doc!"

"I know, son. It gonna hurt. I gots to see wut I can save."

"Keeps it up and you gonna have to save yerself," Quicklip warned.

Guthrak ordered, "Quicklip, shutta up."

"Yessir."

The doc followed muscle and bone up to Quicklip's shoulder. "It hurt here?"

Quicklip answered, "Not as much as down der."

"Dat good, actually."

"Oh ya?"

"Ya," the doc replied. Then, he explained, "Yer shoulder be good. You missin' mosta dis, but da nerves, blood supply, all dat be good."

In pain, Quicklip griped, "Ok, but it hurt lika hell. Wut we gonna do?"

"Nurse," the doc called over. "Get a extra-long left arm fo' me."

"Oh, you gots arms just layin' round?"

The doc nonchalantly stated, "Well yes, as a matta a fact, I do."

He snatched a metallic arm from the nurse. The apparatus was clearly a limb with joints in the shoulder, elbow, wrist, and knuckles. He said to Quicklip, "Dis will work just like yers."

"Oh, boy. I can't wait."

The doc seized Nubbs' mug and downed all the shlogger. "Letta us get started.

"Good luck," Nubbs wished to his wounded friend. He walked away, shaking his head.

Arc added, "Meh, you be fine." He followed Nubbs somewhere.

Quicklip joked nervously, "You leavin' me too, Guthrak."

Guthrak replied, "Go fuck yerself," and left as well. Quicklip smiled.

***

Casualties on both sides were staggering. The Battle at Kockrel Kliffs, as it was later called, knocked Guthrak's forces down to a mere two hundred thousand; half of what it was just four days before. Darkster's casualties totaled five hundred six thousand, bringing his initial army's strength from one million to only three hundred twenty-six thousand.

But another million Darkster troops were on Marshil, settin' up beyond the city. Plus, there were millions of creeps, and more dead to be raised. Things were becoming desperate.

Thirteen
Healing

Nutty rubbed his eyes and said, "It beed three days, but dems still blurry."

The head nurse admitted, "It not good, yet, but it betta. I tink rest a vision comin' back."

"Oh, I gots sumptin' fo' you."

She asked, "Fo' me?" with a cheek-to-cheek smile.

Upon Nutty yelling, "Ok," other nurses entered the room and gathered around.

"Wut all dis?" the flustered head nurse questioned.

"Well, you dids so good savin's me. Anda I nevva called you by name. Fro' now on you be called Doc Smoochie."

The nurses clapped for the first-ever female doctor. Sweetie and Hottie were there, standing behind the other nurses, hoping not to be noticed. They clapped, too, but quietly.

Nutty added, "You in charge now. Der gonna be lots a wounded comin's back fro' Marshil. Start preparin's."

The doc obeyed, "Yessir, Wargod Nuttybomb."

The room emptied, and Nutty went about his business. He made several stops on his way to the launch pad, one of which was his mother.

"Nutty," Muga welcomed with her arms wide open.

"Mama," came from his humble lips as he was wrapped by her warm arms.

"You want sumptin' to eat?"

"You didn't cooks it, did you?" Nutty asked, attempting to be humorous like his father before him.

Muga spat, "Don't start. You gettin' just lika yer fatha." She smiled.

Nutty sat on a crate and quietly asked, "How you doin'?"

A forced smile was accompanied by, "Oh, I ok. Tanks."

"Good. Yer welcome."

Muga explained, "It wasn't lika you stinky-ass dad was always 'round. He was usually off fightin' somewhere. I raised you kids by myself."

"You did good, Mama," Nutty complimented.

"Tanks, But dunno 'bout dat. Da feva and da wars tooks some a you. I tried, though."

Nutty shoved a mouthful of boarcakes into the side of his cheek, attempting to chew and speak at the same time. "I growed up Mama, but I still needs yer help."

Muga asked as she sat next to her prized son, "Wutcha needs, Nutty?"

"Uhra leaves me." His embarrassment heard in his voice.

She rolled her eyes and muttered, "Oh, dat. Sorry."

Nutty questioned, "You knew?"

Muga explained, "No, but I assumed. Der rumors goin' 'round 'bout you and some nurses. Anda Uhra a strong female. She not put up wit' dat stuff."

"Yeah, but Mama...dunno it even happened," he said as he shrugged.

"You no talk to da nurses 'bout it?"

Nutty's hands came up as if to push back. "No way! Dat all Uhra need is fo' me to be talkin's wit' dems."

With a hand extended and resting on her son's shoulder, Muga clarified, "But she already leaves you."

"Ya, no, I can't be seen wit' dems," he rushed in a panicked voice.

Muga asked, "Wut 'bout talkin's wit dems wit yer mind?"

Nutty replied, "Can't. My brain is still brokes."

"Well, keeps tryin'. Dat da best way."

"Tanks, Mama. I off to Marshil."

Muga warned, "You be careful. I hear tings 'bout how powaful Darkster is now."

Nutty hugged his mother one last time and said, "I will. Wuvs you."

"I wuvs you, too, Nutty," Muga whispered as she reached up to accept his loving embrace. The tears she fought back, erupted as soon as the door was closed, and he was gone. She went back to fashioning a blanket in her comfortable chair in the little house she shared with no one.

He passed orcs along the way, always drawing much more attention than he wanted, especially as he walked into light poles.

A bystander asked worriedly, "You ok, Wargod?"

Nutty passed off his health issue as being meaningless with, "Yup. Doc did my stupid eye test today. She puts stuff in my eyes, so she can see in der betta, but I can't see shit for a lil while."

The group of gathering orcs laughed considerably, striking Nutty as odd. Apparently, the words from a wargod meant much more than those from a common orc. Maybe the crowd was just appeasing him to lessen his embarrassment. Maybe they really saw humor in his words, believing wargods weren't susceptible to such trivialities. Regardless, the orcs seemed to buy his story, so he moved on.

A storefront- where crowds were watching TVs through the large windows- stopped Nutty, catching his attention. There was a glass door centered between two sides, each giving view to separate human telecasts.

To the left, orcs were laughing hysterically at human slapstick. Men getting stuck on fences while diving into swimming pools, and others ramming into walls while skating, kept them in stitches.

Nutty worried how the seemingly idiotic humans might adversely affect orcs by lulling them into a sense of security; if they didn't fear humans, they probably wouldn't seriously consider them a threat.

Orcs on the right were growling, some with the hair on the back of their necks at attention. Others mumbled obscenities under their breaths. They were watching newscasts that showed orc torture being reported by humans.

Perhaps humans were a perfect mixture, complex, and to varying degrees. Still, Nutty worried. His concerns over broadcasts some light years away, which meant watching events from the recent past, were miniscule compared to his current fears.

Fears, he thought, rubbing his chin. Orcs weren't supposed to fear anything, but fear they did. It was obvious they had fight or flight reactions. That must have been fear in its most primitive form. And the very thought of creeps gave a feeling of needing to think about something else. Was that fear?

Nutty had felt his heart beat fast and his legs quiver under extreme circumstances unrelated to his health. He certainly felt fear at times. *Damn orcs*, he thought, not understanding the species' need to hide such a thing.

A nod to some bystanders, and he was off again.

He came to a familiar place and stopped outside, pondering whether to go in. The guards stepped aside, allowing him entrance, regardless of his living there anymore or not. All he could think about was Uhra. Would his very presence upset her? His kids were still here; he was their father, after all, and had the right to see them.

He opened the door and entered his old home. It was well-lit, but the opulence struck him as cold and clinical, something he accepted in the past. Now, he scoffed at the luxurious décor.

A nanny, now aware of his presence, welcomed, "Wargod Nuttybomb. Goods a see you."

He stared at her. "Where Uhra?"

"She out, but da kids be here." She pointed to the kid's bedroom and stepped aside, granting passage that he already possessed.

"You know when she be back?" he asked, hoping to see her before he left for months.

"No. Couple hours she said."

Nutty offered, "Tanks," with a grin and walked passed her.

"Daddy," the kids hollered. They grabbed his legs in exuberance.

Nutty said, "Hey, guys. Wow, you gettin' so big."

Crazybomb yelled, "I can 'each food in da closet now."

"Ya," Nutty exclaimed excitedly. "You *are* getting big."

Both youngsters giggled.

Nuttybomb hugged his children one last time and explained, "Daddy gotta go a work. I miss you."

Regrettably, he carried on with his work to save his family, his planet, his armies, and all orcs everywhere; except for the enemy, unless they asked for acceptance or they surrendered. Out the door he went, without seeing Uhra one last time, clumsily banging his shoulder against the door frame.

Short, careful steps brought him closer to his next destination, and final one on Hotta. For it was this place that he would potentially see his homeworld for the last time, casting off into space for a showdown with his arch enemy.

How he wished he saw Uhra before he left. Perhaps it was best; her wishes to avoid him were evident. Maybe he didn't try hard enough to reach out and make amends as well. Either way, he walked passed guards, and up the steps that brought him to the vehicle that would cast him off into nothingness.

He turned the last steps of the climb and met his newest guard at the launchpad. "Gobbygoo," he greeted.

Gobbygoo nodded and said, "Wargod."

Nutty patted Gobbygoo on the back and proceeded to enter the small craft that was to shuttle the orcs to Nuttybomb's newest flagship, *Da Grim*. He was vaguely aware of the nonstop traffic of vessels coming and going, transporting troops and ship crew back and forth from above the atmosphere.

Gobbygoo sat next to his superior and reported, "Our ship be ready, and actuator is workin' good."

"Great," Nutty exclaimed, wiping some sweat from his brow with the material on his forearm. He asked, "What is happenin' on Marshil?"

"Dunno."

Nuttybomb hushed his not too gabby guard with a wave of his hand, and said "Never mind." He buckled his safety harness and sat back, settling in for a rough lift off, which was common in ships breaking free of gravity.

He thought about Uhra and the nurses. He attempted to contact Uhra with his mind, but was unable. The same was true with the nurses. Reality of his physical condition bothered him, for how could he defeat Darkster with such hindrances? He had three days to become the wargod he promised to his people.

***

"Dems know where we are," Gunza stated, punching the arm of his chair.

The enemy scout from Kingskull's fleet disappeared from observable sight to report findings to his leader. Having located Gunza's capital ships, it was just a matter of time before more scouts confirmed, and similarly, reported the ships' movements. And soon after, the foreign enemy fleet would engage Gunza's weaker forces.

Gunza ordered, "Get us to the far side of da actuator."

Moonoak quietly questioned his leader in interim, "But Nutty not der yet. We will be destroyed."

Gunza questioned his perceptive shaman, "You evva work an actuator?"

"No."

"You tink you can get yer mind to talk to it and get us to Hotta?"

Moonoak replied, "I can try."

Gunza snapped, "Tryin' not good 'nuff. Gotta jump us to Hotta." He stood up, his eyes fiery, but also desperate.

A breathy, "Dat not wut I do," came from Moonoak, followed by, "but somehow I will." He scratched the top of his head, beneath his hood.

Another scout came into view and hung around the edges of Gunza's capital ships at a safe distance. It gathered information, and like the first scout, left to inform its findings to Kingskull.

"Ya, dems definitely on to us," Moonoak reluctantly admitted.

Gunza whispered, "Dis not good."

Moonoak quietly excused himself. "I gots to meditate."

"Meditate fo' both a us. I needs some a yer magic stuff, too."

"I meditate fo' all a us," Moonoak obliged. He leaned into Gunza, so as not to be heard by others on the bridge. He said, "I gonna try to make contact wit' da actuator. But you gots to get da numbas so we can jump too. If either of us fail, we dead."

Gunza stared at the shaman. "I fogots about needin' numbas." He rubbed above his brow with his palm and admitted, "Dunno how to get da numbas."

Moonoak pointed to the large viewscreen that wrapped around the front half of the bridge. He said, "You betta figure out da numbas fast."

Coming into view, was a massive fleet. Gunza's eyes widened and leaned forward to take in what he was seeing. He ordered, "Take us starboard. Make all ships do da same."

Moonoak nervously said, "Good luck,' and he left.

"Ucktock, how many mines we gots left?"

Ucktock approached from the rear of the bridge. He lumbered over to a console, pushed some buttons and replied, "Free."

Gunza snapped, "No, not just us. How many our whole fleet gots?"

"Umm," began Ucktock as he tallied the numbers in his head. His face contorted, working to keep up with the calculations his orc brain struggled with. He continued, "Looka like maybe forty. I tink. Or maybe two hundred. No...forty. Ya, forty."

Gunza asked, "You sure? Forty lot different dan two hundred."

"Ya, I sure. Math a lil hard fo' me." He turned to Gunza and shrugged.

Gunza paced and ran his open hand from his forehead, over the back of his head, and down to his neck. "We in trouble. Dat not 'nuff mines."

Ucktock stated, "Dems ships fasta dan us, too."

"I know. And dems won't slow down fo' forty mines." Gunza looked around the bridge. Surely his eyes would find something to halt the enemy in its tracks, but what?

***

Quicklip grimaced. Pain shot into his shoulder each time he closed the metal fingers of his new arm. He fought a terrible headache as a result of the muscles in the shoulder and neck on the side of his prosthetic grabber being tensed.

"Now, twist at da elbow," the doc instructed.

"Sumptin' wrong," Quicklip said, his brow furrowed with pain and concern.

The doc spat, "It turn fine."

Quicklip, still spinning his forearm, argued, "But it backward."

"Backward?"

With his eyes fixated on his meta appendage, Quicklip stated, "Ya. I turn to da right, but it spinna left. I turn to da left, but it spinna right."

The doc corrected, "You mean rotate?"

Quicklip shot, "I gonna rotate dis up yer ass if you don't fix it." He extended it in the doc's direction. He went on with, "Den you will be ass backwards."

Guthrak chuckled. He asked the doc, "Really?"

"Sorry," the doc sighed. "I just gots da nerves connected opposite. I can fix."

Guthrak quizzed, "How long dat take?"

The doc looked at his watch and replied, "Few hours."

"Doc, get him fixed up."

"Yessir!" the doc answered. He hastily grabbed the tools of his trade and summoned a nurse to accompany him. He immediately went to work.

As he looked from the doc, to the surgery site and back, Guthrak instructed, "Tells me 'bout da comas."

"Der not much a tell," the doc explained.

Guthrak asked, "How many now?"

The doc paused with his hands and said, "Round twenty thousand. Der was eight thousand last night."

"Eight thousand? Anda nuttin' you can do?"

The doc went back to work after replying, "Nope."

Guthrak questioned, "Wut 'bout da shamans, or mages, or whatevva dems are?"

The doc sighed as he stopped cutting and reattaching nerves. "Chief, I needs to do dis work wit'out talkin's or I mess it up. Nobody can stops da comas or wakes da orcs so far. Please, lemme work."

Although Guthrak could have easily killed the doctor, he didn't. Regardless of how important twenty thousand troops were compared to Quicklip's single life, he understood nothing could be done to bring back those stricken by Darkster.

Guthrak turned on his heels and brushed past the attending nurse. He sought counsel from Arc. Maybe the young, arrogant orc had some insight into Darkster's abilities, or some way to help revive the orcs in comas.

With the sounds of explosions in the city above, and close combat at the entrances, Guthrak travelled from underground corridor to underground corridor. He gave orders at the entrances to bolster defenses, keeping the enemy at bay, and limiting casualties of his troops by bottlenecking those attacking from above.

But he couldn't find Arc. It was no easy task finding anyone in the dark catacombs that connected the world above to the rails that laid in ruins below. Still, the troublesome bastard had always turned up easier than the current search revealed.

Guthrak gave orders to spread the word; Arc was to report to him ASAP. He returned to his base of operations and ran into Nubbs.

Nubbs asked, "Still lookin' for Arc?"

"Ya," Guthrak replied irritably. "You seed him?"

"Not since last night." Nubbs took a sip of his flask.

Guthrak quizzed, "Any word on Gunza?"

"Nope."

"How 'bout Nuttybomb?"

Nubbs sheltered the flask within his coat. "Nope."

Guthrak shouted, "Dammit! You know anyting?"

Standing in a rather peculiar pose, a lax Nubbs commented, "Chief, der no way to get word in or out. We blocked fro' da surface."

"We can't get Runnas through?"

Nubbs explained, "Not alive. Darkster got evvy entrance cut off."

Guthrak was a warrior by nature. He loathed being stuck in the dark confines of the tunnels, his soldiers being picked off by the thousands, cast into comas while they slept.

As if to add insult to injury, the lights flickered in concert with an explosion from above. Small rocks fell and concrete, now in the form of dust, made its way into eyes, ears, and mouths.

The doctor working on Quicklip was heard yelling, "I can't work in da dark. Anda cover his shoulder. Der stuff fallin' in it."

Nubbs saw distress in Guthrak's eyes. He saw a caged carnidawg, forced to hide in a corner with its tail tucked between its legs, while helplessly waiting for eventual death. He knew the leader wasn't a strong tactician, at least not by choice. Getting passed the enemy and getting to the underground was damn heroic, if not tactically brilliant. But what good was it, if all the Hotta orcs would meet their end while waiting for an opportunity that would never arise? Upon his leader sitting, Nubbs suggested, "Maybe we fight our way out one entrance anda try to get word to Gunza or Nuttybomb."

Guthrak looked up, disgust riddling his face. "Dat why I looka for Arc. He can roast da bastids to clear a big 'nuff path fo' us to get out."

Guthrak and Nubbs turned their heads to face an orc who presented himself. "Sorry, Chief. I just hear dat Arc left last night."

Guthrak sprang to his feet. "Left?"

"Yessir. Hims left da entrance passed da collapsed tunnel in da west." The orc stayed in a submissively, bowed posture. He kept his eyes focused on the floor.

"You know where he went?"

The orc relied wearily, "Not really."

Guthrak asked, "Not really?"

"Nope."

"Dammit, orc! Where is he?" Guthrak was done waiting for the stupid orc to seek the right words in order to thwart his own death. He was just the messenger, but a target for the leader's outburst, if necessary.

"Dunno," sputtered from the orc's mouth. "Hims said sumptin' 'bout Darkster."

***

Nuttybomb said nothing, outwardly, anyway. But his mind was working hard to engage Gobbygoo in telepathic conversation. He had seven minutes to get his crippled brain to work the way it used to; that's how long until he reached *Da Grim*. He put his tongue between the teeth in the side of his mouth and tried again after one failed attempt.

He was about to quit asking Gobbygoo about the orc's parents, when a vocal response of, "Dunno," came from the lips of the unaware orc. Nutty had made contact! He questioned if he succeeded because the two sat next to each other. Perhaps distance kept him from speaking with Uhra and the close proximity to Gobbygoo made contact possible. Maybe Gobbygoo's brain was simple enough to be pried open in Nuttybomb's weakened state. Regardless, contact had been made, so he continued.

Gobbygoo answered, "Dunno. Parents died wen I lil."

Two other orcs on the transport looked over in confusion. They looked at each other, unable to understand who Gobbygoo was responding to. They assumed Gobbygoo had a mental issue, and talking to himself was a result; this wasn't uncommon in orcdom; in fact, rumors told of whole communities speaking to themselves. They shrugged their shoulders and went back to their simple thoughts.

Nuttybomb wondered if it was a problem with Gobbygoo being unable to answer in silence, or if it was himself still broken that caused a verbal response from the quizzed orc. Apparently, Gobbygoo didn't realize he was being talked to through his mind. He kept his eyes closed and answered his usual, "Dunno," a dozen more times before *Da Grim* came into view.

The other orcs glanced over each time Gobbygoo blurted out answers, a habit they found hard to break, irrespective of the repeated chattering.

Da Grim opened her landing bay on the port side, the enormous doors separated at the center, and slid behind the ship's hull. The hangar welcomed the shuttle, landing lights blinking in a pattern that instructed the craft to follow a certain path.

The tiny craft was swallowed by *Da Grim's* monstrous innards. It settled deep within, the landing bay's doors closing upon it's passing from space to the artificial environment inside.

Nuttybomb appeared in the doorway of the shuttlecraft to a heroes' welcome. He quickly waved and walked through the lines of friendly troops. With a fist in the air, he yelled, "Fo' Hotta!"

The troops repeated what he said in deep, male voices in cadence, "Fo' Hotta."

A sergeant took it upon himself to further rally the troops with, "Fo' Wargod Nuttybomb!"

The troops trumpeted in unison, "Fo' Wargod Nuttybomb!" They clapped and cheered.

The unwargod waved in gratitude, briefly closing his eyes in revulsion at his inability to use the powers he needed to even compete with Darkster. At least, he hid his pain well for the sake of all, even on his long path to the bridge.

His troubled mind absorbed as much information as could be held, a saturated sponge, soft and torn. It did tell his feet to spread like a drunk, keeping him from banging into the corridor walls. He was able to traverse the long distance to his throne without noticeable incident.

The surroundings were found to be vaguely familiar. Being the sister ship of *Da Rampage*, Nuttybomb's newest ship was quite similar to his old flagship. Newly commissioned, *Da Grim* had upgraded weapons systems, scanners, and other vital systems, making her superior in many ways to her three-year old counterpart.

Nutty entered the bridge and exhaled a deep, satisfying breath. His crew jumped at attention, awaiting orders. He simply instructed, "Carry on," allowing the orcs to ready for departure.

After receiving disconcerting reports about Guthrak's lack of communication, as well as Gunza's being pursued, Nutty allowed his body to conform to the structure of his chair; slowly easing his bulky frame onto the seat without showing any signs of pain, or concern over the troubled reports he just read.

He recognized the lack of paint and carpeting which would have added thousands of tons to the overall weight of the ship. Lessons learned against fighting humans taught him to strip all unnecessary mass to allow better speed and maneuverability. So, even with added weight in upgrades, his newest ride was faster and more manageable while turning than the other ship in her class.

The few minutes of observation were over. The navigation officer stated, "Ready a gets undaway, Sir."

"Very good," Nutty said, pumping out his chest. "Head fo' da actuator."

"Yessir!" was followed by a deep rumbling sound, along with a slight shaking of the massive battleship. The bright blue wash of the engines lit the space behind them, thrusting *Da Grim* forward.

"Show aft," Nutty ordered.

The view screen depicted Hotta, their homeworld gradually shrinking in size, an optical illusion that told the orcs they were leaving. "Showin' aft," was said by the operations officer.

Nutty asked, "How long to actuator?"

"Forty hours."

"All udder ships undaway?" Nutty asked.

The orc cautiously said, "No. Two ships not ready."

"Hmm," Nutty moaned to himself. He questioned, "Wut 'bout ships fro' Cypra?"

"Booma gots some comin' to meet us at da Marshil actuator."

Nutty smiled. Maybe the battle wouldn't be so lopsided once his mustered fleet came together. He said in a rewarding tone, "Very good," and left for his quarters.

His quarters were simple; bed, locker, and chair were separated by curtains from a desk with a computer. A connected bathroom was something of a luxury, and one he welcomed.

He laid on his bed, rubbing his forehead, and taking slow, deep breaths. He cleared his mind and meditated. But meditation wasn't found; slumber was.

He awoke in a panic, finding himself chanting, "Darkster, Darkster." He sat up, trying to remember the nightmare that found him. Darkster had entered his dreams! But how? It was known that the evil orc was on Marshil, sixty million miles away. So, how was he able to make contact at such a great distance?

Nuttybomb was sitting, rubbing his tired eyes. His body still needed sleep to heal itself from the trauma it had been through, but there was no way it would be allowed to doze; not while the maniacal predator haunted it.

He decided to take time to attempt connection with others he knew. It was clear that he needed to steer clear of Darkster, so he carefully sought out the closest orcs to him. With Gobbygoo aboard, and easily subjectable to mind control, he was the perfect test subject.

Nutty closed his eyes and cleared his mind. He began reaching out with invisible tendrils, seeking a host to manipulate. Gobbygoo wasn't found effortlessly, but another was; an engine room maintenance worker. Nutty greeted the confused orc. "Hello," he said, innocuously.

The orc replied through telepathy, "Hello, Wargod Nuttybomb."

Nutty sighed with relief; a connection; perhaps not the one he wanted, but one, nonetheless. He continued, "You be a great warrior. Tanks fo' yer service."

The orc happily responded, "Tank you!"

Nutty read his thoughts, something that used to happen without much effort. He struggled a bit to make sense of the orc's thoughts, but finally, put it all together.

His mind continued to search, and settled upon a nurse, four decks below. He greeted, "Hello, Nurse Puttak."

She eagerly answered, "Wargod Nuttybomb, hi."

Nutty could feel her joy, as if she had personal contact with one of her gods; never a possibility until now. He congratulated her on work well done and moved on to his next subject.

There were twenty-two connections over the next hour. Gobbygoo was one of his subjects, although it was determined that he didn't need to be a primary target. Nuttybomb's mind had little trouble speaking with any of the crew members.

He took a break to use the bathroom, not only to relieve himself of unwanted fluid, but to rid his mind of unnecessary clutter. While there, he inspected his appearance in the full-length mirror, turning from side to side, lifting each arm and his chin, to get a good look at all his visible issues. He found his body to be scarred, but not as pale as it was days before. His vision was clear, allowing him sight of some added muscle and fat as well. He didn't look like the brute he was a couple years before, but he looked healthier. He was pleased.

Telepathy commenced, now reaching multiple minds simultaneously. Connection was made, but information was randomly exchanged between parties, causing confusion between subjects.

Nuttybomb focused harder, yet somehow allowed tranquility of mind to balance the transfer of information. He and six subjects conversed. They were elated to speak with their wargod.

Each subject's link was severed, and new ones added, allowing multiple lines of communication to enter and leave without incident. And although easier to control, Nuttybomb was becoming exhausted. Due to his brain still being swollen or his overall deteriorated health, he decided to rest, never fully sleeping, but giving himself time to recuperate.

Additionally, after a couple hours of rest, Nuttybomb physically worked in the hangar bays and engine rooms to regain some strength and agility. His crew was happy with his involvement, especially since his size gave added power lifting capabilities, eliminating the use of bulky hydraulic lifts that were tight fits in close quarters.

Unaware how he knew this would rejuvenate him, but certain in its positive effects, he adhered to a rigorous schedule, alternating work, rest, and telepathy, allowing each to best heal him. His memory had been lacking, prohibiting some recent conversations with nurses and doctors to come to light. He wondered if he had been given tools to fix himself while he was ill. Perhaps it was the collective mind, somewhere beyond, that told him through meditation that his efforts would be rewarded. Regardless, he was diligent in his labors; determination leading to accomplishments.

At the end of the day, he was fatigued and a bit sore, but he felt clearer than he had been in months. This further spurred him on to work hard.

Fourteen
The Next Coming!

Gunza ordered, "Swing 'round to port side." He held on to the arm of his chair as the ship banked left, pushing the crew off balance.

Kingskull's fleet fired its guns at long range, hoping to score early hits on Gunza's capital ships. Very few found their targets, but those that did, caused varying degrees of damage.

"Sir," one of Gunza's officers addressed. "Da cruiser, *Gut Jab*, losed her engines."

Gunza watched a hail of energy packed projectiles fly passed his view screen from left to right. Even with the great distances in space granting him little chance of being hit from an individual shot, the collective multitude of gunfire increased the odds by a thousand. He lurched forward as his battleship received two hits. "Keep us movin's along da back row of our a ships."

Navigation complied, "Yessir."

Da Rampage was hit several more times, partially drawing attention away from the rest of the fleet. While she couldn't divert all guns to turn on her, anything she withstood, was less that others had to endure.

Gunza ordered, "Ok, turn starboard. Keep up wit' our udder ships, but stay to der left and behind.

"Yessir," was replied.

"How many ships follow us?" Gunza questioned as he squinted.

A bridge officer, after being delayed while counting, said, "Sixteen."

Gunza asked sharply, "Dat's it?"

"Yessir."

"How bad is *Gut Jab*?"

The officer replied, "She not movin'. Gots fires."

Gunza ordered, "Have all ships drop all der mines and open link wit' *Gut Jab*."

"*Gut Jab* on now."

"Dis Warchief Gunza. Who dis?"

A loud voice was heard over screams and crashing noises from the cruiser. "Dis be Stompa. Captain be dead."

"You da next in line, Officer?" Gunza asked, concern in his voice.

"Yessir."

Gunza asked, "Do you gots any mines left?"

Stompa solemnly replied, "Only two."

"Ok. Try to send dems as close as you can to two different ships. Den shoots da mines to explodes dem near dems ships. Got it?"

"Got it," the dejected, yet determined voice answered.

Gunza said, "We comin' to you. Get ready to evacuate all crew. Send lifeboats in direction a da actuator." He strode down from his chair, toward the front of the bridge. He said, "Come up along *Gut Jab*, but keeps goin'."

The helmsman replied, "Yessir."

Gunza watched his computer monitor as the battleship, *Undatakor*, blew up. "Dammit!" he yelled.

Undatakor was next to launch lifeboats and escape pods. Gunza couldn't save them all, but he would try to rescue as many as he could before his own ship would be destroyed.

Two more ships in the fleet appeared to slow, both cruisers; signs of being crippled. They, too, were ordered to evacuate their disabled hulks.

Friendly mines began tearing into Kingskull's ships, but there were so few that, results hardly changed the high-speed pursuit.

Kingskull's voice was heard throughout every ship that could receive his bandwidth. He said, "Nuttybomb, it time fo' you to accept defeat. Surrendas or all yer orcs will die."

After a pause of thirty seconds, the message was repeated, this time adding, "Wut kinda wargod would lose his whole fleet and kill his peoples?"

Surprising to Gunza, Booma's voice interrupted, "Kingskull, dis be Booma, Wargod Nuttybomb's brudder. You came longa way to die out in space."

Kingskull laughed hardily. He said, "No, it be you who die. Wer be yer brudder, the scaredy wargod?"

Booma jabbed, "Sorry, but it will be you who dies."

"I don't tink so, Brudder of da Warchicklen." Kingskull bellowed a deep annoying laugh that rang out throughout every ships' intercom.

"I undastand you too fraid to fight Nuttybomb face to face. Him nevva losed to anyone," Booma taunted.

Kingskull spat, "I not 'fraid a no one."

"Den stop firin's and meet us on da planet."

"I no fall fo' tricks. You gots sumptin' waitin' down der? I can kills you all now," the pompous Kingskull stated confidently.

Booma said, "I gots ships getting close. You can win, yes, but I will kill mosta yer fleet, anda maybe you too."

Kingskull asked sarcastically, "While da warchicklen hides?"

"No. Him's comin' to kill you anda anyone else who attacks. You can die in space or see him face a face. Your call."

After a short time, Kingskull's fleet stopped firing. He instructed, "Stop runnin' fro' me or I keep shooting."

Booma asked for confirmation, "So, you wait fo' Nuttybomb?"

"Only if he no fire on us, too. Den, we can meet on Marshil anda I kills him der."

"Kingskull, you an orc a honor," Booma stated firmly.

"I outnumba you three-to-one. Any tricks and I destroy you all. You betta have honor, too."

Booma assured Kingskull with, "You gots my word, anda word a Wargod Nuttybomb.

Gunza's fleet stopped and met up with Booma's. The four hundred plus ships stopped short of Kingskull's huge fleet.

Booma asked, "Kingskull, you want I should meet you to talk on yer ship?"

A snarl was returned. "You no tink I kill you?"

"I not a wargod. I just a warrior. I fight good, but I come alone. You wanna kill me? Dat up to you, too."

Kingskull thought about the possibility of killing Nuttybomb's own brother. That would surely bring the so-called wargod right to his door. He was reluctant to eliminate the Hotta combined fleet, for reasons he couldn't quite understand though. He had the sheer numbers; he could destroy the enemy easily. But the lure of facing Nuttybomb was enough to test his pride and a sure victory. Now, he debated whether he should allow Booma aboard his ship or not. He finally decided it best to have Booma close to him, in case the wargod's brother needed to die.

Booma asked, "Want me to come or no?"

"Yes, just you, alone."

Booma left the comfort of his bridge and boarded a shuttle craft. He received instructions, guiding him to Kingskull's battleship, in so doing, revealing Kingskull's location amidst the slew of ships he hid amongst.

Gunza took note of this and relayed it through coded message to the rest of the Hotta combined fleet. He awaited Nuttybomb's presence to give this most important information to.

Booma docked, and when entering Kingskull's ship was thoroughly frisked. His sidearm was confiscated, as was his blade. He was escorted to Kingskull's bridge.

Kingskull met him with, "You either brave or stupid, Booma."

Booma chuckled, "Prolly both."

Kingskull smiled. He studied Booma, his uniform, and his mannerisms. He said, "You pretty big, too."

"Not big as you, but ya. I tink we comes fro' da same planet longa time ago."

Kingskull said defiantly, "You nevva been fro' my planet."

"No," Booma said, and continued explaining, "but Da Rampage did lika thousand years ago. Udder orcs

240

'round here be smaller, but you anda me da same kinda orcs, I tink."

"I heard a dis, Da Rampage. He chased away fro' my world." Kingskull was amused by the possible connection with orcs so far away from his own homeworld. He jabbed, "So you be descendants of da chicklenshit who runned away a thousand years ago?" He honked a big, loud laugh.

Booma said slyly, "Sound funny wen you say it dat way."

"How else you say it?" Kingskull teased.

"Dunno why he came here. Don't matter. Wargod Nuttybomb say we come fro' him, anda part Grim. We gots smart orcs, too, acause a dat."

"Smart, huh? Dat why you standin' alone on my ship?"

"Dat why," Booma said with a devilish smile.

"Lord, Kingskull?" an officer on the bridge addressed.

Kingskull spat, "I busy, wut is it?"

"Mo' ships appearin's outta nowhere."

Booma cut in with, "Dat be Wargod Nuttybomb." He smirked, rolling his tongue in his mouth like a cat that swallowed a canary.

Kingskull raised an eyebrow. He turned to Booma and complimented, "Very good. I get it now. You here to try a kills me if I fire on yer fleet. Dat pretty smart. But not too smart wen you gots no weapons." He moaned a small chuckle in his throat.

"Da ting is, I comes to kill you if I can, only if you fire on my fleet. But also, now all my ships know wer you are. You be da only target." Booma laughed hardily now.

241

Kingskull looked to the floor, his brain working overtime. He looked up and found himself reluctantly admitting, "I give ya dat one. Pretty smart, Booma."

Booma said, "Tanks, Lord Kingskull. I da dumb one in da family. Wait till you meet my brudder."

"I can't wait."

*****

Nuttybomb and his ships jumped through the portal that was opened from the actuator near Hotta, to the one that sat a day or two from Marshil.

Immediately, his head was filled with updates from Gunza, sent via the same coded messages delivered previously. He ordered his fleet to head toward the fleets amassed some fifteen minutes away, and gave control of all ships to Gunza.

His opened mind began probing for Kingskull. He homed in on the enemy's ship, the tentacles of his mind reaching from host to host. At first, he struggled to make any connections at all. But after ten minutes, he linked with someone. It was a simple soldier, no brighter than the toilet in Nuttybomb's bathroom. The conversation was similar to that with Gobbygoo, nondistinct without any real information being exchanged, and frustrating.

Five more minutes brought some loose connections, the links basically failing. Nuttybomb was struggling; the wargod was anything but.

After twenty errant connections, he spoke to the adversary he wanted. Relief washed over him like a cool, moderate rain in the heat of the desert. He sat back and relaxed. He began, "Lord, Kingskull, dis be Wargod Nuttybomb."

Kingskull began responding aloud, confusing some of the orcs around him. He looked around for the voice that beckoned him. Around his chair, he walked; his eyes darted about like a crazed animal.

Booma snickered. He asked, "Sumptin' wrong?"

"I talk wit' you through our a minds," Nuttybomb said.

Kingskull asked Booma, "Wut kinda trick is dis?" He shoved a thick finger into Booma's chest.

"No trick," Booma answered, slowly moving the enemy's hand from his space.

Nutty replied, "No trick," as well.

Kingskull dropped back in his chair. He fought to communicate telepathically, and not expose himself as a blubbering idiot in front of his crew. "How you do dis?" He asked silently, in disbelief.

"I have found a way to learn a path to da gods."

"I don't undastand. Dis some kinda trick," Kingskull scoffed.

"It no trick. Afta last war, I come into space to protect all orcs. I protect yer orcs, too."

Kingskull screamed in defiance, "Da hell wit' you! I protect my orcs." He looked around, panic in his eyes, his brow heavy over his eyes with deep lines cutting into his forehead.

Most of the bridge crew stared at Kingskull, questioning whether he had gone mad.

"It ok. Him trying to talk to my mind," was all the confused leader could say to explain his strange behavior. Then, it occurred to him that he might be explaining something to his crew that he didn't even believe yet- telepathy.

The helmsman looked down, avoiding eye contact. Two other officers stared at each other, wondering what to make of the current situation.

Nuttybomb, feeling Kingskull's uneasiness, and feeling he was now in control, offered, "Letta us meet on Marshil. I show you tings you maybe nevva seen. You decide den."

Kingskull talked from his perception of power. He sat back down and stated, "I can kill yer whole fleet. You will die, too. Why should I goes to Marshil?"

"Because all a my four-hundred eighty-two ships be aimin's only at you right now," Nuttybomb explained.

"Dens Booma, yer brudder will die," Kingskull said, trying to control the conversation.

Nuttybomb stated calmly, "Kingskull, we all will die. You will be dead befo' any a yer fleet can respond to yer orders. I might die in dis battle, too. Or...we meet, just you, me, anda our officers."

Kingskull sat in silence. He gazed around the room, sensing his officers waiting for their next orders. His face was hot, his heart was pounding. He didn't understand what was happening. How was Nuttybomb able to communicate with his mind? Why couldn't he do that? Why weren't any orcs he ever knew able to? He finally demanded some terms. "I land wit' my army. If you brave 'nuff, you come wit' yer officers. I keep Booma as prisoner till den."

"Dat fine. Just land far fro' Darkster till we sort dis out."

He looked at Booma with a frown pasted from ear to ear. He said, "I agree wit' him. But know dat you die

244

as soon as he use a trick. Anda if hims enters my mind again, I fire on all a you."

Booma laughed. He said, "You tell him."

***

They went on to engage in conversations- war, magic, science, and whatever else would be thrown at them- on the cold world.

Nuttybomb was pleased with his progress, but still worrisome over how hard it was to do things since his surgeries. He still hid a limp and pain associated with many of his wounds, and subsequent repairs. At times, he realized the involuntary need to breathe heavily after exerting a fair amount of energy, too. But mostly, his mind struggled to efficiently reach hosts.

So far, he was able to fend off Darkster's prodding. But for how long? Would it be more difficult, the closer he got to the planet and the evil orc? Perhaps it was an impossibility to stave off telepathic meddling. Hell, his mind was all over the place; certainly not the piece of steel it had been in the past.

He wasn't going to sleep; that was for sure! He decided instead to reach out to Uhra if possible. He laid back under dimmed lights and cleared his mind. A calm wrapped him, worries diminished. Soon, complete separation from his body, and distant travel began.

"Uhra," he said, lovingly.

Distressed from a lack of response, he took some deep breaths and tried again. "Uhra."

He began to understand the added difficulty he was having each time he attempted contact with his estranged wife; just thinking of her brought pain and cluttering thoughts to his brain. He lacked the

245

necessary serenity to reach her, having to calm himself with each new attempt.

An exhaustive hour left him depleted in spirit. Seeking counsel any way he good, he devoted his time to reading. It had been ages since he immersed himself in the writings of Grim, the author who spoke of life and death, and everything in between.

Nutty hobbled to a locker, sitting at the foot of his bed. He opened it and captured the first leather bound, written craft that reached to his hand.

The book was old and worn, ancient in fact. Nutty carefully thumbed through the pages until something caught his eye; something relative to his current situation and encounter with Kingskull.

He sat back down, somewhat reclined, and began reading.

***

From a binary star system beyond this one, he came, bringing his kind in a thousand ships. Da Rampage left the beleaguered world of Da Green Planet, to start anew; to spread his knowledge and propel his followers into an enlightened era, and obtain a toehold for civilization to thrive.

Hunted by a billion orcs from dozens of other star systems, he gathered his people, and set out.

Across the vastness of space, a travel that lasted an eventual thirty years, he and his followers suffered every kind of hardship. No amount of intelligence he possessed could save them all, for they fell victim to da feva, which spread like wildfire throughout half the vessels' close quarters. Quarantine left them isolated, and cursed them with certain death. As necessary as confinement was, many orcs resented the leader for sentencing them to death.

Furthermore, spoiled foods were jettisoned, leaving rationed amounts, terribly lacking. Moreover, most food stored aboard ships under quarantine were lost. Starvation for many was common. Resentment was turning to hatred.

Fuel, the final straw, much like food stores, was compromised for the same reasons. The very unlucky were left to die slowly, prisoners in their ships, to the cold, darkness that space provided. Hatred turned to action.

Surely, somebody was responsible for the band's losses. Shared thoughts about the gods' unhappiness traveled as gossip. But as it took hold, the gossip became more of a conspiracy theory. Perhaps the great leader was evil and enacted deception to drag the people from their world. Maybe he was a tool, used by divinity to punish orcs from fleeing, instead of fighting.

Orcs, regardless of the level of intelligence between subspecies, were still orcs. Their inherent need for combat, the want to cause physical harm, the inevitable violence they displayed when faced with survival, was at a moment's turn. And orcs being orcs, emotion tended to outweigh rational thought. The fuse was lit.

While thousands of orcs turned back, and were brutally murdered by the billion that pursued them, many more came together to hunt Da Rampage themselves. They tracked him to the worlds of Tempest, Da White Rock, Orcra, Marshil, and Hotta.

Each new world had challenges, but became homes to most of Da Rampage's followers. Even many hunters settled throughout the system, just happy to have their feet on solid ground again.

Da Rampage had victories against his opposition on Marshil and Hotta. The small bands that remained of his disgruntled hunters were far and few between.

Within a year, the billion who came to conquer everything before them, had dwindled to several million, with most returning to their home worlds, or suffering the same disease and shortages that ravaged their prey.

They would be forced to settle throughout the star system too, based on food and fuel rations; the outer planets were chosen out of necessity because of shortages, the inner planets for those without immediate troubles.

Those settled on Hotta would eventually kill Da Rampage, but not before his people found enough places to secure their future. What's more, the guerilla tactics he engaged in before his death, ended the annihilation of his people by constantly bringing the enemy's numbers lower.

Over time, orcs originating from dozens of worlds, crossbred in the star system. An estimated fifteen subspecies mixed, ensuring the hardiness of the species would continue.

However, certain traits became more prevalent in the new worlds, too. In many cases, descendants of Da Rampage, as well as orcs from his world, became highly intelligent and dominated their areas. This seems to be the truest on Hotta, where more blueblood Da Rampage orcs settled.

Orcs on other worlds, mostly Da Rampage's hunters, remained brutal. They continued being what they had been for hundreds of thousands of years – brutish orcs.

After Da Rampage's death, a dark time fell upon his people. Without him or other stable leadership, disorder ensued, most notably leading to technology lost over time. Additionally, many potential scientists, doctors, and leaders had died. A distinct bottlenecking of science resulted.

Before coming to the star system, it had taken orcs hundreds of thousands of years to advance to space travel and move between the stars. Much of that technology was *lost or was severely stagnated. As a result, travel between the planets stopped for hundreds of years.*

This led to social differences, directly coinciding with the great distances between worlds that caused local variances.

Without fully realizing his accomplishments, Da Rampage succeeded in gaining the toehold he sought, thirty years before.

Fifth Book of Grim, Da Rampage Chronicles

***

Guthrak asked the doctor about Quicklip, "Him ok to fight?"

The doc responded, "Evvyting seem a work ok. Up to him if he can fight."

"Well?" Guthrak queried.

Quicklip moved his mechanical fingers before answering, "It hurt lika hell anda feels weird."

Guthrak clenched his right hand into a fist and threw it toward Quicklip's face, but was stopped by the mechanical claw that caught it above Quicklip's head. "Dat good 'nuff fo' me," the makeshift leader stated with a smile. He continued, "Seems lika you gots pretty good control a it."

A bit stunned, Quicklip said in a little disbelief, "Ya, I tink so. Good ting, too. I hate a pull dis big mechanical beast outta yer ass."

Guthrak cautioned, "Careful. Arc mo' dangerous dens you and I broked his head."

"Arc gots powers, but he no fight lika we do. Him's too slow to defend himself. By da way, you know I only kiddin', right?"

"A course," Guthrak snarled. "You be dead otherwise."

Quicklip asked, "Wer is Arc, anyway? He rolled his head, fighting the tension in his neck.

Guthrak snapped, "Him snuck out."

"To fight Darkster?"

"Or a join him," Guthrak whispered.

The lines in Quicklip's forehead grew. "No. You tink?"

Guthrak said, "Dunno, but it time we find out."

The two orcs made their way through the cramped rail line, barking orders at soldiers to prepare for battle. Furthermore, they sent runners to give word about which entrances to guard, and which ones to break through.

Two entrances to the far north erupted in explosions. Small rocks and dust dropped from newly formed cracks throughout the underground complex, littering the already dirty floors.

Guthrak climbed over dead bodies, casualties from the last couple days, and rushed into the enemy troops that blocked daylight with their cramped bodies. The battle was long and grueling, taking over an hour to get through the carnage that blocked the tall stairway. The smell of accumulated rot was staggering.

Quicklip and Nubbs fought their way to the top, finding the same problems that were inherent in fighting hand to hand in such confined spaces. But fight they did, managing to see daylight for the first time in several days.

The three orcs barely made it to the top when they finally received communication from the outside. Guthrak fell back, allowing his troops to take up the fight to the front. "Nuttybomb?" he asked in excitement.

***

Ships were moved away, leaving a clearing between them. Exposed, was a plateau, chosen for some reason, lost on all, but Darkster.

Great blocks were heaved into place, stacked next to and above the one before, building a wall that retained the rock and dirt that was the plateau. Thousands of workers toiled to construct the raised land. Dozens pushed and lifted each massive stone into place.

Darkster looked to the skies, gathering whatever pertinent information he needed to instruct his underlings in their newest endeavor. His eyes fluttered, rolling back, and exposing the whites. He mumbled a foreign language, not known to orcs.

The skies told him to construct a second layer, upon the first. Dimensions were critical. He conveyed them to his less-than-intelligent workers, killing several because they placed rocks in the wrong locations. Everything had to be precise!

Steps were erected, forced upward to a tall, pyramidic shaped pinnacle. The evil orc's throne would crown the apex.

Near the base of the stairs, the altar was nearly complete. It would soon be lined with precious stones, meant to help ordain what was beyond. Time was nearly at hand for the next coming!

Fifteen
Confrontations

How he travelled among Darkster's troops was amazing. Arc was able to make his way through a hundred thousand enemy troops, the first hundred by means of force, and all after that as a friend.

His movements were like Headhunta, Darkster's own deceased father. When not seen as friend or foe, the shadows concealed him, enhancing his chances of reaching his objective.

He came upon a raised clearing. There, he saw Darkster sitting on a grand throne, casting orders to those beneath him, both physically, and socially.

The plateau was around seven feet high, with a second elevated area, exalting the evil orc. On the first level's periphery were a dozen guards, placed to protect Darkster. Pots of fire lined the steps from there to the leader's chair.

Arc dashed to the wall of the platform and jumped high, his feet landing firmly between two guards, his eyes already changing from yellow to blue.

Lightning bolts shot from his hands, boiling the blood of five guards closest to him. He stood there totally exposed to Darkster, and the remaining guards.

The evil orc broke from his chair and made his way down the steps. He said, "You must be Arc."

Arc replied, "You must be dead."

Darkster cackled. "No, no, no." He gracefully traversed the climb down without worry. He closed his eyes and muttered something under his breath.

Seven guards fell to the ground, convulsing. Troops began encircling the area, a fact not lost on Arc, who was losing his chance to escape, if necessary.

Darkster said, "Dems didn't stop you fro' getting here. I don't need dems. I not sure how you gots all da way here, but dat pretty impressive."

Arc was surprised by the guards being eliminated by his enemy. But being young, and never facing Darkster until now, he was cocksure. He spat on the ground and commented, "Less fo' me to kill."

A high pitch whine settled into a confident cackle. From the lips of the evil orc came, "You be Nuttybomb's student. Dis be perfect. It be fun to kill you."

"I undastand Guthrak's troops broked out and are fightin' der way here. Nuttybomb be here soon, too. But nobody comes a save yer ass," Arc taunted.

Darkster growled, "I don't needs help, boy. I know wut you can do. You too weak."

"I not too weak a kill you." Arc's electricity erupted toward Darkster.

But Darkster's whip cracked and met the younger boy's attack with equal energy. The weapon crackled as it spun, flickering embers of red and yellow around the blue lightning.

Arc ceased his first attack as it had failed. He tried again, using more force. But it, too, was quashed by the evil orc's energy weapon. His assumed invincibility was like a river running dry.

"Wut da matter, boy?" Darkster asked. "Dat all you gots?"

With hands dropping to his sides, the young, inadequate orc replied, "You gonna kill me now?"

"Da thought has crossed my a mind." A smile crept across Darkster's leathery lips. He strode confidently down the steps, and upon his feet settling on the plateau, he gazed around.

Arc fired again. This time lightning danced passed Darkster, briefly confusing him. The metal fire pots that lined the stairs behind the evil orc became conduits, capturing energy and channeling it amongst them. The stairs, unable to absorb, nor channel the boy's energy, sent it back from the direction it came.

Darkster's whip came around involuntarily to protect him from the forward attack. But it failed to anticipate energy reverberating off the steps behind it.

"Guarrr," Darkster howled, as energy engulfed him. He fell to his knees.

The whip still gathered most of the energy from around him, partially shielding him from certain death. But pain still raced through him until he managed to swirl the whip around himself.

Darkster stood up, now enraged. He staggered, stepping toward his young enemy, gradually picking up the pace until he was within seven feet. He snapped the whip.

Arc screamed. The burns to his skin matched Darkster's, the pain he felt, equal. He was thrown to his back with his hands up, fighting to maintain the attack he had mounted. However, he was strictly defensive, writhing, but never quitting.

"Nice try, boy. Bouncing energy to get my ass was good, but you can't beat me. You just not stronga 'nuff." Darkster retracted his weapon, and with it, all energy output.

Arc, exhausted and wounded, finally gave up his attack, too. His body smoked, bloody blisters boiling on his skin. He smoked like a freshly cooked Swinestock.

Darkster's pain and near defeat left him vengeful. His urge to finish Arc was overwhelming. Yet, he fought it. Until recently, he wouldn't have thought twice about killing anyone who even looked at him sideways. But now, he paused, assessing the situation; trying to figure out the best way to use his enemy to his advantage.

Instead of killing Arc, he taunted, "Wut wus you sayin's 'bout Guthrak comin's, and Nuttybomb? Dems can't save you. Only you can save you."

Arc brought his hands behind himself and pushed up to a sitting position. He breathed heavily. He couldn't imagine how he could save himself now; he was totally spent. Then, it hit him.

Darkster ordered, "Join me or die."

Staggering to his feet, the crumpled Arc fought one last time. He couldn't muster enough energy to kill his enemy; no, he could barely stand up. He threw some bolts to Darkster's right, giving flight to several pots that lined the steps. As they rushed toward Darkster's head, the evil orc turned and unleashed his whip. He screamed in anger, knocking the projectiles away harmlessly. He turned to finish his talented, pesky enemy.

But Arc was gone! He disappeared into the onlookers, a small explosion used as a diversion to sneak through them. He was gone.

Darkster reached to the sky and screamed, "Damn you!"

255

The trip to Marshil over the next day gave Nuttybomb ample time to work on his telepathic abilities. First, he engaged crew members aboard his own ship. Then, as he was able to separate his contacts like drawers in a file cabinet, he began connecting to members throughout his fleet.

This was fine, as it sharpened his mind, but it was more difficult reaching the enemy. He still struggled to enter their thoughts consistently. Perhaps it was that they were wired differently. Or maybe, he had a harder time because he was still wounded, unable to fully control his past powers.

Regardless, he carried on with his experiments. His probes did reach dozens of Kingskull's troops throughout the next ten hours. He discovered their neural pathways to be slightly different than his own, giving credence to his earlier belief as to the reason his connections were blocked. However, once he established that difference, regular encounters happened with more regularity.

He found the enemy to be ruthless. Their thoughts were driven by their unadulterated need to inflict harm. Many had raped and killed innocents living in towns they had invaded. Moreover, it was common for them to lock whole populations inside buildings that were burned to the ground, killing those inside in the cruelest way possible.

What's more, some had done the unthinkable-cannibalism. And not just killing and eating, but killing while eating. Even for orcs, ingestion of the species was considered barbaric. Eating women and children alive were crimes against the gods. Nuttybomb was sickened. He would sentence them when he could, regardless of deals made with Kingskull or not.

Nuttybomb had entered Kingskull's mind earlier, but didn't sense the same animalistic urges that drove the leader's followers. Kingskull was brutal; sure, but he was more or less complicit in his troop's atrocities. He allowed their butchery as long as he didn't witness it first-hand. He reasoned that if he didn't see it, it didn't happen; not that he really cared. The populations he conquered were forced to fear him. He walked a fine line between knowing and caring.

Nuttybomb avoided telepathic contact with Kingskull. He wanted to better understand the leader's intentions, but wouldn't risk a battle before reaching Marshil. So, he did the next best thing; he probed Kingskull's officers; they weren't off limits as per the agreement struck between the leaders.

Limited information about the invading orcs' troop sizes and capabilities was obtained, although no concrete findings were obtained; each orc's mathematical abilities limited their capacity to fully understand the true numbers in play. As a result, totals varied. Furthermore, Nuttybomb, in masking his deception, confused their simple minds; they weren't aware they were even contacted, but this restricted his access to all they knew.

Nuttybomb was tired; maybe more so than he could remember ever being, a fact clouded by his spotty memory. He still dared not sleep under the watchful eye of Darkster. He felt the evil orc's presence, and recent attempts to invade his thoughts. No, sleep would wait until the bastard was eliminated!

It was still a mystery why connections with some orcs were made more easily. He was pretty sure there were several factors. Distance was one. How the host's brain was wired was another. He also found that it helped him to make successful contacts with those he already knew or had made connections with before. But sometimes, he just couldn't make a link. He hoped to overcome that obstacle as soon as possible.

He wiped his eyes with his big hands, digging some crust from the inside corners and wiping them on his shirt. He brewed some java, sat, and began probing far beyond, attempting to make the unlikeliest of links.

It was so far away! An hour of forcing his overworked mind found him wearier than when he started his plight. But he trudged on, swiping his brain clean and his emotions too from any unwanted clutter. And then...

"Wargod Nuttybomb?" the silent voice greeted, somewhat surprised.

"Yes," he said. "I far away, but I needs a talk wit' you."

"Oh, boy," she exclaimed nervously.

Nuttybomb asked after a deep breath, "Sweetie, wut happened between us wen I wus in da medical buildin'?"

Her tension was felt as she physically cleared her throat, even though she responded without the use of her voice. She said, "You wer der. You know wut we did."

He gritted his teeth. "No, I don't. I wus very sick."

Sweetie sighed, "Oh, boy," again. She thought at the time he may not have known what was happening. Now, he seemed to confirm her worst fears.

He pressed, "Wut happened?"

With her mind in overdrive, she subconsciously blurted out, "We wus washin' you. We did a good job, cleaned evvyting, ya know? And you gots excited."

"I gots excited?"

She explained, "Well, *it* gots excited. You know, *its*."

Nuttybomb asked further for clarification, "Wus I awake?"

"Umm, yes, no. Well, at first, no. But you wokes up and moaned a lots. I thought you wus. Maybe."

"So, I wus awake den?"

Sweetie backtracked, "Well, Hottie got on tops a you. Then, I did afta. You moaned anda yer eyes opened. You seemed awakes. I really sorry yer wife found out, too." She could feel Nuttybomb's dismay, his feelings of anger, and his total lack of recall.

He took some slow deep breaths and delved deep into his memory banks. He connected with Hottie, hoping to fully understand what transpired and what state of consciousness he was in.

Hottie was now linked with Nuttybomb and Sweetie. She admitted to realizing Nutty's fragile state and his fading in and out of consciousness while she and her friend did stuffin's with him. In her warped view, she had provided herself as a gift to him. He was her wargod, and her body was his to use.

Nuttybomb deeply hurt Hottie when he said, "You not a gift I want. If I wanted you, I would order you to do tings. I no even need a ask. Now, I can finally connect where I wus, and wut condition my mind anda body wus in. I wusn't in control. You did dis wit'out me knowin'."

While Hottie became indignant, Sweetie kept apologizing.

Nuttybomb instructed, "You both goin' to Plenna. You nevva come back to Hotta. Pack yer shit anda get a ride out der on da next transport."

Hottie questioned with disgust, "Plenna? Wut for?"

Nuttybomb said in distain, "So I don't gots to see you no more. You can nurse der."

"I don't wanna nurse der," Hottie exclaimed.

"You nurse der or you die," Nuttybomb said without emotion.

Sweetie said sheepishly, "Ok. Sorry again. I so sorry, my Wargod."

Nuttybomb felt Sweetie's sincerity. He also felt Hottie's anger.

Hottie spat, "Fine."

"Anda if anyone hear 'bout any a dis," Nutty began, "yer lives are ova. Understood?"

Sweetie cried, "Yessir."

He pried, "Hottie?"

She reluctantly answered, "Ya."

A beeping sound and a flashing light brought Nuttybomb back to his current location. He ended the connections with the nurses, pushed a red button by a speaker, and asked, "Wut is it?"

"Sir, Marshil comin's into view."

"Good," Nuttybomb anxiously said. "Give Kingskull da coordinates and letta us begin landin' on da surface.

***

Gunza's anger was almost to a state of madness. His muscles were straining not to explode, but it wasn't quite time yet. The more time that passed, the angrier he became, muttering curses under his breath and pacing wildly.

His troops had never seen him like this. They had no idea what he was waiting for, preparing himself to do. They watched from a careful distance.

Gunza stopped and leered off toward something he spotted. He began to walk, briskly at first. But this soon became a jog; then, a solid run.

It wasn't long before his old, but powerful legs brought him to his destination. His hand balled into a fist and shot out with his extended arm, catching a surprised Nuttybomb on the jaw.

Nutty was thrown backward, a solid punch that knocked him senseless. He got to his feet, unaware what happened. His eyes caught Gunza returning for a second charge, but his brain was too slow to respond. He was leveled again.

Gunza was on top of his wargod, questioning something about nurses and his daughter, Uhra. Nuttybomb was dazed and confused. But instinctively, his hands came up between Gunza's and found his father-in-law's throat.

The younger, but disadvantaged Nuttybomb, released his grip once he realized what was happening. He worked to calm himself down, hoping not to lose control and inflict serious damage to his family member.

Hundreds of orcs had gathered. They were astonished at what they saw. Was Gunza vying for ultimate power? Did he hold a grudge and was stupid enough to attack their wargod? They watched intensely.

Nutty said, "Old Man, calm down." He found it hard to reason with the wild orc effectively.

"Calm down?" Gunza asked passionately, both hands on Nuttybomb's collar.

"Yes. Careful," Nutty urged.

Gunza was growling, his chest was heaving, spit flying from his mouth as he spoke. "Did you do stuffs wit' dose nurses?" He didn't seem to care that he had attacked the wargod in broad daylight in front of troops.

Nuttybomb thought for a few seconds. "Yes anda no."

"Wut da hell dat supposed to mean?"

"Yes, wut you tink happened, happened. But no, I didn't do it."

Gunza spat, "My patience growin' thin, boy."

The crowd gasped.

Nuttybomb warned, "I said, careful. You a my dad anda I respect you. But I yer wargod, too. Get up or I kill you."

Gunza looked around, realizing how many eyes were upon him. He spat on the ground and released his son-in-law. He stood up and offered a hand.

Nutty took Gunza's extended arm and pulled himself up. He said, "Tanks."

"Lemme hear it," Gunza ordered.

Nutty nodded. He began, "I wus sick…"

Gunza rolled his eyes, anticipating this being the start of excuses to help explain the cheating that happened.

Nutty caught the look on Gunza's face. "I know der nuttin' I can say dat make it ok. But I wusn't awake. I didn't know it wus happenin'. I didn't even know

262

until I talked wit' da nurses on da way here. Not even told Uhra yet."

Gunza sought to expose holes in Nutty's explanation. "How do a wargod not know till he talka to da nurses? You da smartest, knowingest orc I evva knowed."

Leaning forward, Nuttybomb whispered, "I died, Gunza. My brain not all da way fixed yet. My body still brokes, too. I still sick. Maybe I nevva get back to how I wus. But I not let da troops know. Morale, ya know? I not let anyone know. I not able to see till a few days ago."

Gunza stopped huffing and puffing. He took a step back and regrettably said, "Sorry."

Nuttybomb asked politely, "You ready?"

Gunza looked down and muttered, "Fuck. I messed up yer face. Fair is fair."

Before Gunza finished talking and preparing himself for the inevitable, Nuttybomb adequately placed him on his ass with a hard, right hook.

Wargod Nuttybomb growled, "Get to work."

Gunza stumbled to his feet and obeyed, his head already swelling. "Yessir." He looked around at the troops and ordered, "You heard yer wargod. Get to work!"

The troops scrambled away to business, not sure what they had witnessed, but somehow ok with the outcome.

Nutty spat a mouthful of blood on the ground.

Ucktock came over and asked, "You need anyting?"

Rubbing his swollen face, and pulling a loose tooth from his mouth, Nutty answered, "Ya, but nuttin' you or any orc can gimme."

***

Quicklip pointed and said, "Der dems are."

Ships entered the atmosphere with thundering sonic booms, passing from the nothingness of space to the thick mix of gasses above the planet. En masse, they came, led by the wargod, to kill Darkster.

Quicklip walked alongside Guthrak. They trudged along an old road, now filled with sand dunes that blocked the visible path at times. They came over a ridge and found some of their brothers.

Guthrak, annoyed with Quicklip's constant playing with the new mechanical arm ordered, "Knock it off. I sick a dat damn noise."

"I not maka dat noise. It da hydraulic pumps, I tink."

"Well, stoppa da hydraulic pumps makin' da noise den," Guthrak said angrily.

Quicklip tried to explain his problem. "But it hard a use dis damn arm. I gots to learn a use it good or I no good to any a us."

Guthrak said sharply, "I gonna stick it up yer ass."

"I don't see how dat help any a us either," Quicklip teased. He smiled as he held up his arm, spinning the hand and making loud whirling noises.

They stopped just short of some colleagues.

Ucktock greeted, "Hiya, guys."

"Hey, Uck," Quicklip said.

Guthrak looked passed Ucktock, watching keenly, the massing of enemy ships opposite Nuttybomb's. He asked, "Wut all dis 'bout?"

Nubbs replied, "Kingskull. Him's meetin' wit' us to talk wit' Nuttybomb."

Gaging how outnumbered his forces were, Guthrak snarled, "Dis should be good."

Nuttybomb, Gunza, Booma, and Moonoak met the others at the ridge. They watched the ships unload armies.

Nuttybomb asked, "Wer be Arc?"

"I here," came from the weakened voice of the young sorcerer.

The orcs turned to see Arc, blistered and skinless in spots. Several of them took a step or two back, unsure of his intentions. They knew how dangerous he was.

Nuttybomb asked, "Wut da hell happens to you?"

Quicklip spat sarcastically, "Prolly playin' wit' fire again."

Arc stared at Quicklip for an uncomfortable amount of time. He found his voice and said, "Darkster."

Ucktock excitedly asked, "You fight him?"

"I tried," Arc said, but then admitted, "Him real strong, tho."

Nuttybomb said, "Looka like we gots our a work cut out fo' us."

Quicklip tipped his head to the side and said, "Der an awful lot a dems," referring to the number of Kingskull troops. "Gots our a work cut out fo' us here too."

Nuttybomb stated, "Dat good. We can use 'em."

"To join us?" Quicklip asked.

"Yup."

265

"Wut if dems not join?" Quicklip scratched his head.

Nuttybomb turned and looked deep into Quicklip's eyes. "Den, we kills dem."

Quicklip was taken aback. "All a dems? Der musta be millions a dems."

Nubbs joked, "I picked a bad day to stop drinkin'." His trusty flask found his lips.

Nuttybomb said, "Oh, I almost forgots. Dis be Gobbygoo. He a guard wit' us now."

The guards offered, "Hi," and, "Hello."

Gobbygoo nodded, but didn't return a word.

Guthrak asked, "You don't talk much, do ya?"

Gobbygoo shrugged his shoulders.

Quicklip teased, "Wer da fuck you get dat name?"

Shoulders were shrugged again.

Booma spoke up for the newcomer. "Hims don't talk much, but him's a great fighta."

Quicklip cheered, "Dat all I needs a know."

Guthrak looked annoyed at Quicklip and said, "Well, dat be two tings you know den. Soona or later we maka you smart."

"I doubt it," Quicklip retorted with a smile. "Busides, ya don't gotta be smart to do wut we do, just gotta fight good."

Ucktock blurted out, "Well, I wanna be smart fo' wen I get back home."

"How's dat workin fo' you?" Quicklip teased.

"C'mon," Nuttybomb ordered. "Letta us go."

Gunza asked, "You sure you up to dis?"

Nuttybomb's eyes surveyed the millions of enemy troops following Kingskull to the rendezvous point. "No," he said with a smile.

266

"Ok den," Quicklip said slyly. He continued, "Dat give me all da confidence I need." He laughed.

The others laughed too. The truth was, Nutty's levity was just what the tremendously outnumbered Hotta guards needed. It gave them faith in their leader and themselves. They walked to the edge of the ridge that overlooked the massive armies.

"Kingskull," Nutty shouted. He clumsily made his way partly down the face of the cliff and stopped on an outcropping that jutted out from the side of the cliff's face. His guards followed him and came to rest at his sides.

Kingskull stopped his troops a hundred feet short of the ledge. He said, "You wanted to talk? Talk."

Nuttybomb began, "I choosed dis spot 'cause we killed mosta da creeps in da area, so it easier to talk."

Kingskull jeered, "'Ere we go. Mo' 'bout creeps. Darkster tried dat trickery too."

"Trickery?" Nuttybomb questioned.

"Ya," Kingskull replied. "Dunno why you tink I be scared a creeps. Dems just kids stuff."

Nuttybomb asked curiously, "Why would I tell you 'bout creeps? How do dat help me?"

Kingskull looked around, noticing his troops awaiting a response from their leader. "I tink you tryin' to scare me or sumptin'."

"But scarin' you don't mean I can beat yer whole army. How do dat help me?"

"You seem to be full a tricks, Nuttybomb. Dunno wut you tink or why. But I tell you dis. I runnin' outta patience wit' you." Kingskull crossed his arms and asked, "You gots sumptin' to say dat important, or just mo' stupid stuff?"

Nuttybomb said, "I told you we killed mosta da creeps in da area. Now, you will see creeps, summoned by Darkster." He nodded toward Ucktock.

Ucktock separated himself from the party and made his way to the bottom. He removed a large boulder that blocked a small cave by prying it with a leveraged tree limb from above. He was safely out of the way.

"Chop off da heads," Nuttybomb instructed. Dat da best way to kill 'em."

Two creeps rushed out of the cave and toward Kingskull's troops.

The surprised troops were slow to react; they had never witnessed such horror. But react they did, coming together to eliminate the putrid, decayed bodies that assailed them. The troops hadn't received much damage.

Kingskull asked, "How da hell? I mean, what are? Are dems dead or alive? Anda why show me?"

Nuttybomb explained, "Dems are dead, but not in da aftalife. Darkster raises dem fro' da ground wit' promises of peace and happiness. He trick dems into walkin' da world again. But dems are so unhappy, dems can only kill a billion times to try anda find dat happiness promised dem. But no matta how many dems kill, dems nevva be happy. We kill dems and let dem rest peaceful like again. Now, I show you, cause you fightin' on da wrong side. Darkster will kill you."

"Creeps not dat dangerous. My troops killed dem easily. You stupid to tink dat showin' me creeps will change my a mind 'bout killin' you."

"Kingskull, dese not da dangerous ones. Dese just regular orcs fro' town. Da dangerous ones are soldiers

268

wit' swords and guns. Der be millions a dose. Dems will kill yer armies."

"Ok, whatevva. You gots anyting else befo' I kill you?"

Nuttybomb pleaded, "If Darkster lives, he will destroy evvyting."

Kingskull said skeptically, "All I hear fro' you and Darkster are words. Words don't maka you strong. Words are fo' da weak. Unless you gots mo' dan dat, it time fo' you to die."

Sixteen
Sides Chosen

Nuttybomb thought out the best tactic to gain favor with Kingskull without showing any weakness. He understood the enemy's understanding of the position of power. With Ucktock rejoining him from below, he stood on the ridge with his seven guards, standing off against several million.

Arc asked Nuttybomb, "Wut you doin' in my mind?"

Nuttybomb hastened, "Shh. I connectin' wit' udders. You tink you can only shoot dem?"

"I can try."

"Well?" Kingskull asked seemingly annoyed.

Nuttybomb spoke, straining to keep his opened catalogue of hosts while talking aloud. "Kingskull, I want to show you real power. My apprentice is going to kill twenty of yer troops. These are orcs who have angered the gods with their deeds. Dems have tortured udder orcs. It not allowed."

Kingskull shouted, "Dems my troops, not yers. You kill dems and my whole army gonna kill you."

Quicklip asked quietly, "Dis a joke, right?"

Nuttybomb said, "Kingskull, you needs to see dis. Dis is ordered by da gods. Anda you needs to know dat I can kill you anywhere at any time."

Arc's eyes changed. Lightning danced throughout the enemy troops, singling out those targeted by Nuttybomb. Twenty orcs screamed and died, a little too quickly, based on their crimes. But die they did.

"How dare you?" Kingskull angrily shouted. "Dat opposed to impress me and show you can kill me? Killin' twenty random orcs isn't special."

"I not done." Nuttybomb said. "Der be orcs dat kill anda eat udder orcs. I gots a hundred a dem ready to die. But I not kill dems. I tell dems to kill demselves."

Kingskull had heard enough. "Wut kinda trickery you tryin' here? You can't maka my orcs kill demselves."

Nutty started making connections, but linking to a hundred was hard, and it took time. He began confusing some links and was beginning to strain.

"I heard 'nuff," Kingskull said. "It time fo' you to all die.

Quicklip murmured, "Now'd be a good time, Chief."

Guthrak instructed, "Shutta up, Quicklip."

Kingskull asked, "Dat it? No mo' words? No mo' magic?" He laughed hardily in front of his troops.

His troops busted a gut too.

"Chief?" Quicklip pleaded.

Kingskull started giving orders to attack Nuttybomb and the guards, when…

A hundred orcs used their own weapons to inflict wounds on themselves. Some were impaled, others slicing deep cuts into their arms and legs. Others spilled their innards on the ground in front of them.

Their comrades unsheathed their own weapons to combat an invisible foe. They looked around wildly, not knowing who to defend against as their brothers dropped one by one. They struggled to understand why orcs were killing themselves.

Nuttybomb said, "Fo' crimes against da gods, fo' eatin' orcs alive, dese orcs are ordered to kill demselves. Anda now you, Kingskull…will you join me, or will you die?"

Gunza whispered to Guthrak, "You evva seen anyting lika dat?"

Guthrak played with the knife in his jaw, rubbing the handle and feathers in astonishment. "Nope," he said.

Nutty was weak. There was no way he could continue monumental tasks of mind to sway Kingskull to his side. He dropped to one knee as he looked up at Gunza. He said, "Dat all I gots." Tears welled up in his eyes; he quietly gasped to catch as much air in his lungs as would be allowed.

Seeing this, Guthrak ordered, "Ready to fight, warriors."

Kingskull ordered his troops to prepare for battle. He seemed unfazed by the spectacle he had just witnessed.

Nutty stood up and delivered the best voice he could, stern and authoritative and complimentary. "Kingskull, all orcs, evvywhere need you to fight alongside me. We need you to help us defeat Darkster."

Kingskull sneered, "Wut kinda wargod are a you, groveling lika dis?"

"Him da bestest wargod in da star clusta!" came from the usually quiet mouth of Gobbygoo.

Kingskull was taken aback. "I know dat voice," he said.

"Hello, brudder."

"Gobbygoo?" Kingskull questioned.

"Yes, brudder."

Quicklip quietly said, "Holy shit, he talks."

Guthrak punched Quicklip in the shoulder and said, "Really? Dat wut you get outta dis? Not dat he's Kingskull a brudder?"

"Well, ya. Dat too, I guess," Quicklip muttered with his head down.

Nubbs whispered, "Fuck. Dis is getting good." He fumbled with the cap on his flask.

During that time, Kingskull thought about his long- lost brother, how he ran away from his duties, and now his apparent treason, joining an enemy army. He said angrily, "It beed ten years, Gobbygoo. You runned away and hid fro' me. Beg fo' forgiveness and I may give you mercy."

Gobbygoo said, "Brudder, you misundastand me. I no run away and hide fro' you. I don't agree wit' all yer killin' fo' nuttin'. I fight you right here anda now if you like."

Kingskull laughed, "Dat sound funny comin' fro' a coward."

"I leaved evvyting behind, went into space wit' almost nuttin', almost dyin' a hundred times, 'cause I believe orcs betta dan wut you maka dems. I not a coward. I coulda killed you anda been leada, but I no wanna hurt you."

Kingskull dismounted from his rhino-like beast, handing the reigns to an underling. He pulled his cape away from one of his broad shoulders, protected by armor, and took up his sword. "Ok, brudder," he said, "now yer chance to be leader and run tings da way you want."

"I accept yer challenge," Gobbygoo answered. He made his way down the face of the ridge, alone to do what he avoided ten years before. He dusted himself off and settled in Kingskull's personal space. He stared into his brother's eyes, a lifetime of hate and resentment culminating in the cold stare that ran a chill up his adversary's spine.

Kingskull didn't anticipate the boldness of Gobbygoo's confrontation without hesitation. Furthermore, before him, stood a large, strong, adult orc warrior, heavily muscled, giving a strikingly fierce appearance. His long tusks and deep ridges in his brow and under his cheeks gave away his true age and hard life. Kingskull muttered, "You growed up."

"I growed old anda tired a fightin' fo' stupidity, brudder. You should try da same." Gobbygoo was ready to fight, although his hands were at his sides. He stood close to his brother with his chest pumped out.

Kingskull wearily took his eyes off Gobbygoo to look passed him. He asked quietly, "Gobbygoo, dis Nuttybomb...why you fight fo' him but not me?"

"'Cause he is good and just. 'Cause he protects orcs, doesn't kill dem just to conquer. Anda him do stuffs I nevva seen befo'. Him da best fighta evva. I believe in him."

Looking around at his troops, Kingskull felt the eyes of his troops waiting for him to order the enemy's deaths; to remove his embarrassment; to save him from possible death at his own brother's hands. But he couldn't give the order. Something told him he needed to rethink his position. He looked at Gobbygoo and said warmly, "I not good at dis. Not lika I can just join anudder orc so easy like."

Gobbygoo used a metaphor the best way he knew how with, "Hardest ting fo' me wus leavin' you, brudder. You wer all I knew afta Mom and Dad died. You took care a me. But it wus time to change. I had to."

Nubbs asked, "Wut da fuck are dems sayin'?"

Quicklip blurted out, "Sounda lika dems talkin' 'bout eatin' you fo dinna. Gobbygoo gonna hand you ova."

"Fuck. Dat sux fo' me," Nubbs said in jest.

Nuttybomb waived them off and ordered, "Shutta up. I tryin's to hear."

Quicklip randomly asked, "You guys evva hear 'bout da cannibal dat showed up late fo' dinna?"

The group looked around at each other, wondering what relevance the stupid question had. A couple smiles were seen.

"He gots da cold shoulda," Quicklip said, a grin forming across his face.

Nubbs' eyes looked up, showing the whites only, clearly not finding humor in Quicklip's joke.

Quicklip spat, "You keep rollin' yer eyes, maybe you find yer brain."

"I find you not funny," Nubbs grumbled.

Guthrak flatulated, loud and long to a thunderous round of cheers and laughter. He shrugged and simply stated, "Sorry, Chief."

How strange they looked from Kingskull's view, laughing and backslapping when their lives were hanging in the balance. He couldn't believe their audacity, their attitudes; they didn't fear him; they didn't even care. He could kill them so easily. Well, he thought, perhaps if the one with the lightning was

275

taken out first, or maybe Nuttybomb was shot…the scary looking one with the knife in his face, or the old, hard-looking warrior, the creepy one in the robe…

They were pretty tough looking. But their odds were insurmountable. Surely, they knew they would die to an entire army, right? Or did they know something he didn't?

Kingskull remembered orders he gave to protect his flanks, the ships, and all materials needed for battle. Fuel and food were guarded, as was all ammunition. It seemed everything was accounted for. It was so strange that Nuttybomb and his guards were so happy-go-lucky.

Even Kingskull's own troops had succumbed to the monkey-see, monkey-do giggling that inevitably followed a good fart, albeit from the enemy. It was so loud that it echoed off the face of the nearest hill, reverberating back into the valley. Contagious laughter rippled through the troops from one end to the other.

And just then…

Quicklip asked loudly and happily, "Gobbygoo, you gonna introduce us to yer brudder, or wut?"

Kingskull fidgeted with the helmet on his head and asked, "Der sumptin' wrong wit' dems?" He patted it down over the top secure it.

Gobbygoo smiled. "Not a ting." There was no weakness to be found in Gobbygoo's eyes. He was tall and proud and ready to fight; ready to die, if necessary.

Until this very second, Kingskull would never have admitted to giving in to an enemy, let alone joining them. He gulped, trying to swallow his pride. He looked around at his troops, feeling vulnerable and

276

silly. But he saw something in Nuttybomb and the guards that propelled him to align.

"Wargod Nuttybomb," Kingskull said in a deep, booming voice, "It be an honor to fight wit' you against Darkster."

Nuttybomb respectfully said, "It an honor to fight alongside you, Kingskull.

The Hotta orcs came down from the ridge and greeted Kingskull properly.

Nuttybomb asked Kingskull to speak with him in private. Away from any ears, Nuttybomb said, "You still have troops dat did crimes against da laws of da gods. You will send dems to me quietly. Dis way I handles dems and you no looka bad in front a yer troops. Agreed?"

"Why would I agree to dat?" Kingskull asked defiantly.

"Kingskull, listen. Dis not da only world we live in. You responsible fo' da souls a yer troops. You allow dems to anger da gods, anda gods be angry wit' you. You do dis, anda it save you."

"Nuttybomb," Kingskull said with a sigh, "no god nevva help me in dis life. Why should I believe in anudder life?"

Nuttybomb explained, "'Cause a da creeps. You see how dems not rest in da aftalife? Dat gonna be you if you no right da wrongs you allowed."

Kingskull bit the inside of his lip and swirled something around in his cheek. "Ok? Wut 'bout da creeps? How dems rest afta we kills em? Dems come back again and again?"

Nuttybomb answered, "Dunno how many times dems can come back, but I gots orcs to put dems to permanent rest. Anda if any a us die, dems put us to rest too. I don't wanna turn into a creep. I send you shamans to clean up afta yer army."

"Ok, Kingskull agreed. "I send you da orcs you want to do whatevva you do to dems."

"I will be merciful."

Kingskull was more than happy to do the heavy lifting; his troops would engage the creep army that was amassing nearby, and throw what he could at Darkster's main force.

Fighters and bombers from both forces would try to pin down Darkster's troops and destroy his transport ships.

Nuttybomb already considered the possibility of losing to Darkster. He arranged the elimination of all enemy fuel and food stocks to keep Darkster from surviving. Stranding him on the planet without resources was the contingency plan.

***

"Wut?" Darkster howled. "Dat bastid joined Nuttybomb?"

"Yessir," the officer replied. "Kingskull troops movin' to da creep army."

"How dare he be disloyal to me! Now I will make him die a thousand deaths!"

The officer didn't know if a response was needed, but he gave one anyway to avoid being killed by his temperamental leader. "Yessir?"

Darkster kicked the officer in the ass with a throaty, "Get da hell fro' me, you imbecile!"

"Yessir!" the officer cried as he ran for his life.

The evil necromancer looked to the horizon. Red and gold banded clouds gave way to black dots that grew. He ordered, "Get our fightas back, now!"

The surroundings bustled with activity as troops began to duck for cover to avoid incoming fire. Those unlucky enough to be caught in the open, were transformed into red and green muck.

Darkster jumped from his platform to the ground below, a dust cloud emanating from his boots impacting the loose soil. He set his sights on a Hotta fighter plane, and just like that, downed it with a bolt of electricity.

His whip deflected the next round of attacks that closed in on his position. He spat a horrific sound, corresponding with the expulsion of energy from his hands. Another plane went down. He cackled incessantly.

Slowly, but surely, Darkster's air force returned to defend his troops on the ground. They had been picking off Guthrak's forces the early part of the day. But now, they faced off against Hotta's best.

Ucktock peeled to his left, avoiding a round that ripped past his wing. He climbed into a cloud bank, and dropped back into the fight, just behind the enemy that had missed him. He yelled, "Rabbit Harrison teached me dat. You don't know who dat is, but don't a matta. You won't live long to find out anyway!"

His bulky plane shuddered under the forces of spin required to dive and catch up with his prey. His finger hit the trigger. The canon shot ripped the enemy fighter into pieces. He yelled, "Dat one fo' Leroy Hardy! You don't know him either." He laughed.

"Nice shot, Uck!", Booma said happily.

"Tanks. Hey, you gots one comin' to yer butt."

Booma replied, "I see him."

"Go to yer," Ucktock began, but failed to finish his plan to keep Booma safe because he struggled to remember right from left. "Wut did Harry Starke tells me? I write wit' my right. Ya, I write wit' my right!"

Booma was hit along his left side as he turned to avoid damage. "Go wer?" He yelled wildly.

Ucktock wiggled the toes on his right foot and said, "Go to yer right."

Booma banked hard right, giving him needed space, and dropping Ucktock into position for a kill.

Ucktock fired. "Yes! Gots da bastid. Dat two fo' me."

"Whatevva you say, Uck." Booma smiled and shook his head.

"Hey, looka. Dat Darkster I tink."

Booma yelled, "Pull up, Ucktock!"

But it was too late. Electricity engulphed Ucktock's fighter plane, erupting the fuel tank into a comet that drove the disabled hulk to the ground.

The wings were ripped away, the canopy thrown somewhere unknown. Shattered glass, metal, and carbon fibers littered the area. Fires were everywhere.

Ucktock sat in pain, pushed up against the dashboard with the control stick in his leg. His head and right shoulder were pinned against the fuselage, which had warped around the front of the plane when it hit the ground. He thought his left arm was probably behind him, hopefully still attached.

The heat from ignited fuel began to intensify in the cramped cockpit. Smoke choked him as his lungs fought to find air.

"Uh oh," Ucktock said nervously, feeling intense heat on his left forearm. He began blowing, like a child would candles on a birthday cake, but this did little to get him out of his predicament. He huffed and he puffed, but the fire was spreading into the cockpit, his arm being taken first. "Yup, it still attached." And it was behind him. No amount of spitting into the air was going to help.

He tried moving his pinned shoulder. "Oh no, oh no, oh no," he said, panicky.

Then, he tried to swing his left arm out from behind him, but that failed, too. He panted like a woman giving birth. "Oh fuck dis hot! I tink I gonna cry. I don't wanna cry, but dis hurt so bad."

For a second, the crumpled mess that was his plane, tightened around him. But then, he felt some leg room, then some space between the fuselage and his head. He heard metal twisting.

"C'mon, Uck. Gimme yer hand."

"Wargod Nuttybomb?" Ucktock's head slipped away from the metal confinement and freed his arm.

Nuttybomb pulled him from the wreck and dragged him away behind some rocks for cover. "Hang in der, buddy."

"It Ucktock. Buddy wus my brudder, but he died in a fire. By da way... I on fire!" He began blowing in spurts again. "Oh, anda Hiya."

Nuttybomb doused the flames and gave whatever aid he could to his guard and pilot. He asked, "Can you move?"

"Umm, no. I tink my legs a brokes. Ugh! Dis arm, too. Ouch. Fuck!"

"Shh," Nuttybomb cautioned. "Ok, stay here. I get sumbody to gets you outta here wen I can. C-ya later." The wargod left.

***

"Move, Move, Move!" Kingskull ordered. His troops lined up against the enormous creeps army. The mass of writhing decay and empty promises buckled his lines, sheer weight pushing his orcs to their knees.

Many a foreign orc contemplated running for their lives during this first encounter. The putrid smells and hellacious sounds alone, were enough to overwhelm the senses. But those were also accompanied by fearless death in rotting bodies, unwilling to yield, unable to die. There was nothing comparable.

The rhino-beasts charged ahead, Kingskull and his Elite Riders on them. They barreled into the wall, casting corpses into the air as they passed, the beasts flinging their heads with impaled undead off to each side. They dug deep into the chaotic swarm of rot, but were ultimately stopped.

Beasts and Elite Riders, now on foot, fought side by side. Several beasts inadvertently crushed their own riders while fighting for survival. But for the most part, they did well, clearing an area for orcs to battle.

Kingskull slashed and slashed; it was akin to human lore about orcs' savagery and how their heroes fought with swords in hand. It could have been any orc battle, or any orc army on any other day for that matter, plastered on the cover of any comic book.

But it was here and now that the foreign orc, on this barren world slayed the darkest of enemies. He was a fearsome warrior indeed, just what Nuttybomb needed to stem the tide and draw Darkster on even terms.

It occurred to Kingskull that he and his troops might have been used as fodder, while Nuttybomb did whatever the hell he did. But the instinct to survive, coupled with the orc driven lust to kill, provided him all he currently needed to concentrate on. Besides, his huge fleet was on standby to assist Nuttybomb's if necessary. The fact that he still had a dangerous armada gave him a sense of security.

It was Darkster he fought to defeat. He found himself angry at the thought of being stripped of the ability to use heavy weapons, fighters, or even grenades against the creeps. Darkster brought to life a freakin' army that could only be shot at close range or killed by sword. Sure, there was some deviation from the truth in his reasoning, but the fact was that he couldn't cause mass casualties and preserve his troops now. No; now, he had to watch his army trade kill for kill with the creeps.

Throughout the day, Kingskull and his armies battled the creeps. The pace was so fast and the carnage so complete, that only red could be seen for miles in every direction.

Half of Kingskull's armies were lost that first day. Night was yet to come.

***

Gunza brought the capital ships to bare against Darkster's fleet. He lacked fighters and bombers that were needed on the surface; he had very few torpedoes too.

But he had at his disposal a modern fleet, with Hotta orcs, hellbent on fighting for their wargod; something the opposition lacked dearly.

He understood that put in any position, orcs have always fought when necessary. But orcs with passion, goals, and understanding of what they fought for gave Gunza a distinct advantage. He used it.

The battleships, *In yer Ear* and *Up Yer Ass*, fired their big guns before ramming *Da Malevolent*. Gunza's *Da Rampage* brought all guns to bare on the super battleship as well. The cruisers, *Big Dawg* and *Da Fang*, fired everything they had too.

Darkster's pride of the fleet, and largest ship any orc ever used in battle, was under siege without him aboard. It fired its main guns, point blank into *Da Fang*, obliterating her and killing everyone onboard.

That was the last Hotta ship she destroyed. Troops from *In yer Ear* and *Up Yer Ass* entered her bowels and soon gained control of most of the main batteries and engine room. Before long, they had the bridge.

Excessive chatter on open bandwidths, typical during war, led to mass confusion above Marshil. Once the massive guns from *Da Malevolent* began firing against other Darkster ships, mass confusion led to utter and complete chaos. Every Darkster ship fired at any other ship they could, not knowing who was friend or foe.

Darkster's fleet, although larger than Gunza's, was in a mere shambles. This allowed Kingskull ships to work diligently, and without interference, to eliminate any and all Darkster ships attempting to leave the planet. They split up, covering every bit of space they could outside the atmosphere. Without being called on to assist Gunza, they were free to cover the expansive area required.

A hunkered-down Nuttybomb received the good news from Gunza, giving him some hope. He breathed a temporary sigh of relief.

He knew the news wasn't good everywhere, though. Kingskull was struggling against the creeps, and most of his own army was lost near the city and underground. Ucktock was wounded, there was no word from Guthrak and Quicklip, and he was pinned down by his own fighters.

At least his fighters took out Darkster's. With complete air superiority, it seemed Darkster and his troops would never leave the surface. There was some comfort in that.

Additionally, Hotta fighters and bombers were wreaking havoc on Darkster's troops and ships. They weaved to and fro, bombarding enemy forces, who were defenseless to their attacks. They blew apart food stores, severed supply lines, and left little doubt about Darkster's capabilities to leave the surface by taking out propulsion systems on every craft encountered.

Arc slithered to his wargod and greeted, "Chief."

Nuttybomb replied in kind, "Arc, how ya doin'?"

"Betta. I ready a fight wen you are."

"Good. How's Ucktock?" Nutty asked.

Arc covered his head and answered, "Not good. He back getting care, tho."

Moonoak, Nubbs, and Gobbygoo threw their bodies down alongside Nuttybomb's and Arc's. The group hid in a crater on the side of a road five hundred feet from Darkster's alter.

Nubbs said, "Wut I miss?"

Nuttybomb answered, "Not much. Waitin' fo' our a planes to finish up. Den, we move. I wanna surround him and all a us charge him fro' different directions. He can't stop us all."

Nubbs asked as he squinted, "Is dat him?"

Nuttybomb answered in disgust, "Ya, dat's him."

"He don't look so tuff," Nubbs scoffed.

Arc said, "I beed here lika two minutes and he killed three a our planes. And all dis shit on my face anda arms fro' him. He tuff!"

Nubbs nodded, "Ok, ok. He tuff. Don't get yer undies all twisted. So, letta us just shoots him fro' here."

Nuttybomb said, rubbing his tired eyes, "Can't. Been watching bullets bounce off da whole area. It lika shield or sumptin'."

Moonoak, after studying Darkster and the platform with altar, offered, "Him gettin' ready fo' sumptin' big. Ya, sumptin' big comin'."

Nuttybomb concurred, "I tink so, too. But wut?"

Seventeen
Nukes

Guthrak and his remaining forces fought their way from the west. With help of air support, they were able to push back Darkster's larger armies and move closer to the necromancer's location. "Gods dammit," Guthrak screamed, as shrapnel from a nearby explosion entered his side. "Dis my last fight. I done afta dis. I way too old fo' dis shit anymo'."

Quicklip was getting the hang of his new appendage, using it to bash in the faces of his enemy, utilizing its heavy, metallic bulk. Proficiency wasn't found, yet, but it was damn close. "I like a spring chicklen," he gloated.

"Fuck you," Guthrak insulted.

"Not on yer best day, Ole Man." Quicklip laughed before ducking beneath an enemy's blade.

"You sure? I tought lil gurls liked olda males." It was Guthrak's turn to laugh.

Quicklip retorted, "Ya, olda, not dead. You so old, you fart dust."

"Here sum dust for you. Shutta up anda fight."

The tunnels, now vacated by Hotta troops, became the sole location for the wounded. Sewers were used in the surrounding areas to move casualties to the safety of their cover from above.

Darkster's troops were totally unaware of the activity going on around and beneath them. While Hotta orcs were delivered to safety, they were being decimated from air attacks. The evil orc was either incapable of leading, or simply didn't care about any of his losses.

He was a bit busy, too, downing planes and making offerings to his god. With hands raised above his head, and his opened mouth spewing ungodsly words to the heavens, Darkster caused the elements to change. The winds whipped nearby materials to be lost in the distance. Sand and dust were picked up, and grains not deposited in orifices of orcs, were carried far away.

Clouds separated, then assembled into a swirling maelstrom that circled above, a rushing cyclone, eager to unleash Hell. Claps of thunder clamored above the sounds of distant battle. Lightning danced in the sky.

Nuttybomb and his guards were mesmerized; all orcs were. The spectacle was more than they could comprehend. Understanding was completely lost when the fabric of space and time was ripped apart, opening a tear that connected the physical world with the heavens.

Nuttybomb said in disbelief, "I tink it time we move, fighta planes or no."

Wiping dust from their eyes and removing debris from where they laid, the group scattered and worked their way around Darkster.

A magnificent shockwave shot out in all directions, everyone within five miles in each direction was thrown to the dirt. The ground tremored, undulating waves, plowing through the rock and sediment.

Nutty was knocked nearly unconscious, his body hurled against the remnants of a transport ship. He saw Moonoak similarly thrown to his left.

The other Hotta orcs, beaten and battered, crawled for better cover as they, too, were tossed like ragdolls.

One of Nubbs' arms hung uselessly, misshapen and disconnected from the shoulder. He groaned in pain as he scurried on his belly into a ditch.

Arc was severely shaken, blood coming from his nose and ears. He staggered behind a pile of rubble and dropped to the ground.

Guthrak picked himself up, grabbed Quicklip and charged toward his wargod's location. There was little fighting along the way, as Darkster troops- also wounded and concussed- stared up at the ungodly spectacle.

Enormous cracks opened, sucking into the bowels of the planet everything in their treacherous grasp. The winds calmed, the dust hung in the air, and in their wake, a vision of horror appeared.

A monstrosity emerged from beyond. A demon, almost twenty feet tall, clad in ancient armor, and sporting great horns from its head, sprang in front of Darkster, its enormous weight rocking the ground yet again.

Nuttybomb and Moonoak looked at each other in bewilderment. Nutty cried, "Oh my gods!"

Orcs picked themselves up and ran in horror, away from death's bringer. Some, watching the monster, didn't see that they were running right into chasms, opened by the necromancer. They fell to their temporary deaths.

The Hotta orcs wanted to run; they needed to; everything in their very essences begged them to. But they couldn't. They knew they had to do everything, even dying themselves, to stop Darkster.

The ground began to shake violently at random with aftershocks that caused resettling of the ground that was whipped up like churned butter. Wave after wave tossed the orcs for minutes at a time.

Orcs still tried to run away, screaming frantically. They ran into walls and each other, total panic ruling their movements.

Dead bodies were everywhere, the result of a week's worth of battles. But they began to stir.

Darkster swayed back and forth, the winds howling to and fro in concert with his body. What he said is anyone's guess, but it was aimed somewhere beyond the physical.

Creeps picked themselves up from the dust whence they came. Hideous moans filled the air, strong winds howling devilish sounds, the bowels of the planet moaning in deep upheaval.

Darkster lowered his arms. The demon took up position beside him at the altar. They were ready to rule the universe!

What was read to the guards by Nuttybomb wasn't forgotten. Indeed, the words never rang truer than ever.

***

The mind is a world of wonder. More complex than the secrets of the universe, its possibilities are unlimited. However, due to its complexity and our crude understanding of it, it is greatly misunderstood and widely misused. Therefore, we have barely begun to understand its true potential and power.

For some, it can be controlled to accomplish unimaginable feats. Those that learn to connect its pathways will understand essence in its truest form…to know what knowledge is…to fully understand understanding…to know all and nothing. No longer will we be bound by physical form, limited by bone, skin, and muscle; no longer will we feel pain, nor will we die; we will become beings that transcend space and time.

I have begun on a path to the gods. Through years of alchemy and ingestion of substances, I have learned to enter a state of limited understanding. Even in these relatively benign trances, I have seen events in the past, as well as images of the future. I have been visited by the dead and warned by the gods. I have learned to leave my body and take journeys to distant worlds. I have begun to communicate with others, from my mind to theirs. I am only able to accomplish this while the others are also in a state of sleep. I can see their dreams and enter their visions. I have found that I can alter their dreams by casting illusions and manipulating their thoughts. It is my goal to be able to converse telepathically while they are awake. I am confident that I will be able to control their minds. They shall be subject to my will, helpless to make their own decisions or perform actions by their own doing. One that can control multiple subjects could very well cause mass hysteria or brainwash subjects into total subjugation…a very powerful implement to have on a path to the gods.

As dangerous and sinister as mind control may seem, there are other forms of physical manipulation of objects that are possible. There are forces at work all around us that are more misunderstood than the brain itself. Energy and matter are connected in ways like thoughts controlling movement in the body. Energy, like thought processes or visions, is a somewhat intangible entity. However, it can control physical properties within the body. I have found the ability within myself and outside myself to move objects without the use of touch. No longer do I need to push an object with my hand; nor do I need to touch it to know what it feels like.

The gods have warned me about this last topic. I am reluctant to incorporate this for fear that its inclusion may cause, rather than hinder, its use. However, I will, even with unrivaled trepidation and unmatched uncertainty, for it is directed and warranted by the gods.

Take heed! Goliath will return upon the sign and the heavens will fall! Thousands of years of suffering under his vehemence will mark his reign!

I am, as are all, forbidden to raise the dead! This goes against the fabric of the universe and is absolutely forbidden by the gods. Death may be unjust, but natural, whereas undeath isn't natural, but is demonic. The soul of one that plays with this evil will die a thousand times, times a thousand times in unmerciful anguish.

The Third Book of Grim/the Early Years

***

Darkster screamed an awful scream, sending chills into his enemies.

The demon howled.

Moonoak asked, "Wut we do?"

Nuttybomb sighed, "Dunno. My legs a shakin's so bad, dunno if I can stand."

Darkster's voice cut through the sounds of impending doom. He said sarcastically, "Wargod Nuttybomb, you can come out now."

***

Something was amiss. Even fighting against creeps, the unlikeliest of enemies, Kingskull saw the angry skies just to his north, and heard the shriek of winds and the planet's cries as it rumbled under foot; something big was happening.

Another strong aftershock put him on his back. The land lifted and fell, shook and crumbled in spots. Dust, picked up from the planet's constant vibrating, kept a rusty haze in the air.

Kingskull ordered, "We gots to work our a way north. Fight hard. Kill, kill, kill!"

His exhausted armies did what they could. Some arms were too tired to even lift the weight of their weapons. The mass of mutilation was epic. The carnage spread over miles.

The creep horde was thinned enough that they could trek north though. And as they moved, Nuttybomb's shamans offered peace to the fallen, so they wouldn't fall prey to Darkster's deviant intentions.

Kingskull ordered his wounded into the city underground to the west, so they could rest and receive much needed care. He and Gobbygoo got within a few miles of Darkster and the Hotta guards.

As they approached, they felt what every other orc in the vicinity felt; nausea, vertigo; not from the smells or the sounds; not from the concussive forces that assailed them. There was a pressure difference that tore through them; the same tear that ran through space and time; the very same tear that was opened to allow Hell's behemoth to enter the physical world. It sickened; it weakened.

Darkster was immune to this sickness. He still stumbled when the ground shook, but he seemed accustomed to the infliction that haunted the others.

He said, "Wargod Nuttybomb, it time."

But Nuttybomb was afraid. He knew not how to defeat Darkster, and no clue how to engage the demon. Exposing himself would surely mean a meaningless death.

Nutty asked quietly, "Moon, wer be dat armor we had made?"

"Da carbon, human stuff?"

"Ya," Nutty confirmed. "Might be my only chance."

Moonoak said, "If I can get to it, take me maybe fifteen minutes to get it anda come back."

Nuttybomb ordered, "Go get it." He stood up and darted out into the open. Following their leader, the guards took the cue from Nutty, and stepped from their cover and into vulnerability too.

Darkster cheered, "Yes! I tought you would hide foevva."

The demon howled so loud, the guards jumped. Vocalization was like a thousand trumpets in deep baritone, playing for all to hear. It held a great sword that scraped the ground, sparks flaking from the rock that it scratched. It looked back and forth at the guards, waiting to kill them; its eyes watched intensely.

Nubbs muttered, "Yup, dis a bad day to give up drinkin'."

Nuttybomb took a deep breath and screamed, "Darkster, I condemn you back to wer you came." He hid his fright from the guards. They struggled to focus on anything other than the monster before them anyway; they didn't see him shaking.

Arc attacked with all the energy he could muster. Blue and white electricity shot toward the evil necromancer.

Darkster countered with his whip, equaling the force needed to counter the attack.

Nuttybomb entered Darkster's mind. He tried over and over to get him to lower his hands, so Arc could fry him, but it was to no avail. It did keep him busy though.

As the demon jumped down from the platform and in front of Arc, the guards rushed the beast. Its muscles pulsated from the electricity that engulfed them as it entered Arc's energy zone. It reared back, bringing the sword it held in its huge hand over its head, ready to swing downward.

Guthrak slashed its calf. The demon swung down and back, disarming him, and sending his weapon flying fifty feet away. He rolled away from immediate harm, helped by Nubbs cutting the beast above a knee.

The monstrosity swung a backhand, faster than expected, and smashed Nubbs into a nearby ship. The guard laid there, gasping for air.

Moving around the demon, Arc again concentrated his power on Darkster. Even the evil orc found it hard to destroy the pesky sorcerer while Nuttybomb distracted him.

Nuttybomb traversed the few steps to the platform, and as he climbed, Darkster's hideous being revealed itself more clearly; first, his head; then, his torso; and finally, legs and feet.

Nutty thought he looked different than the first time they met. Time, battles, and madness shaped him into something other than an orc. He was young, but hunched and pale. His eyes were menacing.

Darkster thought the same thing about his enemy. The one who killed his mother stood before him, looking like anything other than a capable warrior at this point.

A sharp pain grabbed Nuttybomb in his heel. A rogue creep bit into the back of his ankle. A quick thrust downward with his sword, and the creep's skull was lanced, sending it back to the beyond.

But Nutty's mind was lacking, his focus shaken, his weakness exposed.

Darkster's brief respite from forced mind control freed him to send much more power into Arc. As soon as the young sorcerer screamed and fell, he turned on his arch enemy.

Nuttybomb felt the whip surround him with electricity. His muscles spasmed, his nerves afire. But his sword raised and cut the whip, severing the electric current from its user. He suffered minor burns.

He stepped forward and thrust his sword into Darkster. The necromancer sidestepped and parried with the shortened weapon he held, saving him from sure death.

However, the sword buried itself deep into Darkster's shoulder. He cursed and hissed between screams.

Somehow, Nuttybomb was on fire. It was willed by Darkster and allowed by Nutty's subconscious. Through the blaze that was him, he saw Guthrak fly passed him, swatted like a fly by the demon.

As Nutty stepped backward, he stumbled over Quicklip, another demon casualty. He fell off the platform and rolled to put out the fire.

Darkster pulled the sword from his shoulder.

The ground shook, the air cried, souls begged for mercy. One of the largest quakes yet knocked down all, even the demon. Evil's cruel reality was enacted, even against its own kind.

For anyone watching, there was nothing graceful about the struggle that was transpiring. For all their combined power, fluidity with weapons, and experience, the orcs and demon took potshots at each other, hoping to land a decisive blow.

Kingskull and Gobbygoo engaged the demon. A slash here, a stab there, and the same general results ensued. The demon bled some more with a new cut, and the orcs were tossed like toys with broken bones.

Booma landed his fighter, and fought to achieve what the others couldn't. He ended up lying on his back with his legs crushed after removing some demon fingers.

Occasionally, a creep would enter into the fray and cause minor wounds to the Hotta orcs before being felled. These were more or less distractions that interrupted their primary objectives.

The dance continued between Nuttybomb, Darkster, and Arc as well. Each vied for dominance while being unable, due to equal force being applied by the enemy.

The planet belched hot liquid metals and pumice high into the air through large cracks that ran away from the platform like rivers to the sea. Although the planet was cold, Darkster's surroundings were a boiling cauldron.

Troops watched from hundreds of feet away, colors dazzling them. The fireworks were fantastic to watch.

A great boom, from within the planet, pushed rock formations hundreds of feet into the sky. Orcs lost their footing, their legs unable to hold them under such monstrous forces.

Nuttybomb fell to his knees. His senses were confused. He and the guards were in some slow-motion nightmare. Time was warping around them and space was changing in size.

The tear above the platform, near Darkster's throne, appeared to begin closing. Winds began blowing toward it. What if the tear closed while the demon was on this side?

Nuttybomb, still keeping Darkster at bay, ran to meet Moonoak, who had returned. He ordered, "Goods. Keep Darkster mind busy."

Moonoak rebuked, "Dat not wut I do."

"No? Den, we all die."

Moonoak nodded. H closed his eyes and transcended the physical, into a plane that allowed connection with Darkster.

Darkster greeted, "Moonoak. I amemba you."

"As I you," Moonoak answered. "You da troubled boy in da cave, da same bastid I fought three years ago."

Darkster attempted to pin the responsibility for his evil ways on the shaman. Anything to manipulate his enemy, and cause him to lose control was key. "Dat fire ting you tought me worka good. Tanks fo' dat. Dat really help to send me to wer I am now. Anda, ya…three years ago. I much stronga dan I wus den."

Moonoak was losing his connection. He said, "Hurry, Nutty. I can't do dis much longer."

"I hurryin'," Nutty said frantically. He was nearly dressed in the protective gear when he remembered there was a communication device built into the suit.

He set the bandwidth and said, "Gunza, you hear me?" He fiddled with it and talked again. "Gunza?"

"Dis Gunza."

Nutty ordered as he tightened the last strap, "Ready da nukes."

Gunza questioned, "You sure?"

"Hurry," was shouted from Nutty's lips as he raced from his current place of cover and back toward death. He closed his eyes and reconnected with Darkster.

"Der you are," Darkster said with great satisfaction in his voice. "You put out da fire. Nice job."

Nuttybomb never could have conceived that the evil orc so thoroughly enjoyed their confrontation. He jumped to the top of the platform and picked up his sword. "Now, Moonoak," he screamed in desperation.

The shaman made the leap to telepathy again and found Darkster, Nuttybomb, and even Arc connected in a strange power struggle.

Darkster was outmatched in mind control for the briefest of moments. The ground shook and heaved upward again. Nuttybomb leaped forward as the evil necromancer stumbled upon the shaky ground.

Nuttybomb yelled, looking squarely into his enemy's eyes, "I killed yer Mom anda now I kills you! Darkster, I condemn you back to wer you came." He pushed his sword through Darkster's breastplate and between his ribs, piercing his heart, and sending blood out his back.

A gruesome scream sent a shockwave away from the necromancer.

The skies opened. Hail, the size of grenades, came crashing down in the billions. Marshil's parent star was lost in darkness behind thick, menacing clouds. Winds roared across the landscape.

Arc was relieved; relieved and dog-tired. He released his powerful electricity from Darkster and unleashed it on another. He reached back and hurled his power at the demon, just twelve feet away.

Nuttybomb yelled, "Evvyone push him dat way."

Guthrak hollered, "You big, oogly bitch!" and grabbed a leg. Kingskull and Gobbygoo were pushing on the other with all their might.

Quicklip joined Guthrak.

Nuttybomb jumped high into the air and let loose his blade, severing the demon's hand from the wrist before it swung down with its fury upon the guards.

The beast howled in agony. It screamed in anger. It swatted Gobbygoo and Kingskull from its leg. Then, it kicked their beaten bodies back with its free leg. But it was burning from Arc's bolts of energy.

Those in contact with the beast, received burns and were shocked by the associated voltage. But they carried on.

Moonoak rushed into Guthrak and Quicklip, helping to unbalance the monster. It stumbled slightly, but not enough.

Nutty threw himself onto the demon again, this time driving his sword into its throat.

Gobbygoo and Kingskull were up for one last push. They rushed the demon's free leg.

Nutty watched the tear shrinking. He had seconds to expel the demon. He yelled, "Evvybody one lasta push."

They pushed one last time, tripping the beast over the stairs that ran up to the throne. It stumbled backward and fell on its back.

Nuttybomb was grabbed by the demon and held firmly in its one good hand. The grip was so tight that he struggled to breathe. His ribs cracked one by one; he was slowly being crushed to death. He reached for his sword, but couldn't get to it. He hoped the armor wouldn't compress as much as it did under the monster's immense power, but there was nothing he could do now. Blood was forced away from his body and into his head. He felt as if he would squirt out the top like stepping on one side of a bug.

The demon crushed Nutty under its weight as it used its hand to steady itself on the ground. It began to stand up, it's legs straddling the stairway. The beast wobbled and fell back on the stairs.

Nutty couldn't hear anything; he couldn't see. Weakness enveloped him. The throbbing in his midsection was terrible. He hoped beyond hope he was in the right place to order, "Gunza, now!" He cried out again, "Gun...Now."

He opened his mouth wide and bit down on the demon's finger, still fighting with everything he had. He needed to free himself from the demon and the tear they had fallen into.

Nutty didn't open his eyes, but he saw his kids...and he saw Uhra. The last thing he thought was...that he never told her that he didn't do stuffin's with the nurses. He was sad.

Thoughts escaped him now. There was no more pain.

...

....

.....

306

A blinding white flash, brighter and hotter than a thousand stars, turned night into day. Winds, five hundred miles an hour, shot out from ground zero; then, sucked air in at a phenomenal pace, feeding the great ball of fire that mushroomed high into the sky.

Everything exposed to the blast within several miles was vaporized. Large ships were tossed away from the explosion. The dusty residue from soil, pumice, glass, metals, materials, and bodies rushed around until they drifted lightly as a fog.

Gunza watched from the bridge, saddened by the horror he unleashed on his guards and his Wargod, his son-in-law. It mattered not that the order came from someone else. He executed it; he executed them.

He hung his head in sorrow and shame.

Eighteen
Found

Gunza had the unenviable task of taking over for Nuttybomb, and everything that the job entailed. First, there was the dreaded search for survivors at and around ground zero. Without signs of Darkster or the demon, that commenced almost immediately.

He came from the comforts of his ship to the epicenter that changed the outcome for him, and all orcs everywhere. His mind began going over a checklist of things to do, but it was interrupted by his senses being attacked.

The hatch from his transport opened, and he walked out into the grayish day. He was at the edge of an enormous crater, gouged out by the nuclear blast.

The skies spoke of death and destruction, their ominous clouds ready to burst. They were dark and hazardous, the gentle winds fighting against the materials caught up in the towering cumulous.

Periodically, lightning struck the ground, illuminating the wasteland it assaulted. Thunder clamored, rolling away, its echoes reminding all of the destruction around them. Ferocity beckoned the eyes to see, the ears to hear.

The mother star hid behind the atmosphere, decorated in gray and black. The morning was cold, a sharp contrast to the superheated areas that remained, smoke scantily rising in small plumes here and there.

The trees, already long dead, were merely stumps burnt and decayed; their once glorious limbs filled with green life were swept away by the blast that leveled everything. Remnants of ships laid about, not resembling what they had once been.

Mostly, there was a chemical taste that assailed the tongue. It was an acidic aroma that left an aftertaste like some type of metal.

Gunza smelled the odorous air, rolled the taste around in his mouth, and fought back a gag. He unrolled some paper and shoved tobacco in his mouth. His eyes surveyed his surroundings.

The tear had closed, leaving the space around it, stable. The ground still quaked for weeks as it settled, but overall, it was much like it was prior to the demon being summoned.

Darkster's troops were offered citizenship. If they chose not to join the Hotta orcs, they were executed. They were rounded up and their loyalties questioned. Furthermore, populations from their worlds were welcomed as part of the Hotta empire. It was an ongoing job which would probably take years to complete as they relocated and retrained the new populations.

As far as Kingskull's troops and his crews in space, many of them joined Gobbygoo, who was found right away. Gobbygoo survived the blast by dashing into the sewers that led him away from most of the damage that occurred above.

When asked if he would travel back to his home world to bring order under the Hotta flag, he nodded and shrugged his shoulders. He simply said, "I guess."

His trek would take years.

The balance of Kingskull troops were the main force in gathering Darkster's troops. Without them, Gunza's job of capturing the enemy's forces, would have been nearly impossible. As Darkster troops joined them, cleanup and searching were made easier and quicker.

One of the unfinished tasks at hand was destroying whatever creeps still roamed Marshil. When the search and cleanup were completed, the combined armies would go back to battle against the lost souls.

Moonoak's shamans continued to heal creeps' souls, and would continue doing that for months to come as well.

Next, and most importantly, the all-out search for Darkster was begun. Although the chances of his survival were slim, it was conceivable that the evil orc could have found a way to escape. It had to be considered after witnessing his other marvels.

Another job Gunza had was sending ships to Hotta with the wounded. Their returns would bring more supplies and help, and fairly quickly too. The newly manufactured actuator cut off months of travel time from Marshil to Hotta. He tasked several shamans with properly sending the ships between actuators. Not many were capable, but thankfully, a few were found that were able to operate them.

The old man was tired and weary. Cave-ins within the tunnel system were widespread, complicating search and rescue missions. Every aftershock collapsed more sections of tunnel, trapping additional orcs with those already buried.

He wandered around, mumbling to himself helplessly, "How da hell did I get stuck wit' dis? I not da one to unite all dese worlds. I not a wargod or da head advisor. I don't gots equipment to dig up all da tunnels. I ain't got many a my own troops. Dis a lot to ask of a old man.

But in his heart and in his mind, he knew why he fought to save everyone he could and bring orcs together. It was his daughter's husband, Nuttybomb, who gave him the job to do so the first time; he gave him unequaled authority over all matters orcish. Now, without Nuttybomb or any senior guards able to carry out the wargod's wishes, it fell on him.

The long day met the seemingly innocent night, and with it, more creeps. They seemed to just appear, even after the area was just cleared of them; akin to roaches when the lights were turned off.

Small skirmishes cropped up here and there, either against rebellious Darkster troops or creeps. They caused minor disruption in finding survivors, but even the lightest delays meant life or death for those clinging to the former.

Another quake and cave-in dropped the ground into a tunnel. Along with a few of his orcs, he found himself near possible survivors.

"Ova der," he pointed while coughing dust from his lungs. He was aware of the radiated soil falling down on him and the others. He reasoned that his exposure was no more important than those he attempted to save. He spat some tobacco and saliva, and returned to his job.

Groaning beneath debris was a familiar voice. "Get me outta here," Guthrak growled.

"I comin', old friend," Gunza exclaimed. He and the others hurried to remove heavy blocks that covered Guthrak's legs and torso.

"It 'bout time." The chip on Guthrak's shoulder was speaking for him.

Gunza asked, "Any udders in here you know 'bout?"

"Dunno. Prolly Quicklip and Nubbs. Dems wus ahead a me."

"Dig ova here," Gunza ordered.

The tunnel was completely collapsed beyond where he stood. Just a few feet further into his escape, and Guthrak would have been crushed to death by tons of material.

Gunza instructed, "Ova here. Dig out dese blocks. Dat should make a hole to get through. Looka, dese udder blocks are held up by dose ones." His troops worked feverishly.

Large stones were cut away and handed past Gunza from orc to orc, like a fire line. Buckets with dirt and small rocks were handed off as well.

Gunza ducked down and crawled into the opening made by his orcs. "Anyone here? Anyone alives?"

"Help. I stuck," was moaned with heavy choking.

Gunza laid on his belly and pushed with all his might to move a mountainous rock, but he couldn't. He crawled back out of the confines that constricted his movement and said, "Guys, move dese outta da way."

The fire line handed huge stones off and away. Fifteen minutes allowed part of somebody's arm to be exposed.

Gunza crawled back in, this time less hampered by clutter. He said, "Use dis arm to help lift dis. Can you do dat?"

"I try," came from the weakened voice beneath the rubble.

Gunza pushed, now able to move a large stone off the crushed body of the survivor he fought to free. "Arc,' he said with elation. "I gotcha."

Arc didn't speak. He laid there quietly, moaning at times while he was wrapped and carried away from the collapse.

Gunza crawled a little farther into the cave. He discovered a foot, without a shoe. It moved slightly when he touched it. "I gonna get you out. Hang on."

He dug as fast as he could. Orcs behind him began removing debris that he loosened. But as they did...

More shaking occurred. Rocks fell from above, pummeling Gunza and his team. Thankfully, the ground didn't settle on them. Coughing up dust became common.

A leg was free now. More digging uncovered some metal that appeared to be blocking Gunza from freeing the orc's torso and other leg. It became apparent after some time, that the metal was the orc; it was Quicklip's prosthetic arm.

"Quicklip, can you hear me?" Gunza asked frantically.

There was no response. The leg and foot stopped moving.

Gunza was tired, too tired to move around like he was able to in his younger years. He ordered his orcs to remove Quicklip from his burial as soon as they were able. He cursed the gods for sticking him with his thankless tasks.

He made his way back to a place where he could climb to the surface. Upon ascending to the cobblestone road, he was met by an officer.

"Sir?" the officer greeted.

"What is it?"

"I tink you should see dis."

Gunza slogged some hundred feet where he was shown two bodies. "Oh no," he muttered, recognizing the first body as Booma, Nuttybomb's brother. "Dead?"

"Yessir."

With his legs shattered and unable to find shelter quickly, Booma fell victim to the blast. It was unclear which guard pulled him into the sewers, but it appears it may have been Kingskull. He apparently gave his life in an attempt to save Nutty's brother, for it was his remains found next to Booma's.

Gunza hung his head. What else would he find? Three dozen other dead bodies were reported to have been found; none of those being guards. He took a deep breath, spat out some tobacco from his cheek, and went about the business of playing wargod.

He returned to the area where he first found Guthrak. Quicklip had been extracted and brought to the city. He was triaged above ground as collapses ravaged the subway tunnels.

Nubbs was found alive, but crushed. He, too, was carried off along the road that lined the cliffs to the destroyed population center.

Black rain began to fall, as was predicted. Gunza's orcs were somewhat protected by the gear they wore, but others, trapped by the ground itself, were vulnerable to the deadly toxins that washed down around them.

Gunza gathered himself and took cover near the cliffs. He saw outlines of orcs who once were. They had no remains to find, just silhouettes left behind as the blast's radiation permanently implanted their likenesses on the rock's face.

He didn't know everything about nuclear explosions and their effects on orcs. The blast was massive, that was for sure. The unseen radiation was what concerned him. It was in the soil that sprinkled down into the tunnels during each quake. It was the rain that attempted to quench the arid land and bring life. Perhaps the air itself was still contaminated too.

There were far too few masks to protect everyone, and time was of the essence. More would be delivered when ships returned from Hotta. That would be in just less than a week. So much of the ground would be disturbed by then, so much rain falling.

Gunza, not much of a praying orc, took a few minutes to initiate a one-way conversation with the gods. He hoped to find answers to questions he didn't even know to ask, but mostly, he prayed for salvation for what he had done.

Feeling empty in the process of talking to something he couldn't see, touch, or hear, he talked himself into returning to the miserable chore of digging up dead bodies.

As he walked, looking at the ground for anything that might lead him to survivors, he found a metal cover that had been welded to the frame in which it sat in the cobblestone road. It was a cover to the sewer system, now noticeable as rain water washed it clean of soot. Apparently, it had been welded by heat from the blast.

He pried it open and climbed down. As soon as he reached the bottom, he turned and found Moonoak. The shaman was unconscious, but alive.

Gunza threw Moonoak over his shoulder and got to the surface. He sent other orcs back down to search for others, while he carried Moonoak to the city, but they came up empty. So many passageways were still blocked by fallen debris.

The day was ending, the gray clouds being replaced by starless black. Work progressed by the weary orcs, albeit slower, as darkness prevailed.

The cursed world still had secrets it refused to reveal. It was pretty clear that the guards that survived were below ground, just outside the blast radius that cratered the surface. But could Nuttybomb and Darkster still be found? Or were they shadows, left on the rock face, vaporized like some of the other unfortunates?

So far, only two orcs had been found above ground and alive within two miles of the explosion. They were so badly mangled, they weren't believed to survive the night though. Odds weren't promising.

Gunza walked passed the unbelievable destruction on the way to his shuttle. His day wasn't' done, but he needed to not only escape the surrealism of the devastation, but also study the location of his comrades during the explosion. When he arrived, he ordered video of the area to be sent to him from his flagship. He hoped to see what may have happened to his wargod.

He kicked off his boots and wiggled his aching toes, several poking through his torn socks. The smell of his feet welcomed him; it was a far better than the stench of death and burnt metal. A yawn accompanied the stretching of arms above his head and his legs fully extended. The video appeared on his screen.

He fast-forwarded to the point right before the blast. The guards had already dashed off, out of view. Cloud cover made details impossible to see. He scrolled forward and back, but the only time clouds separated enough to see anything, was during the blast itself. He turned off the monitor.

Written reports were all over his desk, drawing his attention. He muttered, "Six thousand found dead on da first day." He shook his head unhappily. "How many mo' tomorrow?"

His answer at the end of day two came in the form of another written report. "Anudder twelve thousand dead fro' da blast," Gunza sighed.

Day three was much worse. As he and his orcs spread out from ground zero, they found many more dead and dying. Things weren't as completely leveled that far out from the center of the explosion, as was the case closer to the blast. Instead, orcs were subject to every kind of shrapnel imaginable, sent through their bodies from the violent winds. Severe burns were common as well. All told, seventy-one thousand were found dead that day.

When the parent star showed on the horizon, a new day brought new hope. Black rain had stopped falling during the night, and nary a cloud resided.

Gunza was already up and about, giving orders, and searching for survivors. While the star was still low in the sky, he heard, "Sir?" frantically screamed in the distance. It repeated and got louder. He turned to receive.

A runner approached at top speed. "Sir?" he said between breaths.

"Yes?" Gunza replied.

"Da wargod, Sir."

Gunza asked urgently, "Wer?"

"Dis way."

Gunza followed the runner for a half mile. He asked with hope in his voice, "Him alive?"

The Runna answered, "I tink so."

As they approached, they saw heavy equipment tearing metal from metal, the extreme heats from the blast fusing them together.

Gunza came to a stop and asked loudly, "Is da wargod alive?"

A few voices answered, "Ya."

"Move outta da way," he ordered. Bodies separated, allowing access to the clump of metal that entombed Nuttybomb.

Gunza knelt down and held Nuttybomb's hand. He asked, "Nutty, can you hear me?" He peeked his head into the mangled mess to see better.

Nuttybomb's breathing was shallow and labored. His pulse was weak and very slow, but he was alive. For how much longer, nobody knew, but he was alive! He didn't answer.

He was two miles from the epicenter, wrapped in steel and carboncrete, ripped from a ship in the blast. He was unconscious and severely wounded...and unconscious.

As the metal was removed, it was determined by a doc to leave some in place, for it was buried, deep inside the wargod's body. Even the depth and severity of the wounds were suspect; the body armor Nuttybomb wore couldn't be cut away; it was a carbon composite, made of some of the strongest materials known.

Copious amounts of his blood surrounded him and the workers that freed him. His condition didn't look good.

The wargod was rushed to Kockrel, along with the other wounded. Gunza stayed with his leader and son-in-law, hoping for the best, but preparing for the worst.

Doc Mucker, who operated on Quicklip, was summoned.

"Get outta da way!" Mucker yelled as he pushed Gunza aside. "Yer in my light."

Nurses scrambled to gather tools for the doc to use. They bumped into each other as they rushed to save their wargod. They hooked him up to wires and tubes.

Mucker glanced at Nuttybomb's vitals and studied the wounds he could see. They were bad, but probably not life threatening. It was the wounds he couldn't see that concerned him.

"Gunza," he said, "Pull dis metal outta hims stomach while I pull his armor ova his head. Da metal holdin' da armor in place. Gotta get it out befo' I can get it ova his a head." He turned to his bustling helpers and said angrily, "Shutta up anda listen. You nurses gots to stop bleeding wen we taka out da metal. But stay outta my way so I can fix him."

Gunza put a foot on a crate for leverage and pulled the huge chunk of metal from Nuttybomb's torso. Mucker fought to remove the body armor and the nurses applied pressure to the gaping wound that was revealed.

Mucker yelled, "Get some blood into him!" He poked around and found tears in vital organs, veins, and arteries. "You, sew up here." He looked at Gunza and nodded in apparent disbelief.

"Wut?" Gunza asked.

"Him's got mo' holes dan a Wivvaflow whore." Mucker had a nurse temporarily plug a gusher with her thumb.

"Wutcha think?"

Mucker sighed, working quickly. He answered, "Dunno. Heart anda lungs looka ok, I tink." He removed an iron slug from somewhere in Nutty's body and flung it toward the floor. It clanged as it hit the concrete.

For an hour, they worked on their wargod. Transfusion after transfusion resupplied him with blood lost in the field and while they operated. More metal was removed, exposing more damage after the armor was taken off. Finally, Mucker instructed, "Close him up."

Gunza asked, "Well?"

"Well," Mucker paused. "Well, hopefully we gots all da holes. I tink all da organs be ok. Dunno 'bout his brain or if he bled too much dat it be damaged."

"His brain?"

Mucker replied, rubbing his forehead with his forearm, "Ya. Him's all bruised behind da right ear. I gonna get some scans to maka sure der no damage fro' impact. But blood loss...dunno."

320

Patients were vomiting everywhere. Gunza saw their yellow eyes and pale green skin, marked with patches of discolor. "Wut wrong wit' dems?" he asked.

Doc looked around and realized what was being asked of him. He quietly replied, "Radiation."

"Oh."

Mucker added, "Mosta be deads in a week."

Gunza sighed, "Fuck. Wut 'bout da udder guards?" his concern was obvious, considering taking radiation into account.

"All in bad shape. Not sure which ones gots radiation sick."

***

Nuttybomb laid in a tub of warm water. A helper came with a pot, steaming of vapor, and poured a hot mixture of water, salt, and remedies from plants into his bath. He smiled.

Gunza had told Uhra about Nutty's innocence regarding the nurses. She accepted the information and concluded to nurse her husband back to health.

Nutty watched a TV that set on a table of sorts against a wall opposite the tub. He laughed as he saw humans hitting each other in the face with pies. The recollection of similar instances happening when he had attended school as a boy weren't retained. This was new and funny, and it stirred his hunger.

His son burst in and asked for the channel to be changed so he could share view of a cartoon. Uhra obliged, and to Nutty's astonishment, great colors in two-dimension were accompanied by music and sound that was unique to humans.

Nutty's eyes were fixated, his ears attuned to the silly characters that dotted the screen. This was funnier than the pie skit. He was hysterical.

Gunza stood nearby, waiting for his wargod to calm down so he could gain his attention. Finally, he began giving account to goals accomplished and those yet to be achieved. He said as he paced, "Still nuttin' on Darkster."

"Nuttin' on Darkster?" Nutty asked.

"No. The tear closed, so I tink da demon stuck on da udder side."

Nuttybomb acknowledged, "Ok." He looked back at the TV and smiled.

Uhra asked her husband with a note of assurance, "Dat good, right?"

"Right," Nuttybomb exclaimed, playing with the bubbles that ran down his arm from his hand, a vacant look in his eyes.

Gunza added, "Anda it good dat Gobbygoo go back to get udder orcs to join us."

Nuttybomb nodded, "Good." He studied his arm, now in front of his face.

Uhra asked, "Der anyting else, Nutty?"

He answered, "Wut dis on my a arm?"

Uhra nervously looked at Gunza and looked back at her husband. She said, "Honey, dat fro' da esplosion on Marshil."

"An esplosion on Marshil?"

Her eyes fell to the floor, but she smiled and replied, "Yes. You were near da esplosion. It leaved marks on you later."

"Lika da ones on my chest anda back?" Nutty asked, touching the dark green spots that took over his torso.

"Yes, Nutty," Uhra said quietly, her eyes looking back to her father for guidance.

Gunza explained, "We talked 'bout dis, Nuttybomb. It fro' da radiation."

"Da radiation?" Bubbles popped in the foam that was the wargod's pleasant soaking.

After sharing another glance with Gunza, Uhra said quietly, "Yeah, Nutty. You sick fro' da esplosion."

Nutty said, "Ok."

Gunza added quickly, "You doin' good, tho. You no throw up right away fro' da radiation. You get sick later. Means you gots less radiation, so dat good."

"Good." A smile followed.

Gunza mulled over what he wanted to say. Apparently, Nutty's awareness of things was lacking. He began anyway with, "Nuttybomb, I can't be warchief. I too old and all dis takes a toll on me. I not strong lika I used a be."

Nuttybomb blew the foam from between his fingers and simply stated, "Ok. Too old."

Gunza looked at Uhra. "I gonna go."

"Ok," she replied. She wiped a tear from her eye and said to her husband, "C'mon. Letta us get you outta da tub.

"But I wanna watch TV," he said in a panic.

Uhra assured him, "You can watch in bed until you fall asleep."

Nutty smiled wide and said childishly, "Ok." He left the tub with a towel partially wrapped around him.

He hurried to the bedroom so as not to miss too much of the cartoon he was watching.

Moonoak greeted Gunza in the grand living room of Nuttybomb's opulent home. "Any improvement?" he asked.

Nutty was spotted, running like a kid, leaving water in his wake.

Gunza nodded, "Nope. Wut we gonna do?"

Moonoak looked up, beyond the high ceilings, hoping to be answered. "Dunno," he said, discouraged. "I can't connect wit' his mind. He don't amember dat his father and brudder are dead, either."

Gunza sighed, "He ain't gots no mind."

"Ya." Moonoak hung his head.

"Did doc say he will gets betta?" Gunza asked.

Moonoak answered with reluctance in his voice, and a low volume so Nutty wouldn't hear him, "She don't know. Maybe dis part a da radiation."

Gunza peeked down the hallway toward Nutty's bedroom and hesitantly asked the inevitable, "Him gonna live?"

"Dunno dat either," Moonoak admitted.

Gunza stated firmly, "Tell you wut, tho, stoppin' dis TV shit. I gonna see wut channels are ok, and wut ones I tink are no good fo' orcs. Nuttybomb wanted to do it, But well...you know."

"Gotcha," Moonoak said. "I gonna start his language stuff. He talked 'bout it three years ago, but wus too busy fightin' and goin' to different planets. Anyway, I hear orcs sayin' yer and a you. Dems mean da same ting, but we only need one. Stuff lika dat."

Gunza admitted, "Ya, I do it sumptimes too. Dat good to fix."

"Maka it easier to talk wit' humans, too."

"You see da Guthrak gots himself a big ol' bitch to taka care a him?" Gunza asked with a smirk.

Moonoak answered, "Ya. Him's happy. Sick, but happy."

Gunza's smirk faded. "He quittin' da guards. No mo' fightin' fo' him."

"You be quittin' soon. We figure out who to be in charge."

"Well," Gunza said, "I gotta get goin'. Dis leadin' ting takins a toll on me. I gots to do it fo' now, so…"

Moonoak patted Gunza on the back and said optimistically, "You bein' warchief a lil longer ain't so bad. It be easy. No war wit' Darkster; just some stuff against da humans."

"Ya, but I gots lika ten worlds pullin' fo' Nuttybomb. I just a fill in. Dems aren't listenin' to me lika dems wus." Gunza frowned and shook his head.

Moonoak said, "I help you howevva I can, and again, at least der no Darkster."

Nineteen
The Future, Uncertain

Nuttybomb was in bed. He was clean and ready; his mind was clear of concern.

His kids jumped up on his bed, shouting, "Daddy."

"Heya, kids!" he howled happily. He shouted "I wuvs dis TV stuff," followed by patting their heads and words of, "Goodnight. Wuvs you chitlins, too."

A helper urged their departure, then followed the scurrying children to their bedroom, where they were put down for the night.

Uhra crawled up with her husband. She hugged him and laid an arm over his chest. She smiled when she saw happiness in his eyes. This was what she wanted; for him to be around; to be with her and the kids.

But she never wanted him to be in the condition he was in. She would have never wished him to be around as a result of what he had been through and his body's failings. She silently cursed the gods and mumbled, "Be careful wut you wish for," a human saying that was all too relevant, learned from watching TV.

"I wish fo' TVs in evvy room," he blurted out with exuberance.

She said, "We'll see." She briefly thought about having TVs in every room and how that might hamper the children's readying for school each morning. Other than that, she saw no harm in obliging her debilitated husband.

"Goodnight, Younut. Wuvs you," she said, leaning into him for a kiss. But he was already sleeping. She watched his eyes move behind the lids, slowly at first, then darting from side to side. Although it felt a little creepy, she watched over him.

Nuttybomb's facial features took on a look of curiosity, and then, concern. He shook, not so violently at first that Uhra was concerned, but enough to get her attention. She watched him closely.

His mouth opened, trying to say something. His eyelids blinked, his arms and legs throwing themselves around.

Uhra yelled, "Nutty!" She sat up and grabbed him by both shoulders. "Wut wrong?"

Nuttybomb convulsed. He spat, his lips fighting to speak. He sat up and awoke from a dead sleep. His speech- haunted while memories unfolded of evil revealed- fought to come. He grabbed his head, the swelling misery of the past and present coming to light, the future, uncertain. His mind was invaded.

Uhra questioned with fear, "Wut is it, Nutty?"

He yelled, "Darkster!"

The end.

If you enjoyed this work, please leave a positive review where you purchased it, if possible. Thank you for your involvement in the Hyadeswars universe.